Newman's Gym, San Francisco

SHADOW BOXER

A BILLY NICHOLS NOVEL

EDDIE MULLER

SCRIBNER

NEW YORK LONDON TORONTO SYDNEY SINGAPORE

SCRIBNER
1230 Avenue of the Americas
New York, NY 10020

Frontispiece illustration by Howard Brodie

SCRIBNER and design are trademarks of Macmillan Library Reference USA, Inc., used under license by Simon & Schuster, the publisher of this work.

For information regarding special discounts for bulk purchases, please contact Simon & Schuster Special Sales at 1-800-456-6798 or *business@simonandschuster.com*

Designed by Colin Joh
Text set in Janson

Manufactured in the United States of America

1   3   5   7   9   10   8   6   4   2

Library of Congress Cataloging-in-Publication Data

Muller, Eddie.
Shadow boxer: a Billy Nichols novel/Eddie Muller.
p. cm.
1. San Francisco (Calif.)—Fiction. 2. Boxers (Sports)—Fiction. 3. Sportswriters—Fiction. I. Title.

PS3613.U45 S43 2003
813'.54—dc21
2002026816

ISBN 0-7432-1444-7

For F. X. Toole

Author's Note

As in the initial Billy Nichols story, *The Distance*, real people appear in these pages. Be assured they act in an entirely fictitious manner: Jake Ehrlich, Artie Samish, and Edmund G. Brown did not participate in the activities depicted in *Shadow Boxer*.

In much the same way the Mount Davidson Trust was dropped into Billy's lap, so too was the grist for this novel unexpectedly dropped on me, years ago, by Ron and Maria Blum. They'll be surprised to learn it, but I thank them nonetheless. Many thanks as well to Bill Selby, Christine Okon, Marc Kagan, Russel Pleech, Lisa Greene, Dennis Parlato, and my wonderful wife, Kathleen.

Much appreciation also to my agent, Denise "The Manhattan Mauler" Marcil, and my editor, Susanne "The Truth" Kirk. As always, the lion's share of my gratitude is reserved for Erik "The Well-Read" McMahon.

The difference between a moral man and a man of honor is that the latter regrets a discreditable act, even when it has worked and he has not been caught.

—Henry Louis Mencken

THROUGH THE ROPES
By Billy Nichols

Hack Escalante is hanging 'em up.

The heavyweight battler, a fan favorite around these parts for years, called the other day to report that he's quitting the ring and moving to Southern California.

Against the wishes of his manager, Smilin' Sid Conte, Hack snubbed an offer to fight Joe Louis, part of the Brown Bomber's comeback campaign. The purse was a paltry five grand—same as Escalante got for challenging champ Chester Carter.

That battle royale, which almost leveled the Cow Palace back in August, is in the books as one of the best ever.

Can't say we blame Hack for pulling a fast fade. Has any boxer absorbed more punishment *outside* a ring? First, his manager, former lightweight Gig Liardi, took a powder last spring. Not wanting to miss any paydays, Hack signed up with gadfly Conte.

Then Liardi's body was discovered in Golden Gate Park. Murdered, it turned out. Plenty of people, including the police, suspected that Hack was mixed up in it. Before he'd had a chance to recover from that body blow, the fighter's wife, Claire Escalante, was found dead in their Sunset district home.

Most of us would never recover from such a tragedy, or the attendant suspicion. Incredibly, Escalante fought for the title only weeks after his wife's death. He almost scored the biggest upset in recent ring history.

Hack's only reward? Having the SFPD arrest promoter Burnell Sanders for the murder of his wife. After that came the stunning revelation, detailed in a written confession prior to her demise, that it was Mrs. Escalante who'd killed her husband's manager.

Any wonder the kid wants to start fresh? Wouldn't we all?

*   *   *

1

1

She craned her head out the passenger window and gave me the once-over. Dark-eyed dame, olive-skinned, lush-lipped: a one-time dream-boat steaming toward the shoals of middle age.

"You the guy they call *Mr. Boxing*?" she asked.

Female fight fans aren't as rare as you'd think. They grew up listening to title bouts on the radio with their fathers. It got in their blood. I stepped toward her car and turned on the guarded grin I reserved for curious strangers.

"That's me—Billy Nichols. *San Francisco Inquirer.*"

Long black lashes flapped once. Then her eyes darted somewhere behind me. I was shoved up against the machine. Before I could register a beef, the torpedo crammed me into the front seat, the broad sliding over behind the wheel. She went heavy on the gas and we shot away from the curb.

"What the hell is all this about?" I squawked, trying not to sound completely terrified. We slanted across Market onto Kearny, weaving in and out of midafternoon traffic.

"I'm taking you to jail," she said.

Okay, it was a gag. Dewey Thomas pulling another of his pranks. Renting a couple of shills to "kidnap" me, haul me to the Royal Athletic Club to preview talent in the 1948 Golden Gloves tournament. Dewey must have handpicked the ghee squeezed in at my right. Perfect casting. Swarthy like the woman, but skin pocked like a cantaloupe. Reminded me of somebody . . . a boxer, years back.

"What's the charge, Officer?" I snickered, playing along.

"Not taking my husband's letters seriously," the dame snapped. "Never returning his phone calls. They only let him make one a day, you know. All things considered, wouldn't hurt you to show a little decency."

"I could say the same. Who the hell are you?" She bypassed the left that would have led to the Royal. Shit, we *were* headed toward County Jail.

"Florence Sanders. It's my goddamn husband they're trying to frame for murder. He's sent you fifty million letters and can't reach you. A note practically every day for a whole month, begging you to come see him. What's your problem? No time for your old pals?"

"Sorry, Florence. I've had a lot on my plate lately. Can't say your husband's a priority."

"Not a *priority*? A murder rap? What *would* be a priority, Mr. Big Shot?"

"Polishing the silverware. For my wife."

"Screw you! You think this is funny? First he won't quit ranting and raving it's your fault he's in this spot. Then he starts in on how you're the only one who can help him. I'm sick of listening to him. You don't want to go see him? Fuck it, I'll drag your ass over there—if only to shut his yap. You're gonna go there and talk to Burney, is that clear? My cousin here will make sure you don't take a detour on your way in."

She smoked. Not right this moment, but every other chance she had. Tobacco permanently roughened the edges of her words. Fumes seeped from the fabric of her jacket. No doubt a nervous habit, seeing as her spouse was a killer.

I needed to talk to Florence Sanders's husband like I needed another hole in my head. True enough, it was my doing that Burney Sanders, only months ago the top fight promoter in San Francisco, was facing this murder rap. Not that I gave a damn. I'd like to see him rot in a prison cell, for life. Better yet, maybe the state would see its way clear to give him the gas.

I examined Florence's cousin, calculating how I'd ditch him once we reached Washington Street. The muscle decided he wanted a speaking part in this rolling farce. "It's no big deal," he mumbled. "You can talk to the man for ten minutes, can't you? What'll it hurt?"

"Pardon me, Buddy," Mrs. Sanders barked. "Anybody ask to hear from you? I'm not paying for your commentary. So dummy up."

"Your name Silva, by any chance?" I asked my ugly, sullen seat mate.

He lit up, looked almost tickled.

"You remember me?"

"Bud Silva. Middleweight. Lotta fights in the early thirties. Then you dropped outta sight."

"Doing other things. I wasn't bad, though, huh? Tell her. Tell her 'bout the night I beat Lawless. Remember that fight?"

"Oh, sure. Unforgettable. To say the least."

"Hear that? He remembers my figh—"

"Shut the hell up, I said! You're supposed to scare him, not ask for his goddamn autograph. Moron. Shoulda known."

"Hey, Florie," Silva spat. "Why don't you watch that mouth, huh?"

We all simmered silently for a couple of blocks. I wondered how much Burney Sanders had confided to his struggle-and-strife about the blackmail racket he'd been running, and my connection to it.

I turned her way: "What'd Burney mean when he told you I was the only one who could help him?"

"Haven't got the slightest idea," she replied, with an overblown sigh. She wheeled onto Clay Street without checking street signs. She'd memorized the route. "Little while ago, he wanted to kill you. Claimed you'd set him up. Swore he was gonna get even. Now everything's out the other side of his mouth—you're his last hope, he keeps on saying."

"Any idea what he's talking about?"

"Listen—my husband's been playing dirty pool long as I've known him. Think I'm blind? Does he let me in on it? Think I *wanna* be in on it? All I know is—this time his tit's really in the wringer. He gets nailed for one this serious, I'll have to figure out how to fend for myself."

She swung the car up Dunbar Alley and braked abruptly at the rear entrance to County Jail No. 1.

"I can tell he has your unflagging support," I said.

"Everybody's rope's got an end. Outta the car."

"You're not coming?"

"I told him I'd get you here. You're here. I got better things to do."

"Thanks for finally coming," Sanders began.

"Definitely wasn't my idea."

He nodded toward the gate of the visitors' pen. "Florence bring you?"

"She's got a persuasive manner."

"She waiting outside?"

"Beauty parlor appointment. What's the pitch? I still got a column to write today."

I expected the familiar hair-triggered hothead. Worse yet, with a murder rap hanging over him. But Burney didn't give off much heat, staring through the steel cage. Harsh light bouncing off bilious green institutional walls made his pasty skin even more sallow. City-issue dungarees flapped on his spindly frame. He'd dropped pounds he couldn't spare. Might starve before they could serve up the cyanide.

"If the guard starts getting nosy," Sanders warned in a whisper, "go right into fight talk, okay? They probably figure you're here about what happens to my action if I go up on this bullshit charge."

He drilled me with an urgent gaze. I owed the little prick less than nothing. All he got was a weak nod. Sanders flashed a look at a uniformed bull propping up the wall about twenty feet away, on his side of the wire. The guard's eyes locked on his prisoner and never strayed.

"Pretty rich, huh?" Sanders said, voice dropping as he leaned closer. "That you're the one I gotta go to in this spot."

"How's that?"

"Listen—this blackmail scheme I'm supposed to have cooked up? The pictures of you with Claire? Let's be realistic—I'm not exactly innocent. But it's chickenshit compared to what's really going on. The blackmail dodge was a sideline. Tip of the iceberg. I'm just a mechanic for the real operators. You did them a big favor, shoving me front and center. Keeps them out of the picture."

I took off my specs, polishing the lenses with the fat end of my tie.

"Pay attention," he snapped. "I can't just lay it all out for you. I think this place is wired. They hear what I tell you, then they'll be up *your* ass—and you'll be no help to me at all."

"Why the hell would I help you? Case you haven't gotten the signals, I'm rooting for you to take the pipe."

The old Burney would have tried socking me for such provocation. But if he was offended, he swallowed it.

"I got no right to expect anything from you," he said. "I know that. It was a lousy play, setting you up like I did. You did what you had to, to get even. Maybe we're square. I fucked with you and you fucked me

6

back twice as hard. But this is too much. I didn't kill Claire. I'm taking the rap for something I didn't do. The people behind this, they've got the fix. With me gone, they get away with everything."

"Am I supposed to understand what you're talking about?"

"Just listen. Three lawyers have dumped me, for no good reason. The DA had nothing—*you* know that—and any shyster worth his shit should have been itching to take this on. Then they cut this deal with Daws to finger me. So here I am—like a leper—with a snot-nosed public defender and no bail."

Larry Daws was a so-so light heavyweight Sanders employed for personal security and occasional acts of persuasion. I'd heard through the grapevine he was going to offer testimony that'd cinch Burney's conviction. Cops uncovered a neighbor who'd spotted Sanders and Daws leaving the house in which Claire Escalante was found dead. For Daws, it was an immunity trade. Anybody who took a good look would see something didn't jibe. Daws was a professional hitter. Sanders was a runt. It was ass-backward and carried plenty of stink.

"How the hell do I rate 'no bail'?" Sanders asked.

"You'd skip first chance you got."

"Drag my wife and kid around, playing fugitive? No chance."

I could have informed him Florence wouldn't shed a tear if he hanged himself in here. Long as he had life insurance. But I thought better of it. He was a father, after all. Never knew that. Not that I cared.

"Look at you," he sputtered. "This is news? I been married six years. My boy's gonna be five next month." His mercury was rising. He edged too near the grate and the guard shouted for him to heel. "Rate this is going, I'll be in San Quentin when my boy's blowing out his candles."

"I feel for you, Burney." I held thumb and index finger half an inch apart. "About this much. You're a liar, a pimp, an extortionist, a killer. I don't give a shit what happens to you."

Why would I? I'd put the cops wise to him. Sanders had operated an extortion racket, using Claire Escalante as the bait, and he'd killed her after she'd turned over to me photographic proof that he was blackmailing people. People like Eddie Ryan, owner of Golden State racetrack, among others.

I was one of the "others."

"You sold the cops a story 'bout how I was shaking Ryan down," Sanders said. "You really believe that's what this is about? It's way bigger than Ryan or you. People with serious pull in this town are mixed up in it. I was just a guy who didn't mind doing a little dirty work for his share. But once you go down that road, there's no going back. Everybody you meet, you're working an angle, trying to get 'em in your pocket."

"Why'd you set me up?"

"I'll tell you why. Somehow you and Claire and Hack were all mixed up in Gig Liardi's death. I didn't know exactly what was going on, but I could see that Mr. Above-It-All was neck-deep in shit. I saw a chance to nail you. When you're in with con artists, everybody's ripe for a touch. I was like a fighter, you know? Started to feel I could take down *anybody*. That I *had* to. That was the game. I started out doing it for *them*. When they tried to ace me out, that's when it all went south. Thought I was looking out for myself. Now look at me."

The guard shoved off from the wall and slow-stepped toward us.

"You can check things out without looking suspicious," Burney whispered. "You're a newspaper guy. You know your way around. I get me a PI, they'll be on him like stink on shit."

The guard strolled behind Sanders, right hand fondling the billy club strapped to his hip.

"Saw in your column where Hack's quitting," Burney vamped. "I guess it'd be pretty tough for him to stay around here, after they hung Gig's murder on his wife." He gave a glance that was supposed to penetrate me, down to the marrow. When I didn't flinch, he added: "That all seemed damn convenient, you ask me."

"Nobody asked you." I changed the subject. "Let your wife be your legman, Burney. She seems formidable enough."

"I don't trust her."

I snorted. "But you trust *me*. That's a good one."

The guard strolled out of earshot and Burney shifted gears. "They got Daws turned against me. He's gonna say I beat Claire to death. That's not true and you know it."

"Sort of defeats the purpose of having him on the payroll."

"I didn't kill her, Bill." He played it sincere.

"Right—you just used her like a whore in your shitty little black-mail scheme."

"So try me for that! There's a big fucking difference from where I'm sitting. I didn't kill her. Neither did Larry. But he's the one that hit her. I've said that all along. But they don't want to believe it—they want *me* for it. They'll do anything to bury me."

"Burney, you sound like every loser facing hard time—*they* did it, not *me*. Fuck you. Along with this mysterious *them* you keep bring-ing up."

"Listen—I can't say outright who's involved. But, Bill, c'mon—you don't have to be a genius to put it together."

He waved at the dingy, depressing surroundings. A few fellow hard-luck cases hunched nearby, spinning pathetic spiels before sinking back into the sewers of our justice system. This criminal corral was the bailiwick of District Attorney Edmund G. "Pat" Brown, the only city official powerful enough to scare off lawyers and broker testimony.

"It makes no sense, Burney. Why would the DA have it in for you?"

His eyes fixed on me, gleaming. "That's what I need to find out."

Whatever amusement value there was in this cryptic nonsense, it evaporated. I was angry, more than anything. Not just because Sanders was a shitheel. He was a time-wasting, annoying, unprofessional shitheel. Here was a guy with a *real* deadline, who couldn't—or wouldn't—place the crucial facts up in his lead.

"You want the truth, pal? Claire's dead. To hell with details. She left three little motherless kids. Somebody's gonna pay for that. You're the one."

"That ain't justice."

"She's dead. You're breathing. *That* ain't justice."

"Okay, call Jake Ehrlich. Phone's right outside. You two are big buddies—tell *him* to take my case. He'll see it's a frame-job right off the bat."

I laughed out loud. I was supposed to use up chits with the city's top criminal lawyer to help Burney Sanders, a lowlife grifter who con-spired to blackmail me and then killed the woman I loved?

"You're dreaming, Burney."

"Think so? Couple things break different, it could be you in here trying to save *your* ass. See, that's why I went to *you* for help. *You* know the truth. *You* were mixed up with Claire. Managed to pull yourself out of the picture when she died. Gave a tidy story to the cops. But like I said—it's the tip of the iceberg. All I'm asking is a chance to fight this rap. I didn't kill her. It was an accident. We go to trial and they bring in phony testimony, manufacture evidence—I'll start spewing names like the goddamn phone book. Everybody that's messed up in it—including *you*. What'll I have to lose? Do me this favor. Help me flush out the real chiselers, then I could forget to mention in court how you were banging the wife of our local heavyweight hero."

I'd hidden all traces of my connection to the deaths of Claire Escalante and Gig Liardi, manager of her husband, heavyweight Hack Escalante. There was little chance I'd be held to account for anything. But if I've learned one lesson as a newsman, it's that you don't need facts to destroy somebody. Should my name get bandied about in court, attached to such popular pastimes as blackmail, extortion, adultery, and murder, *Mr. Boxing*'s reputation as the cleanest guy in a dirty racket would be shot to hell. Once that was gone, it was a fast fall from top of the heap to the unemployment line.

"I can't buy into any of this," I said, ignoring Burney's implied threat. "You haven't told me a damn thing that explains whatever it is 'these people' are getting away with. I wouldn't know where to start—*if* I wanted to."

"Check out last Tuesday's obituaries—an associate of mine's in there. Dexter Threllkyl. We did some things together. Remember the gal who used to work for me—the one whose name you're *not* going to mention in here? Remember her? You should—she musta helped Claire swipe those photos of the two of you from my office. Only that's not all she got. She's got what *they're* after. Find her. Find her and lots of things will make sense—'pecifically about Threllkyl."

The guard poked his club in Burney's back. "Time's up," he announced.

Sanders was trying to arrange his features into a convincingly pathetic expression as the bull prodded him back into the jail's bowels. I looked at my watch. Burney'd only gotten half of his allotted twenty minutes.

2

Memory, more than wordsmithing, accounted for my success as a reporter, and my ascension to *Mr. Boxing* status. Off the top of my head I could recount bouts more accurately than a radio replay. I'd put a name to a face when the guy's own mother didn't recognize him. I remembered all the angles, who played them, and how well. Who knocked out who to win the welterweight title in such and such year. I'll tell you the round, the punch combination, and what they had for breakfast that day.

It's a gift. Guys tell me that all the time, usually when I'm settling a bet. Only you don't feel so blessed when you're trying to forget.

Before Florence Sanders hauled me over to the County Jail, I was diligently trying to wash away the misery of the last few months by diving back into the circuit. I'd learned, however, that memory doesn't do your bidding. At work, Claire's raspy laugh would suddenly rattle around my head. At the Communion rail, I'd smell the hollow of her throat, taste her skin. Riding on the streetcar, the mundane details of my life would suddenly be obliterated by crime scene photos: Claire, laid out lifelessly in a pool of blood, her eyes still open.

So, of course, I remembered Virginia Wagner. The gal who'd worked for Burney Sanders. Her phone number was stamped in my memory. I'd dialed it dozens of times over the past few months, after I'd discovered the connection between her and Claire Escalante—that the two of them had busted up Burney's play by heisting his stash of blackmail photos.

After Claire died, I was afraid Virginia Wagner had gone the same route, compliments of Burney. But she never turned up in the obits. Never turned up at all.

When I got back to the office after the fights that night, I dialed her number. I listened to it ring for about a minute, then got spooked and chucked the receiver back in its cradle. *Why the hell was I calling this Wagner woman?* Because Sanders asked me to find her? God forbid.

Wondering, that's all. Wondering what became of the brusque, sharp-featured blonde with the overflowing briefcase, whom I'd met once at Sanders's office. Never saw her again. That briefcase, however—I'd noticed it in Claire's house, empty, after she'd been killed. Maybe it contained what "everybody was after." And who the hell was *everybody*?

Swiveling the chair around, I returned my attention to the typewriter. The column was begging three more inches, and they sure as hell weren't going to be about Burney Sanders's pending trial or some vamoosed vixen. *Let it lie*, I told myself.

I decided to tag on yet another pitch for the upcoming Golden Gloves, the annual amateur tournament that started in three weeks. I'd become a virtual one-man band when it came to promoting the Gloves, since none of the other dailies touched it. The *Inquirer* sponsored the two-week competition, during which professional boxing played second fiddle to the simon-pures. Reminded me that I needed to get more entry forms. The new printer wasn't as reliable as my original source for all the forms and programs: Burney Sanders.

He'd built himself a solid little union shop on York Street, turning out placards and posters for a long roster of local clients, mostly sports-related. Sanders had a hand in everything. Every player in the fight game has the safety net, some other stable, legitimate business. Helps them survive the knockdowns.

I was looking for the new printer's number when I glanced up. All three hundred pounds of Manny Gold advanced through the sports department, big as a battleship steaming to port. That's one thing about working for a paper—they always know where to find you.

My desktop darkened, consumed by Manny's immense shadow. "William, my friend! Look at you! Look at you!" That was Gold's standard greeting, a salesman's safe gambit, appropriate for any occasion: Hit the exacta? *Look at you! Look at you!* Hit by a truck? *Look at you! Look at you!* Manny was a mainstay in the local menagerie, and the only one of the bunch who called me William. His chalk-striped suits had to be custom-sewn by Omar the Tent-Maker, and he always wore his hat brim-up, like the ancient bocce ball players in Washington Square.

"Didn't see you tonight, Manny. Not like you to miss a card."

"Business first, I'm afraid. And you're the lucky beneficiary. We just got these in and we're going to do huge business. I wanted to give you the very first ones."

He came around the desk. From within his coat he produced a slim rectangle of white plastic. A moment of panic welled as Manny's bulk hovered over me like the *Hindenburg*. He delicately plucked three pencils from my shirt pocket and deftly replaced them with the doodad. It had a flap that extended over the mouth of the pocket. Emblazoned on it in blue Old English type: *Monarch of the Dailies*.

"Never again will you soil a fine shirt with streaks of pencil lead. And speaking of pencils—" Manny opened his fist to magically unveil a dozen freshly sharpened KEN Extra Soft 722s, my pencil of preference. Embossed on each in silver lettering: *Billy Nichols—Dean of the Fistic Fraternity.*

"Manny—you shouldn't have."

He carefully arrayed the pencils, points down, within the sheath that now lined the breast pocket of my dress shirt. His paw patted them in place. "My compliments," he said. "As many as you want. You just tell me."

Emmanuel Goldstein, aka Manny Gold, was a partner in a promotional novelty company called C. J. Enterprises, operated out of a nondescript warehouse on Sixteenth Street, at the foot of Potrero Hill. What else moved through that facility was open to speculation. What the "C. J." represented was also a mystery, although it'd long ago unanimously been decreed by Gold's comrades and clients that it stood for "Colossal Jew." Manny had his mitts in rackets all over town. I'd known him more than ten years and in all that time I couldn't recall an instance, not the briefest respite, when Manny wasn't in there pitching. On fight nights he was the busiest guy in the arena, schmoozing his way from ringside to rafters, sniffing out scores.

His biggest takedown, everyone agreed, was when he somehow slipped a wedding ring on the finger of Elizabeth "Peggy" Winokur. She was a hometown fashion model, who in the years before the war was one of the most photographed women in San Francisco. Studio people from Hollywood scouted her on runways and at cotillions. Her destiny shone beyond the city line. Or so it seemed. We all joked that Manny Gold's courtship of the eligible beauty ranked with the century's toughest sell-jobs. So when Peggy Winokur said "I do," she wasn't only making an honest man out of Manny—she was making him a local legend.

"William, how is *your* beautiful wife? And the boy? He's going to be a movie star with the parents he has. All's well on the home front, I trust."

"Ida's fine. The boy's good."

"His name again? I'm sorry . . ."

"Vincent."

"How old is he now?"

"Six months." I shoveled stuff around the desktop, hoping Manny'd take the hint and drift. Not Manny. Not a prayer. Not when he's working a play. He was good for about five more minutes of the well-spoken gentleman routine. If it hadn't cut him any mustard by then, he'd revert to his genuine self.

"What took you two so long? Peggy and I were starting to think you'd never have kids."

"Guess you never know, huh?" I gestured to the seat beside my desk, knowing he'd decline.

"Oh no, thanks. I'll stand." Damn right he would. His ass *may* have fit in that chair, but it'd take a winch and crane to hoist it out.

"Has Ida got her figure back?" he asked. "Because I want you to bring her over to my place one of these days. A shipment of dresses just arrived from Thailand that I was lucky enough to get in on. Beautfiul, beautiful items. She can pick out any she wants. They're silk, for the most part. Would cost you an arm and a leg in Magnin's, I'm telling you. I got in dirt cheap. Don't tell anybody, 'cause I'm working a deal with the City of Paris, and they don't need to know my source. Or, God forbid, my price. But come by and I'll take care of you. And stop over the house. Peggy'll make dinner. She'd like to see Ida and the kid—Vincent."

I tapped one of Manny's gift pencils on a stack of daily detritus and smiled at him. *Be amused*, I reminded myself for the hundredth time that day. No denying that Manny was always good for a laugh, in small doses, promoting his endless stream of bullshit and all his ceaseless scams. But it was quarter of eleven, I was still three inches short of done, and Tony Bernal would be waiting outside for me in fifteen to provide the lift home.

"What do you think of the pocket protector? Clever item, huh? Very classy for a professional situation such as a newspaper office."

"I noticed the inscription."

"*Monarch of the Dailies*—strong but subtle, don't you agree?"

"Did you just use the word *subtle*, Manny?"

"I can get sixty thousand of 'em, just like that one. Twelve hundred bucks for the load, all in. Breaks out at two cents apiece. Outfit the whole staff and use the rest as a promotional inducement to new subscribers. Who do I talk to?"

"We just finished a subscription campaign."

"What'd they give away?"

"Two free months."

"Ridiculous. That's real money. This here is two cents."

"This here is a little slip of plastic—not that I don't deeply appreciate mine."

"Wait till you see the difference it makes in your cleaning bills!"

"I don't know if it's something they'll go for, Manny. I don't even know—"

"Two cents apiece! You're telling me Hearst can't afford two cents of appreciation for his staff and new subscribers? For fuck's sake—he shits gold bricks after breakfast!"

The office boy showed a keen sense of timing, choosing this moment to reappear. I'd sent him to the morgue more than a half hour ago. The kid never got his ass out of first gear—hence his perpetual presence on the lobster shift.

"Here's the edition you asked for, Mr. Nichols. Last Tuesday." The boy gaped at Gold as if he were some extinct dinosaur come back to life. I grabbed the back issue from the kid and flipped him a nickel, fished out of the desk drawer.

"Manny, I don't mean to be rude, but I gotta wrap this column." I shot a look at my watch. "And I've only got about five minutes before I gotta get out of here. So . . ."

"You say you're going out in five? I'll wait. I'll walk down with you."

"Suit yourself," I said, turning back to the typewriter. I hated people standing behind me while I wrote. In Manny's case it felt like a battalion lurking. But I hammered away, best I could, stringing together final tidbits for Thursday's space. I was tugging the scroll from the carriage when Gold piped up:

"So you went to see Burney?"

He was holding one of the notes I'd gotten from Sanders. He'd excavated it from the mess on my desk. Goddamn snoop.

"I did," I admitted. "Briefly."

"How's he holding up? I hear they're building a real case against him. Hard to believe, isn't it? That he killed Hack's wife. What'd he have to say for himself?"

"Not much," I lied. "We just talked about business stuff."

"Hard to believe," he repeated, dropping the note back onto the piles. Yeah, my lie *would* be hard to believe if he'd just read Sanders's plea for an audience. The desperation in those scrawled words had nothing to do with "business stuff."

Manny looked at me and shook his head. "Hard to believe that little turd could actually kill somebody. What a world."

3

Manny and I rode the elevator down with a gaggle of production gals cut loose after a long shift. Manny's corpulence dominated the descent; one girl executed a few furtive sidesteps to avoid contact with his bulk. Many times I'd seen the man Panzer-tank through a crowd, throwing his girth around, so I was surprised to see a flush of embarrassment creep up his face. One additional indignity to cap a lousy day, I suspected. My dismissive manner hadn't helped.

"Hey, sis," I said, loud enough to draw a glance from the girls and Manny. I pulled back my overcoat and jacket lapels to display the embossed pocket protector. "Pretty slick, huh?" There were mildly baffled expressions. But one gal, God bless her, leaned in for a closer look: "Neat! Where'd you get it?"

"My friend here is the city's leading distributor of promotional premiums, and he might supply these for the whole staff—if we're lucky."

Manny brightened, enormous hand dipping into the magic pocket. Out came a trio of gleaming pocket protectors, still carrying the chemical scent of freshly pressed plastic. He eyeballed the group like he was about to pin each with a corsage, but the bustiest of the bunch burst his bubble: "Girls don't have pockets there," she pouted, straightening up and emphatically exhibiting her points.

A serious oversight—I could tell from the way Manny's bright eyes dimmed. In a heartbeat, half his market had evaporated. His promo pitch needed rapid renovation.

"Give 'em to your boyfriends," he proposed, trying to regroup.

Doors opened onto the lobby. Two gals sauntered off empty-handed. The sweetie who'd picked up my cue snatched the three pocket guards from Manny's meathook, chirping, "Thanks a million, bud."

"I'll get the name of the right guy to see in Promotion," I said. "Best I can do is get your foot in the door. After that . . ."

"That's all I can ask, my friend." Gold clapped an arm around my shoulders, bucking himself up, ceremoniously escorting me to the exit. "Just give me a leg up. I'll take it from there."

The girls shoved through the heavy doors onto the corner of Third and Market only to be brought up short by a precipitous drop in the temperature. They huddled closer, chattering noisily and scampering across the street, goosed along by the wind, howling down the main stem. Haloes of swirling mist embraced the street lamps. The few shivering souls queued up for outbound streetcars would remember their topcoats tomorrow. Indian summer was over early this year.

"Where can I drop you?" Manny offered. "I'm parked over on Sutter."

"I'm good. I got my guy meeting me here. Thanks anyway."

"You'll call me with that name? The guy in Promotion?"

"Don't worry."

"Thank you, William."

I gave him a farewell whack with the folded archival edition I toted. Last I saw him, Manny Gold was gingerly mincing across Market, looking uncharacteristically unsure of himself.

I gazed down Third, expecting to see Tony Bernal perched on the fender of his coupe, right at the mouth of Stevenson Alley, dragging on his twentieth tar-bar of the day. He wasn't. My watch said eleven-ten. Not like Tony to be late. I positioned myself conspicuously under the lamppost and waited.

I shook loose the paper and fingered the corners. No need to look at page numbers; I knew the *Inquirer* backward and forward, inside and out. A quick fold and snap—the streetcar rider's specialty—and I was scanning the death notices.

> THRELLKYL, Dexter—Age 63, returned home to rest, at peace with his Lord, October 25, 1948, in San Francisco, Calif. Died of a heart attack, according to Astrid Threllkyl, his beloved wife of 37 years, who discovered the body Sunday night in the family's Vallejo Street home. A well-respected attorney who specialized in corporate law, Mr. Threllkyl numbered among his clients many of San Francisco's most prominent businesses. Born in Gutherie, Oklahoma, 1885, Mr. Threllkyl's precocious intelligence earned him a scholarship to Princeton University, from which he graduated with honors in

1903. Prior to moving to San Francisco, he worked with the Federal Housing Administration and the Bureau of Land Management in Washington, D.C. He is survived by his wife and two daughters, Devin and Dulcie. Funeral services are private.

How the hell Burney Sanders was connected to an uptown contract-scribbler like Threllkyl, I had no idea. Neither could I feature what Burney thought I'd glean from the guy's obit. He and Sanders clearly ran in different crowds. I was hard-pressed to imagine any angles they'd work together. But then, I *could* miss things. Hadn't pegged Burney for a family man, after all.

I reread the item a few times for good measure, squinting at the fine print under the meager lamplight. Must have been studying it pretty hard, not to have heard the crash.

When the shouting started, I pulled my snout out of the paper. A whiff of apprehension suddenly warmed the night air. Some youngsters were scurrying down Third with that anxious *don't wanna miss it* dash in their stride. Then came the siren. Two blocks south I saw taillights congeal at the intersection of Third and Howard. A flash of light—magnesium—and I made out the steaming shapes of a wreck. I'd have bet anything the Johnny-on-the-spot camera jockey was Jack Early of the *Call-Bulletin*. That detestable, unscrupulous bastard was pure genius when it came to snagging sensational shots. You'd swear he staged them.

I ambled toward the commotion. In the flash pop, I thought I recognized the green paint job of Tony Bernal's car. Another blast of light made it clear—a green coupe turning onto Third from Howard had taken on a delivery truck and lost.

I broke into a trot, keeping pace with the frat boys in front of me. By the time I reached the intersection I was at full gallop. Shattered glass everywhere across the asphalt. Screams inside the auto. A cop was trying to get the passenger door open while his partner spread flares around the perimeter. They'd angled the patrol car across Third to block traffic. Jack Early was up on the truck's bumper, setting up another shot, aiming down at the crumpled coupe. I blew past the scattered gawkers as Early fired his flash. In the burst I saw Tony Bernal's face, spiderwebbed with blood and twisted in anguish, behind what used to be the windshield.

Tony was a right guy. His brother Mitch worked in Circulation, had been a Golden Gloves bantam champ back in the thirties. Tony had three kids, one of whom he brought to work regularly. The boy wanted to be a writer. Newspaperman, specifically. You could see on his face that he loved the hustle, soaked it up like a sponge. In fact, I'd let the boy stand behind me, ringside at the Cow Palace, while I banged out my story of the Carter-Escalante heavyweight title fight. His dad had been setting type at the *Inquirer* for almost two decades, and driving me to and from bouts, or home from the office, for as long as I could remember. Tony loved chauffeuring me around, shooting the shit.

The cop coaxed open the passenger door but came up empty on his next move. "Hang on, buddy" was the best he could manage. He backed into me, swearing under his breath. His partner climbed up on the truck's running board to check on the driver, who was dazed but conscious. *Major Liquor Company* was stenciled on the side of his rig.

More sirens bellowed toward the intersection. I leaned in to offer Tony words of encouragement and saw his left leg twisted in a terrible way, pinned where the side of the car had been crushed in. Glass was all over the front seat, the floor. His head may have bashed the windshield and broken it. He was lucky to be alive.

"Take it easy, Tony," I shouted. "They're gonna get you out!"

His tear-filled eyes locked on mine, and I can't say he knew, or cared, who I was.

"My fucking leg" was all he said during the next twenty minutes, as a rescue crew worked to dislodge him from the mangled metal. By the time the cops got around to interviewing witnesses, those who'd actually seen the accident were long gone. Only some morbid late-comers remained. All I could provide was an ID on the injured driver.

Jack Early was gone too, off prepping an exclusive for the bulldog edition of the *Call-Bulletin*. His prints, sensational for sure, were probably dry by the time the ambulance hauled off what was left of Tony Bernal.

4

Ida could see I was miserable when I finally dragged myself to the breakfast table, twenty minutes later than usual. None of the parlor tricks I'd lately been using to tame a guilty conscience had held up during the night. A shave and shower had only freshened my exterior.

"What's wrong?" Ida asked, deftly pouring me a cup of coffee while she fed the baby, writhing around in his high chair.

"Friend of mine got in a car accident last night," I muttered. "On his way to pick me up."

"Is he all right?"

"Don't know. He looked awful bad when they took him away."

"You *saw* it?"

"Happened just a couple of blocks from the office."

Ida considered the grid. Calculating how close this tragedy had come to disrupting her own world. I understood her mental mechanisms all too readily and well. The operating manual wasn't complicated.

"You could have been *killed*," she said suddenly. She clutched her baby's fragile forearm when she said it. "Another few minutes and *you'd* have been in that car!"

There was nothing to be gained by pointing out the selfishness of such a response, or its absurdity. No percentage sparring with the spouse at the top of the morning, so I settled for "Yeah, I'm damn lucky. I'd have missed your coffee."

She gave a smile. My friend's mishap had already vanished from her mind.

Part of my recovery regimen was to go easier on my wife. Truth be told, she was a more pleasant person now that she had a child. If she learned to keep the claws sheathed, we might make a go of our tentative setup. Way I figured it, if I could learn to extract amusement from everyday calamities, I could train myself not to see the face of the baby's actual father every time I looked at him. *Don't take it out on the kid*, I reminded myself. *It wasn't his choice to be here.*

"I saw Manny Gold last night after the fights," I mentioned. "He wants us to come over some evening for dinner. The three of us."

"How's Peggy?" she chirped, then, "did you want eggs or something?"

"Sure. And maybe some toast." I topped off my coffee while she clattered around the kitchen. "He said that Peggy's anxious to see the k— Vince. How old is their boy now? I didn't even ask Manny about him. I couldn't remember his name."

"Daniel," Ida called from the other room, without a pause. I heard her crack a couple of eggs into a skillet. "He must be eight or nine now." Stepping into the doorway that separated the breakfast nook from the kitchen, she smiled slyly. "Remember what he gave us for a wedding present?"

"Oh, Jesus." I laughed. "Did he go on enough about it?" Manny had bestowed a stock certificate purported to represent preferred shares in some silver mine in the far reaches of Stanislaus County. He silenced our reception with an oration about letting us in on a once-in-a-lifetime opportunity and how we'd never have to worry about putting our kids through college—

"—thanks to this little piece of paper," Ida proclaimed, waving the spatula in a parody of Manny. She'd been reading my mind.

"Do we still have that thing?" I asked, bemused as she puffed her cheeks to Manny-sized proportions.

"I stashed it away," she sighed, letting out her breath. "Someplace. Think it's really worth anything?"

I made a sour face. "Would Manny Gold be hawking personalized pens if he'd tapped a silver lode?"

The faint ember of hope in her eyes expired. She returned to the stove. "Up or over on the eggs?"

"Up's good." Sound of the toaster being pushed down.

I sipped more coffee as the kid gleefully rubbed a fistful of food into his bib. It occurred to me that I'd neglected to slip my new *Monarch of the Dailies* pocket protector into that morning's fresh shirt.

On the way out, I picked the morning *Inquirer* off the stoop, pried loose Sports, and left the rest inside the door for Ida. Since I'd filed it so late yesterday, Fuzzy hadn't tampered with it much.

THROUGH THE ROPES
By Billy Nichols

"What's the worst decision you ever saw?"

I get asked that regularly, on the phone or in the circuit. Runs a close second to "Who's the best fighter ever, pound for pound?" That one's easy: Joe Louis—I don't think twice. The reason I go with Louis is that he took care of business early and efficiently. If a fighter wants a place in the annals of the all-time greats, he's got to settle matters himself. Leave it in the hands of judges, you're asking for trouble.

Worst decision? Saw it early in my career. A rising welterweight named Sammy Lawless boxed a 10-round main event at Oakland Auditorium against Bud Silva, a journeyman. Silva pursued methodically, once in a while landing a shot to the body. For the most part, Lawless boxed circles around his befuddled opponent, who didn't know whether to fish or wind a wristwatch. By the seventh, I didn't just have Lawless ahead on points—I had him ready to take on welter boss Jimmy McLarnin.

But all three judges scored the fight for Silva. Not even close. Lawless bawled in his dressing room, door closed to the press. I buttonholed every judge, and each issued straight-faced justifications, from "Silva pressed the fight" to "He did better work inside" to the inconceivable "Lawless ran all night." It was tough to bat out a story, pondering how experienced arbiters could score the bout so differently from what I'd witnessed. Still a squirt in this dodge, I refrained from calling them the Three Blind Mice in print.

Over the following months, I got educated. One judge, I learned, had a long-standing grudge against Lawless's manager, going all the way back to their fighting days. Another "objective" scorer was in the pocket of the auditorium's new promoter, who had no intention of paying Lawless his worth as

23

a headliner. The third guy *was* blind, as he proved years later by walking in front of a streetcar. Lawless, thoroughly dejected, took his consummate boxing skills and drifted south. Last seen, he was working oil rigs off the coast.

None of the judges ever fessed up to robbing Lawless, no matter how I ribbed them over the years. So adamantly did they defend their scoring, I came to understand that they actually *did* see a different bout that night.

Seeing, you may have heard, *is* believing. The problem is that everybody, for various reasons, has their own biased view. Truth, like beauty, is strictly in the eye of the beholder.

You might conclude from what I'm saying that fights are sometimes fixed. I'd contend that your perspective is far too narrow.

Life is fixed.

That's why I always offer simple advice to any amateur turning pro: Kid, don't leave it up to judges. Get yourself a knockout punch.

* * *

"Interesting column this morning," sports editor Fuzzy Reasnor told me, standing next to my desk, the original copyedited scroll dangling from his hands. "Here—I thought you might want to save it for posterity." He draped it over the chaos of my desktop.

Fuzzy's blunt and hasty editor's marks only went halfway down the sheet.

"I'm probably gonna catch hell for running it," he said. "But I got caught there. Didn't know what the hell to do with it. You shifted gears on me. Thought you were touting the Gloves or something."

"Inspiration struck."

Fuzzy wanted to prop half his ass on the desk, to assume the proper stance for one of his heart-to-hearts. No space was available. He elected not to shift any of the precarious piles.

"Last time I looked you were on top of the world," Reasnor elaborated. "Didn't you just get a bump? Pretty healthy one, I heard. So why bite the hand that feeds you? You know the score, I know the score— but what's the point of *this*?" He gave my latest effort a disdainful backhand.

I didn't bother arguing. Instead, my pencil tapped out a nervous beat on a pile of papers.

"And another thing—we don't need people thinking we're doing political editorials in the sports pages."

My expression was genuinely puzzled: "What the hell's that supposed to mean?"

"All this confusion with the election? They might think you're insinuating something about corruption in the electoral process."

"Oh, for chrissakes." I threw down the pencil. The polls had closed two days earlier, but the *Inquirer*, cautious for once, hadn't jumped the gun and proclaimed a winner. Tom Dewey had entered the ring looking like a shoo-in, but Truman rallied late. The battle for the White House was a dead heat, still too close to call.

"That column has nothing to do with the goddamn election," I scoffed.

"'*Life* is fixed,'" Reasnor quoted, his finger tracing the words on the sheet. "Maybe you just got carried away. I could give a shit. So get with it—sports reassures people. You want to grouse about the state of the world, go write a book. You want to make a confession, take it to your priest. Here, you write about boxing. It's what people want, it's what they expect, it's what you do best. Why bite the hand that feeds you? Shitcan the philosophizing and give me some fight dope, okay?"

I cabbed it from the office to S.F. General around 3 P.M., soon as I got word that Tony was out of surgery and in the Critical Care ward. I'd have been wiser to keep my nose to the grindstone.

"This is all *your* fault," Tony's wife hissed as I stepped hesitantly through the curtains and joined the Bernal family's bedside vigil. "If he'd drove home regular instead of chauffering you all over town this never would have happened."

She was a wisp, a bread stick in a dowdy housecoat, her face pretty but worn. A purple wool scarf hid a tangle of unbrushed dark hair. Her eyes gleamed agate-hard. She contemptuously slung my bouquet and Whitman's Sampler offering into the arms of one of her three silent sons.

Tony lay corpse-still beneath the antiseptic linens, artfully arranged to cover everything but one gruesomely mummified leg, elevated by a

Rube Goldberg confusion of pulleys. "What are you going to do for him now?" Mrs. Bernal said. "Huh? Some tickets to the fights gonna fix it so he can walk again? Why don't you come push his wheelchair around—maybe that'd even things up."

My head felt like it was being held over a boiling kettle. On the other side of the bed, Tony's eldest boy—my big fan, whose name I couldn't recall at the moment—was chewing his lips like luncheon meat. He couldn't look at me or his mother, so he stared, dead-eyed, at the pasty face of his father, sunk into the starchy pillows. Me and the kid both worried the brims of our doffed hats.

Suddenly the boy's eyes came awake. "Mama," he whispered urgently, nodding toward his old man.

Tony's parched lips moved, his fingers gripped the sheets. Mrs. Bernal practically threw herself on the bed, pressing her face close to her husband's. The brood drew closer. I discreetly backed away.

"What did he say?" one boy asked his mother.

"Could you hear that?" asked another.

"No," she said, withdrawing. "He's too weak."

"He said, 'Shut the hell up,'" offered Nate, whose name resurfaced right then. Nate's mother threw him a wicked look and pantomimed a backhand.

"Well, that's what he said," Nate insisted, as a dutiful reporter would.

Stepping through the curtains I sucked in a few drafts of hospital air, that wretched mix of disinfectant and distress. The ward was a vast open space under a high ceiling. Oversized lamps hung from the center beam. Farther below, a grid of steel rods and drab green drapes divided the collected misery into separate chambers. Plenty of them contained stories worse than Tony's, I reassured myself.

Heavy footsteps turned my attention around.

"Hey, *Mr. Boxing*—what are you doing here?"

Woody Montague extended his hand, which I eagerly shook. He was a former colleague, a first-rate cityside reporter. The byline *By Woodrow Montague* ensured that you were about to read the most diligently researched journalism, not just in the *Inquirer*, but in all of San Francisco. He looked exactly as I'd last seen him: long-limbed as a birch tree, in the same nondescript gray suit and tie he wryly described as his "disguise." His lengthy mug sported heavy black horn-rims and was topped by a crew cut so severe you could see his scalp. Woody reminded me of a pale, professorial jazz musician, hopeless rube amid a quartet of ebon hepcats. Until he showed his stuff. Woody's "stuff" was his investigative skill. The stories may not have been ornamental, but you could build houses on his facts.

"Woodrow! It's been years," I said, grateful for the camaraderie. Casting a glance at the hushed environs, I added, "Nothing wrong, I hope."

"I came to see Tony Bernal," he said.

I hooked a thumb at the space I'd just vacated. "I didn't know you were friends."

"We're not. I'm working a case involving the Major Liquor Company. I heard Mr. Bernal was in an accident last night that involved one of their trucks."

"Yeah, I was there."

Montague pushed the bulky specs up his nose and eyed me eagerly: "You were a witness?"

"Not exactly. I got there a few minutes after it happened. Why do you say 'working a case'? You're not a lawyer now? Please, don't tell me that."

"Well, I passed the bar—give me some credit. But mainly I'm an investigator. Private. Still digging out the truth."

Montague made his reputation with a series of *Inquirer* features exposing fiscal chicanery in a slew of civic building contracts. When he took on the military for the same type of schemes, he had top brass breathing down Hearst's neck. But he'd left the paper unexpectedly two years back. I was shocked his byline didn't immediately turn up in a rival sheet. I figured he'd gone big-time, maybe New York or Chicago.

"You were the best reporter we had," I said. "The paper hated to see you go."

His squint of skepticism suggested a long, involved story.

"I stopped by to offer some advice to these people," he said. "Based on my familiarity with Virgil Dardi."

Dardi owned the Major Liquor Company. It'd been rumored for years that he was mobbed-up. I knew he was good for a quarter page in the ring weeklies, but other than that my file on the man was empty.

"What's the family likely to face?"

"The worst. Especially if they try to file a lawsuit. Dardi's arrogant. Doesn't even carry insurance, if you can believe it. He feels protected already, if you get my drift."

"You mean by Samish? Or *the* boys?"

"There's a difference?"

5

Artie Samish, the big man himself, attended the fights Friday night, basking in a ringside pew at the Civic beside attorney J. W. "Jake" Ehrlich. Local business must have dislodged Samish from his Sacramento roost. Bloated by all the juice he'd absorbed over the years, Artie's belly strained against the vast canopy of his houndstooth trousers. Arms were nonchalantly folded over the mountainous girth. He gave a hearty chortle as Ehrlich whispered in his ear. Stanton Delaplane of the *Chronicle* had recently described Samish as a "Sydney Greenstreet character," suggesting a nefarious nature cloaked in a deferential demeanor. To me, "The Secret Boss of California" resembled a well-fed, florid tavern keeper, a cheerful dispenser of simple truths and heavy pours.

It was the right image for a guy who'd distilled his political punch through booze. The California State Brewers Association was the first commercial group Samish repped as a lobbyist, back in 1935. The state's beer tax hadn't increased since Samish set up shop near the Capitol. He fought to hold alcohol content to 3.2 percent. It meant lousy beer—but beer that could be sold anywhere, not just saloons. He made brewers a fortune. He then wrote and introduced new taxation laws that picked the pockets of out-of-state beer makers, creating a virtual monopoly for his California clients.

That was only the start. Samish became a political boss without a party. He did it by forming trade associations—labor, liquor, railroads, trucking, racetracks, stagehands, child care, you name it. These groups then hired Samish as their agent in Sacramento. And since each member of his many affiliated associations counted as a vote, Samish was soon using a simple strategy of "select and elect" to handpick candidates around the state and turn out the vote for them. That was how Samish, like me a guy without benefit of high school diploma, created his own gestapo in the state legislature.

Before claiming my regular perch on press row I detoured over to

Jake Ehrlich. He'd been a fixture at the fights for years. "Master, good to see you," I said.

"Master" was the barrister's moniker, earned through a slew of highly publicized courtroom victories. The owner of San Francisco's highest profile rose to shake hands. Although he'd moved to the city as a youth, Ehrlich retained impeccable manners learned from a family of Confederate plantation owners.

"*Mr. Boxing*," Jake obliged.

His French cuffs were starched and snowy, festooned with chunks of gold. Jake's trademark was his ever-crisp sartorial splendor. Collar, cuffs, and display handkerchief always blade-sharp and blazing white. Physically, he was Samish's opposite: lean and lightweight, with shrewd, reptilian eyes peering past a pronounced beak. His deceptive, sleepy-lidded gaze had mesmerized countless judges and juries.

"Billy, you must know Arthur Samish," Jake said, gesturing to his seat mate.

"Only by reputation." I gripped the big man's mitt.

"Arthur, meet Billy Nichols, our finest fight writer."

"Don't believe everything you hear about me," Samish said. "Only what I tell you. *Ha!* Just kidding. Been reading your stuff for years. I go way back with the fights in this town, believe me. I remember when Jack Johnson came out to fight Al Kaufman. I was in Fremont Grammar School. And Johnson drove past every day with that big flashy convertible he had and every once in a while he'd stop and talk to us kids in the school yard. What a dude! The fur hats and the fancy jewelry? Brother, did he make an impression on me!"

It's hard not to get full of yourself when you're greased by "The Man Who Gets Things Done." I suppressed a grin. "You ever box?" I asked Samish.

"I wouldn't call it boxing. But I sure as hell fought, especially selling papers. Your *Inquirer*, in fact. When I lived with my mother, God rest her soul, I used to get up every Sunday morning at three and take a car from Clement down to the Ferry Building. I had this apple box with wheels and I'd pull it up to the *Inquirer* building and load it with papers. Then I'd haul the whole thing back home and sell papers to my neighbors. Sometimes I had to slug it out with the other newsies. They'd try to steal my papers, or muscle me off the block."

"How old were you?"

"I was maybe nine. Yeah, about that. We'd moved out there after the fire. I needed to make a couple of bucks to help out my ma. Henrietta, that was her name, God love her. Raised me by herself after my father walked out. I'm Arthur *H.* Samish, you know—I took the H for her. Changed my middle name to Henrietta and that's the God's honest truth."

"You should write a book," I told him. Nothing strokes another human like being told he should write a book.

"Someday I will, and then everybody will know where the bodies are buried. But I can't write. I can talk. Maybe I'll get one of you pencil pushers to write it out for me. I get on great with you newspaper guys. I'd be nowhere without the papers."

I couldn't help but notice the glittery group holding court in the second row. A preening, swarthy shrimp in an exceptional blue chalk-striped suit surrounded by a gaggle of dolled-up dames. I pegged him for a foreigner off the bat, with the wavy black locks brilliantined in place and the bushy ridge of eyebrow. The women were draped in furs and dripping ice; must have cleaned out some swank shops on Union Square. On *his* bankroll, judging by how they fawned over the squirt.

Ehrlich caught me staring. "That's Mohammad Reza Pahlavi—the shah of Iran," he said. "Soaking up a little local color. Leaving a little dough behind."

I nodded, like I knew who the dignitary was. I couldn't point to Iran on a map if you spotted me five continents. "Is the harem on staff," I asked, "or by the hour?"

Samish laughed and gave my thigh a slap with his meaty right hand. "Let me tell you this, my friend," he confided. "If I've got one skill: it's that I know whether a man wants potatoes, money, or a girl." He nodded toward the royal personage. "And that boy's got no shortage of spuds or simoleons."

Ehrlich snickered. It was abbreviated; he'd noticed something on the far side of the ring. I followed his gaze.

"This is something new," the solicitor declared. "I've never seen *him* at the fights before."

Across the canvas I spied a nonregular floating in the ringside stream, a guy unremarkable except for the awkwardness with which he, and a couple of trailing toadies, threaded warily through the initiated. I figured the newcomer hailed from Jake's turf down at the Hall of Justice.

"William Corey." Ehrlich ID'd him. "The deputy DA. Way out of his element."

"Doing a little campaigning?" I suggested, trying to trade badinage the big boys would appreciate.

"What's he got to run for?" Ehrlich said. "Not Brown's job. Certainly not a judgeship. Arthur, you see this?"

Samish noted the officious interloper and shrugged. Corey apparently rated no estimation.

"You ever go against him in court?" I asked Ehrlich. Jake liked to equate his legal bouts with pugilism. He'd boxed professionally back in the twenties to put himself through law school.

The attorney's thin lips spread into a cruel smile. "He hasn't had the privilege. I'd embarrass him. Corey's strictly a meat-grinder. No panache."

We palavered several more minutes. Briefly, I entertained the notion that my balls were big enough to quiz Samish about Virgil Dardi. Impress Woody Montague by gleaning some inside dope. But when the appropriate conversational lull came, Dardi's name stayed in my mouth. *Not my can of worms*, I told myself.

Just then a group of photographers swarmed us like bees. Ehrlich subtly directed them, with a finesse DeMille would have envied. Jake knew how to work the papers. He wasn't only the city's best barrister, he was its savviest press agent as well. In seconds he'd shaped up five jostling rivals into a orderly phalanx poised to document the shah's night out.

"Hey, boys—up here!" came a terse command.

All eyes swerved up to the ring, where Jack Early had staked out his own angle. The magnesium burst caught everyone before they could don their official public faces. "That's the winner!" Early cackled, leaving his competitors to Ehrlich's direction.

"Who was that guy?" Jake asked me after the fusillade of flashbulbs finally dimmed.

"Jack Early, *Call-Bulletin*," I said.

Ehrlich consulted a slip of paper withdrawn from his coat pocket. "He wasn't even on my list. That guy's pretty good."

It wasn't until just before the main event that the "meat-grinder" approached me at ringside. He attempted to sidle, but was bouncing too insistently on the balls of his feet. His hands dangled too casually in his pockets, rattling loose change. He'd never been one of the boys, never would be.

"Billy Nichols, right?"

The glare of ring lights exposed a grotesquely forced smile. "Deputy District Attorney William Corey. I'm a big fan of yours."

If trying to sell this bald-faced lie was an example of his persuasive skills, it was a miracle he ever got a conviction. We shook hands and I grew even less impressed. Disdain wafted from him.

"Good to meet you," I deadpanned. "Funny I haven't seen you around before. Big fan and all."

"I don't get out from under the work often enough. Reading your accounts in the paper, though, I'd swear I was right there."

"Who do you like in the main event?" I eased shut the program in which I'd been keeping score, preventing him from a quick study.

"Too close to call in my book," he improvised. His book was out of date; Moore would take it within five.

"I noticed you speaking before with Jake Ehrlich," he went on. "You friends?"

"I've known Jake a few years," I replied, newsman's antennae rising. "I don't suppose *you're* pals," I couldn't resist adding. When it came to murder cases, Erlich had nearly an undefeated record against the DA's office. The trials he lost were unwinnable; Jake was paid to downgrade murder to manslaughter, which he managed routinely. If you shot somebody in cold blood within the City and County of San Francisco, you needed to remember only two words: Get Jake.

"Discussing the Sanders case by any chance?"

Now my antennae were fully extended and tingling.

"You visited the County Jail the other day," Corey said, like he was talking about the weather. "Paid a call on Burney Sanders, I've been told."

I swiveled in my seat and gave him a lengthy reappraisal. "So I did."

"What did you talk about, if you don't mind my asking?" Corey toyed with coins in his pocket, right next to my ear. I wanted to stand, but he was crowding me.

"I'm not sure I get you," I said. "What difference does it make?"

"In my experience," he said, hunkering down slightly and dropping all trace of the casual, "prisoners are paid visits by lawyers, family, and sympathetic friends. In preparing the People's case I noted that some of the key evidence tying Sanders to the victim was provided to the police by one Billy Nichols. Your calling on him therefore strikes me as a trifle odd."

"You too?" My carefree tone didn't even convince me.

The crowd noise perked up as the fighters entered the arena and headed toward the ring. Corey edged in closer, resting a hand on the back of my chair.

"I may have to call you as a material witness," he said. "I'd like to avoid any surprises gumming up the works."

"Such as?"

"Such as Jake Ehrlich, for one."

The deputy DA was apparently scared shitless of the Master's litigating prowess.

I'd laughed when Burney begged me to Get Jake, and I scoffed again at Corey's suppositions. "Counselor," I said, turning away, "I think Mr. Ehrlich's frying bigger fish."

"I fry the fish," Corey stated. "*He* throws them back. And I'd hate to see this matter treated inappropriately in the Sports section," he continued. "It's not a pretty situation, and it reflects poorly on the sport. One of your own being a murderer, I mean. It hardly casts boxing in a glowing light."

"You got all this from me saying 'What's new' to Jake?"

"If you were to be summoned as a prosecution witness I don't imagine you'd relish the prospect of being cross-examined by Mr. Ehrlich."

"If you've got a solid case against Sanders I don't imagine you'd care one way or the other," I said. Too rash. My instant antipathy had gotten the better of me.

"Sanders is guilty," he said. "And I'm not going to have any trouble proving it."

I rolled a sheet into the Royal and banged keys. I tried to type his words as cleanly as possible, since I knew he'd lean in for a look.

"I can quote you on that, right?" I asked, even though I had no intention of printing anything of the sort. I got no answer. The combatants were now milling at center ring and the bell was clanging the crowd to attention.

"Pleasure to meet you, Mr. Nichols," said the deputy DA before moving back to his seat.

"Delighted," I responded, just as sincerely.

6

THROUGH THE ROPES
By Billy Nichols

Inside or outside the ring, I appreciate watching a master at work. I've just seen a battler worthy of the mantle, and his name is Jake Ehrlich. He's a lawyer, but don't hold it against him.

Yesterday Ehrlich represented Oakland impresario Leo Leavitt, a brash young man who calls himself "Leo the Lion." His opponents call him "Leo the Lyin'." His rivals claim Leavitt wants to monopolize Bay Area fight cards. His strategy, they contend, involves acting as both promoter and manager—a double-dip forbidden by regulatory commissions everywhere.

Leavitt's competitors spread word that his show last year headlining Cleveland's Eddie Simms against hometown hero Phainting Phil Brubaker was maybe fixed. Leo, it was suggested, was slipping Simms 20 percent of the gate and a $750 blowback to tank the fight, so as to boost his boy Brubaker's flagging fortunes.

Hep to all the hullabaloo, Jake Ehrlich was ringside that night, rubbing shoulders with former Notre Dame gridiron great Slip Madigan. The main event was a bust, devoid of any intentions, bad or otherwise. The ref, Honest Billy Burke, dogged by the crowd's insistent catcalls, waved the whole thing off in the seventh round. It was declared "No Contest" and the purses withheld.

As the stink enveloped Leavitt, he decided to Get Jake.

At yesterday's State Athletic Commission hearing inside the Palace Hotel, Ehrlich offered a pugnacious defense of Leo the

37

Lion—tossing legalese around the way Sugar Ray Robinson throws combinations. For almost an hour, Jake prowled the hardwood like it was his personal canvas, literally shadow boxing as he recounted the history of pugilism, from Julius Caesar to Cesar Brion.

At one point he displayed blown-up photos of sore and swollen hands: "What was he hitting if not Simms?" Ehrlich shouted. "The ring posts?"

So thoroughly was the audience transfixed, nobody asked for proof that those abused appendages actually belonged to Phainting Phil Brubaker.

Jake served Sophocles and Shakespeare to mugs who could barely digest Mother Goose. By the time he was done, local scribes were boosting him as the next boxing commissioner.

"That would be *very* bad matchmaking," Ehrlich assessed.

That write-up, from 1946, earned me a place at the rail next to the Master whenever we alighted in the same watering hole. But that's all it earned, I assumed. The notion of discount counsel being part of the deal never occurred to me.

Jake had long since shaken off leeches who wanted his services on the cuff. Part of his legend was a yellow stripe he'd painted across his desk. Once his patience for the pro bono was exhausted, Jake would simply start tapping the enameled equator. Time for the prospect to "lay it on the line" or drift.

How would Jake have reacted Friday night if I'd entered a plea on Burney Sanders's behalf? Would I have rated his indulgence?

I wasn't eager to find out. Hell, I was afraid Sanders might scare up sufficient scratch to Get Jake. The notion of Ehrlich sinking his hooks into the case frightened me as much as it did Deputy DA Corey. Jake would debunk the "evidence" against Sanders before the jury even got their asses comfortably arranged. I wanted no part of the dandified and deadly celebrity in this morning's paper, the one staring sternly into Jack Early's lens.

Morning editions of the *Call-Bulletin* gave Early's fight-night photo three-column play in News. It was a hell of a halftone. The photographer's sneaky backdoor approach caught the calculation in Ehrlich's eyes. Likewise, he caught Artie's abundant effluence before he could suck it in. The poodles packed around the Persian playboy showed the stony stares of working girls waiting to be booked. The surreptitious camera angle, the starkness of the flash, the subjects' captured candor—a vaguely sinister light suffused the proceedings. I'm glad the *Call* cropped me out. By contrast, the *Inquirer*'s version was benign: a standard, eye-level souvenir drawn from an evening among the sporting elite, including yours truly.

The camera doesn't lie, they say—but it *can* editorialize.

The phone rang, sparing me any more dire brooding.

"Sports," I spat.

"I wish to speak with Billy Nichols, the writer." A female voice, not a regular.

"This is Nichols."

"Mr. Nichols, what time do you normally leave work?"

"That depends. Who wants to know?"

"Just listen to me. I want you to board the first outbound streetcar to leave the Third and Market stop after five P.M. today. Is that clear?"

Her tone was curt and clipped. I'd heard it before, somewhere. "What the hell are you talking about?" I protested, buying time while I tried to match a face to the demanding voice.

"I don't like talking on the phone, Mr. Nichols. Board that car. I'll find you. We'll talk then."

"Virginia?" I inquired weakly.

The line was already dead.

Short-stepping among jostling commuters boarding the coach at Third and Market, I figured she'd selected this hour for a reason. Anonymity and safety in numbers, most likely. My watch showed 5:06 P.M. I scanned the throng for the delicate, angular features and tousle of blond hair that were my only recollections of Burney Sanders's secretary. That and the legs. More than nice, if memory served.

Fortunately, the car wasn't sardine-tight. Earlier that year the city had torn out the tracks closest to the curbs, making room for a new fleet of trackless trolleys on the boulevard. The green-and-white vehicles, although still tethered to overhead electrical lines, ran on rubber, not metal, wheels. They also hauled more passengers than the old White Fronts, which now seemed sadly antiquated compared with their gleaming new counterparts.

As we shoved off from Third with a shudder, I quit trying to locate my mystery woman and plunked down onto a rock-hard wooden-slat seat, hoarding more room than was polite. She'd tag me first, anyway. My mug was plastered daily in the paper, the sketch atop my column, "Through the Ropes," being a good-enough likeness to spur a few glad-hands from strangers every day.

She still hadn't shown herself by the time we reached Fifth. A flood of citizens spilled across Market from the J C Penney Building, swamping the car stop. I recalled something about a dedication that day: Louis Lurie, our town's top property-holder and Penney's landlord, had installed escalators in the booming department store. Hundreds of shoppers and gawkers had turned out for the ribbon-cutting and a free ride on the electric stairway.

Scuttling ahead of the fresh wave of passengers was a ferret-faced teenager, further punished by a rash of rampant acne. He deposited himself next to me, oozing adolescent orneriness. So much for saving Virginia some room.

"Give a girl a seat?" came the request from above.

The sullen youth glared up at Virginia Wagner. Her blond waves were gone; she'd either ditched the peroxide or done a dye job. A black embroidered toque topped cinnamon tresses, and she sported black sunglasses. All I recognized was the small scarlet pout and the curt chirp in her voice: Betty without the Boop.

"I was here first," the kid groused.

"Take a hike, Junior," she instructed.

Okay—Betty Boop by way of Jimmy Cagney. When the kid stood up, trying to muster some menace into his scrawny frame, she brushed him off with, "Learn some manners on the way."

She settled in and situated the folds of her dark wool cape. I said, "Virginia Wagner," like a student proudly proclaiming the answer to the big test question. I offered a smile and a handshake. She ignored both, gloved fingers clutching the purse in her lap, gaze fixed dead ahead.

"Mr. Nichols," she whispered, "do you think it's safe for me to come back to the city?"

Her profile was outlined against the weaving, business-suited bodies, its porcelain prettiness strained and drawn. Along the curve of her throat I noted rapid pulsing. My diagnosis: a case of the galloping heebie-jeebies. I broke off my study, squinting through the grimy window as the Rainier Ale billboard drifted by.

"If you're afraid of ending up like Claire," I said, "all I can tell you is that Sanders is behind bars. And it's doubtful he's getting out any time soon."

"If he thinks I betrayed him by stealing those things from his office . . ." She broke off the thought, lurching against me slightly as the car resumed its westward haul. "You're right—I don't want to end up like Claire."

"I tried like hell to reach you after she died," I said. "I assumed you were the one who . . . lifted that stuff off Burney. Your briefcase was at Claire's house. I thought Burney might have . . . done something to you, too. How 'bout filling in the gaps?"

She turned my way, her eyes barely visible behind the black lenses. Her voice dropped lower, dead serious: "All I want, Mr. Nichols, is to get on with my life. You're in this mess even more deeply than me, yet you seem to be suffering no ill effects. I, on the other hand, don't have a job anymore. I haven't set foot in my own apartment in over two months. I can't sleep at night. I don't eat in restaurants. I don't go to shows. I don't see the few friends I have. I'm sick of being scared. All I want is for you to tell me that Sanders has no chance of beating this rap. Tell me he's going to prison. Tell me I can walk the streets again without worrying about one of his goons blowing my head off."

Virginia Wagner required reassurance. Telling her I'd seen Burney in the jailhouse—or worse, that he'd begged me to find her—was the last thing she needed to hear. She wouldn't understand it. Hell, *I* didn't understand it. Better to reveal that the deputy DA was dead-set on ramming her former boss into a prison cell. But she might simply take that happy news and bolt, never to be seen again. For some reason, I didn't want that. My mind weighed the options while the streetcar ground to a halt in front of the Orpheum Theater.

"What do you know about Dexter Threllkyl?" I asked her.

She blanched. Like I'd asked what she knew about enemas. Several hot seconds passed. Knees, elbows, hats, shoving on and off the coach at the bustling Hyde and Market intersection.

She turned toward me once more. A shaft of late-day sunlight fell across her face, almost revealing eyes behind the opaque cheaters. "What do *you* know about him?" she countered.

"Not much. He's dead. That's what I know."

This was breaking news. She hastily snapped open her purse and began rummaging inside. Amid the typically feminine clutter, jutting up as delicately as a headstone among daisies, was the butt end of an automatic pistol.

"Goddamn it," she groaned.

"Whatr'ya looking for?"

"A scrap of paper."

I pulled the slim, spiral-bound reporter's notebook from inside my jacket.

"And a pen," she added mildly, snapping shut the purse.

I withdrew a pencil from Manny's pocket protector. His gift was now a mainstay of the wardrobe. Virginia flipped open the pad, found a blank page, and scrawled an address. A stout businessman, claiming an ample portion of the aisle, observed our interaction, bemused.

"My apartment," she explained, returning the pad and pencil and hoisting herself upright. "Come tonight. After nine. I've got things to show you."

She edged past Mr. Portly, who watched her thread into the line of passengers exiting via the rear steps. His enormous untrimmed eyebrows lifted in an appreciative manner as he sank down beside me.

"Smooth work," Portly said. "Quite impressive."

Lying to Ida required guile. Her internal Fib-O-Meter was finely tuned; she could catch the scent of fish in the most innocent exchange. Excuses such as *Still a few things to finish up at the office* or *I've got to stop by the gym,* offered at the wrong moment, could spark suspicion. Proper bait was needed if she was to take the hook.

I used Ehrlich.

"Sorry I can't make it home for dinner, hon," I told my wife from the pay phone outside Jimmy Ryan's Daily Double. "Jake Ehrlich wants to talk about a case he's working on. Says he needs some background dope."

"He's taking you to dinner?" she gushed. "I could be ready in about an hour."

She bit hard, as I'd figured. Big-shot celebrities had that effect on her.

"It's just drinks. One of his Tenderloin dives. But he can't get away until nine. I'm gonna hafta kill time till then."

I could sense her disappointment across the wire. Once that faded she'd get back on the horn, bragging to her sisters about my confab with the Master. I didn't worry about being found out. Ida and her kin had as much chance of crossing paths with Ehrlich as I did of winning a Pulitzer.

I detoured into the Royal Athletic Club on my way to dinner. Golden Gloves season had begun: The place was filled with smooth-skinned fledglings, muscles unformed, movements tentative. The professionals had taken a powder. Maybe they didn't want to be reminded of lost innocence, or how eager they'd once been to prove themselves.

Managers and trainers outnumbered the kids. Fathers, uncles, brothers—amateurs all—birddogged the unblemished tyros, torn between guarding them and shoving them from the nest into the pit. Plenty of the regulars prowled around, looking to scoop up any prospect that flashed instinctive footwork or a meaningful jab.

I watched the action beside Dewey Thomas, who ran the place. A battered brown felt hat covered his silver mane. He wore his usual outfit, windbreaker over a cardigan, and his hangdog expression never changed.

"Any standouts?" I asked.

"Nobody's shown anything yet. But if those clowns over there keep leaning on the apron, they'll get a nice surprise."

Dewey hated for anybody to sit or lean at the foot of the ropes, on the edge of the canvas. So he ran a wire outside the ring, barely visible. From his office he could throw a switch and shoot juice through the wire. Shocked the shit out of people. Dewey laughed like hell. And Dempsey, he loved it. Whenever he came through town Jack spent an hour or two in Dewey's office, giving guys the juice. Once everybody'd wised up, Dewey had to pay guys to take a jolt, just so the champ could leave happy, tears of laughter staining his face.

"Seen Larry Daws lately?" I asked, just making conversation. That's right, just making conversation.

"I'd be happy if I never saw that bastard again," Dewey said. "I got him a good match with Whitlock after Burney went down, with a fair purse, but he wouldn't take it. Same old shit. Ask me, he's done. Damn shame. Remember when he turned pro? Holy fuck, he was *mean*."

I'd seen Daws from his start in the Golden Gloves. After taking a few shots to the head, he went wild and attacked his opponent with berserk ferocity. The ref had to pull him off. I'll never forget how red his face flushed or the crazy look in his eyes. The problem with Daws was that he refused to get in the ring with colored fighters. Claimed they fought dirty, which couldn't have been further from the truth. It was Daws who was colored: *yellow*. Just the type of no-count loser to betray a guy who'd been getting him fights, and piecework, for years.

"Daws is the prosecution's big witness against Sanders, you know," I said. Just to see what Dew would say.

"Do me a favor. Tell me nothing. That whole story breaks my heart, guy like Hack losing his wife that way. But you know and I know that if Daws and Burney was in it together, it was Daws who did the dirty work. Other way round makes no sense. Don't you think?"

"Sorry I brought it up, Dew."

* * *

The Pine Grove Apartments was seven stories of Deco stucco situated between Franklin and Gough, in not-quite-Pacific Heights. A short-enough walk from Polk Street to savor the pleasant effects of a light supper at Maye's Oyster House and a couple of cocktails at Jimmy Ryan's Daily Double. A woman on her way out held the heavy, wrought-iron door for me, offering a trusting smile. The lobby had tall mirrors on both sides, creating the illusion of expansiveness. This neighborhood had enjoyed a building boom just before the Crash. The high ceiling was a sultan's dream of elaborate gilt filigree, the lush carpet was alive with Byzantine patterns. But the place wasn't big or swanky enough to rate a doorman. Probably one reason Virginia Wagner had cleared out.

No elevator operator, either. I worked the cage myself and ascended to the fifth floor. The ride was brief, affording no chance to second-guess what I was getting into. The corridor, barely illuminated by ceramic sconces, curved into darkness at either end. I went right, following the numbers. Panels on each door featured a variety of machine-tooled nature scenes: a moose here, a crane there. The kind of extra adornment they don't bother with anymore. At the end of the hallway, I rapped twice on a horse decorating the door of apartment 506.

"Who is it?" came her distinctive voice, muffled behind the door.

"Nichols."

"Anybody follow you?" she asked.

"All by myself," I assured her, looking around.

Stepping inside, I immediately noticed the books. Piled along the baseboards, the teetering stacks resembled a city skyline erected precariously of various-sized volumes.

She closed the door, after taking a peek down the corridor for herself. Tapping on a central panel in the door, she drew attention to its hinges. "This used to open," she explained. "Like in a speakeasy. You could see who was at the door. Isn't that neat?"

"They knew how to build 'em," I said. "Least they used to."

"Someone told me a tenant got shot when he looked out, and after that they nailed them shut. What a shame."

"City's not like it used to be, that's for sure."

Faint strains of a clarinet curlicued through the apartment. Following her down a short hallway I noted that, below the hem of a casually cinched white cotton robe, her feet were bare. You'd have thought I'd shown up unexpectedly. It wasn't a warm night, but she'd cranked open a couple of lead-paned windows in the cozy living room, causing the gauzy drapes to swell like a ship's sails. Bookcases, crammed chock-ablock, lined the walls. She'd converted the cloistered one-bedroom apartment into an annex of the main library.

"You'll have to excuse me—I only got out of the bath a few minutes ago," she explained. "I've been dying for a good soak and I guess I lost track of the time." Several damp tendrils dangled in evidence. She secured the robe when my gaze began straying.

"Reading in the tub, no doubt," I quipped, redirecting my attention to an open suitcase on the couch, and its cascade of tangled garments. I gathered she'd been away from Pine Street quite a while. I gathered as well her fresh scent, mingled with a flowery bath oil. The whistle of a kettle pulled her toward the kitchen.

"I'm making tea," she called. "Would you care to join me?"

I stealthily opened what I'd hoped was a small liquor cabinet, only to discover the green-glowing tuner of a radio console, source of the soft swing. Artie Shaw, it sounded like, though I wouldn't have bet two bits on it. I shut the doors on him.

"Sure, I'll have a cup," I said, settling down next to the suitcase on the pink-cushioned love seat. Couldn't help spotting several lacy "unmentionables" in the jumble. I scouted for the purse, just to locate the pistol, but didn't see it anywhere. I distracted myself with one of the books on the coffee table: *The Loved One*, by some gal named Waugh. On the inside flap was a picture of the author. I'd be wearing a sour scowl too, if I was a guy whose parents named me Evelyn.

Virginia returned balancing a hand-painted teapot and matching cups on a tray. She dipped to a knee to set it on the table, managing to keep the robe closed. "We'll let it steep a bit," she said. Her face was flushed and damp. From nerves or steam, I couldn't tell. "I suppose I should put something on."

Doing my best impression of a gentleman, I made no comment. Never easy for me. She edged around the table and hastily restuffed the suitcase. I watched vapor rise from the teapot's spout. She padded off with the bulging, unlatched case hugged to her hip. A rectangle of light appeared on the wall beyond an archway, curving into the coved ceiling.

"What's with all the books?" I asked, raising my voice over the radio. Once she was suitably clad, I doubted we'd share small talk.

"Majored in English Lit at Berkeley," she called back, a measure of pride in her voice. Then she added, with an equal measure of disdain: "For all the good it did me."

She was back in no time. Still barefoot, but now wearing a beautifully embroidered jade green kimono. She'd put a satin camisole on underneath, that's all that was different. That, and a bulky accordion file, bound with ribbon, which she set atop *The Loved One*.

"Is that what you wanted to show me?" I asked, nodding at the file.

"If you'll hold your horses," she said, pouring and evaluating a splash of tea, "I'll start at the beginning." Satisfied, she doled out two cups. "Like to take off your overcoat?"

"Am I going to be here that long?"

She looked sheepish. "I thought you'd be more comfortable."

I steadied the saucer and cup in my hands and gazed blankly at her. The topcoat stayed on. "At least take off your hat," she insisted, gesturing for me to hand it over. I doffed the fedora, but placed it crown down on the cushion beside me. Never give up your hat, I'd learned several bent brims and costly reblockings ago.

"Have it your way." She shrugged.

From the pocket of her robe she extracted a dwindling pack of Old Golds. She fished one out with two fingernails, pointing the rest at me. I waved them off. I didn't like cigarettes and I was saving my last Macanudo for the journey home. She lit up, then slipped the matches under the cellophane wrapper.

"If you change your mind," she said, tossing the pack on the table. The matchbook was from Croll's Gardens in Alameda, across the Bay. It was once a thriving resort, back when Alameda boasted an amusement paradise called Neptune Beach, "The Coney Island of the West." The fun stopped with the incursion of the Navy in 1939. A corner saloon—filled with fight pictures—was all that remained of Croll's, and Neptune Beach.

"First," she said, "I want to explain how I got hooked up with Mr. Sanders."

She perched on a plump ottoman that matched the couch and took a drag of the tar-bar, her knees drawn together demurely: Little Miss Muffet's more experienced sister. The tea's aroma had a pleasant trace of oranges. I peered expectantly over the rim of the cup, mimicking an eager first-nighter waiting for the curtain to rise. Trying to resemble someone who actually gave a shit.

8

"A couple of years ago I had this boyfriend," she began. "A real four-flusher—but we won't go into that. He went partners with Mr. Sanders on a parking garage, over on Mason. The city was pulling out so many streetcar tracks, they were convinced garages were the next big thing. And making money without working—that always had appeal for my boyfriend."

"Your boyfriend have a name?"

"It's not important. *He's* not important."

"Maybe I know him."

"You should be so unlucky. We'll just call him Cad. After the garage is open a few months, Cad wasn't seeing the profit he expected. He suspected Mr. Sanders was skimming off the top. Now Mr. Sanders, he didn't know me from Eve. So when Cad learns his partner is looking to hire a bookkeeper, I happen to show up—before Mr. Sanders even placed an ad."

"This is at the garage?"

"No, no, no—at his office on York Street. Mr. Sanders never went to the garage. He had a printing business, too, and ran all his boxing promotions out of there. Before he bought the new building at Sixteenth and Capp. Where we met that time."

I nodded, familiar with Burney's recent roosts.

"Anyway, I pretended to be looking for work. He tossed me his checkbook and had me balance it. That was the interview. Didn't ask for references or anything. Hired me on the spot. Very gullible, I thought."

She sipped tea. She had an endearing way of cradling the cup, like it was a snifter. No pretentiously extended pinky.

"He could've found you easy on the eyes," I suggested.

"Is that supposed to be a compliment?" She clinked the cup back in its saucer.

"If you like. It was meant to say more about Bur— Mr. Sanders."

"He never tried any funny business, if that's what's you're implying."

I checked the heft of the accordion file. "When do we get to this?"

She pulled it from my grasp and wedged it under her bottom, out of view.

"I'd been working for Mr. Sanders about six months when I started to notice something fishy. Of course, by that time I'd broken up with my boyfriend—"

"Cad."

"Right. But I decided to stay on with Mr. Sanders. He paid a decent wage, always on time. In fact, the job was the only good thing that came out of being with that jerk. That and the car."

"So what was fishy?"

"I was handling lots of paperwork that—far as I could tell—didn't have anything to do with Mr. Sanders's businesses. At least the ones I knew about. He was always sending me to get things notarized. It was shocking how much dough was in those documents. Deeds, stock certificates, promissory notes, under all kinds of different names. Corporations, trusts, holding companies. And one name kept cropping up over and over—"

"Dexter Threllkyl."

"Correct." She leaned to the table, tapping ash into a tray shaped like a swan.

"Where's the stink in that? So far, it all sounds legit. Unlikely, knowing Burney's background, but still—"

"He had me start answering the phone. He was getting angry calls from people who, I had to figure, were involved in deals with this Threllkyl. It got pretty bad."

"So Burney made you stonewall?"

"I have a disarming manner. Or so I've been told."

"Handling business in a kimono and bare feet? I suppose that could be considered disarming."

"I'd apologize, if I thought you really minded."

She'd obviously noticed how my glances darted automatically to the brief flashes of flesh. Guess she didn't like it. But I wasn't clear on her intentions, either. It wasn't part of my regular routine to have young women invite me to their apartments, let alone have them expose calves and cleavage to me.

Then I remembered an important fact. Virginia had been a friend of Claire Escalante—and she'd probably heard all about our affair. Maybe she'd pegged me as a low-rent Lothario, trying to charm dames into the sack. Maybe she was rating me, to gauge if I was on the level, or a lecher.

Maybe I was just an idiot, concentrating more on her ankles than the story she was telling.

"Where'd Claire fit in the scheme of things?" I asked, an attempt to shift the mood.

"We'd worked together before."

"Where was that?"

On the radio, a female singer crooned a slow ballad. The place was small enough that Virginia could lean over, flip the console doors, and turn up the volume. In the process, her robe slipped open. She crossed her leg and drew the kimono around her, cloaking the briefly bared knee.

"I love this song," she said. "But I always miss the name of the singer. Do you know who this is?"

For a moment we just listened. Curtains gently waved. The song had a quavering, mournful quality, something about dreams and haunted hearts. Frankly, it gave me the creeps.

"Not a clue," I cut in, interrupting the musical reverie. "I'm not up on the new tunes. Where'd you and Claire work?"

"It was a law firm," she answered, visibly disappointed I wasn't interested in the rest of the song. "I started there in forty-five, right after the war. I worked at Bethlehem Steel before that, you know." She said it with great pride, and I didn't blame her. I tried picturing her in the kimono, wielding a rivet gun.

"Anyway," she continued, "I was at the firm about a year before Claire came on. We hadn't seen each other since high school. We'd both gone to Mission."

"Which law firm was this?"

"Stout, McNally and Katz. Why?"

I shook off her query. If she'd said it was Ehrlich's outfit, I'd've torn out of there, spooked.

"I was a legal secretary. Claire got hired as a docket clerk. Didn't last too long, though. As you may know, Claire could be a little headstrong. She didn't like being bossed around, and those lawyers rubbed her the wrong way once too often."

"Quit or fired?"

"Quit. We meant to keep in touch, but you know how it is. I didn't see her again until the day she walked into Mr. Sanders's office."

"Why'd you leave Clout and Spatz, or whatever it was?"

"I didn't. I only worked for Mr. Sanders part-time. I still had the other job."

"You must like to keep busy."

"*Ha*. I like taking long baths and reading big thick books and not going out for days at a time. But that's tough after your 'sweetheart' talks you into a loan and then runs off with some cheap twist in a sparkly Cadillac. Lousy son of a bitch."

"It was *your* money that went into the garage."

"Mostly." She plugged the cigarette between her lips and pouted, searching the room for a remnant of Cad to curse.

"Why didn't you tell Burney the truth?" I asked, immediately feeling stupid. In a moment of empathy, I forgot what world we lived in. She didn't even bother with an explanation, just frowned and blew a derisive gust my way.

"So what'd Claire say when she showed up at Burney's?"

"Nothing at first. We laughed about it, you know—*what a coincidence!* But I could never figure out the connection. She claimed she was picking up money Mr. Sanders owed her husband—you know, the fighter, Hack Escalante."

She gave me a quick, blushing smile, one that said *Sorry, of course— you're* Mr. Boxing, *the big columnist.*

"Anyway," Virginia continued, "she was there only a couple of times is all, and Mr. Sanders wasn't happy about it. I got a bad feeling about the whole thing."

"Did Burney know you were friends?"

"Claire didn't want me to say anything. She clammed up soon as he came in the office."

"Contributing to your 'bad feeling.'"

"It did. But I didn't see her again for maybe six months or so, until she called and asked me to meet her at her house."

"That's when she told you what was really going on?"

"She said Burney was running a shakedown racket. He had pictures and things that he was using to blackmail people. That helped explain where the money was coming from. I mean, what he was spending on that new boxing arena he was building? It didn't jibe with any books I was keeping."

"So she asked you to steal the photos. Did she say what she was after, exactly?"

"She was in the pictures. Or so she told me."

"You look at them?"

A moment crawled by, the only sound a barely audible lament seeping from the radio. "A friend asked me for a favor," Virgina said. "I was happy to oblige. That doesn't make her private affairs any of my business."

But Virginia Wagner couldn't look at me now, after showing me big eyes all night. I took it as proof that she'd seen the pictures—shots of me and Claire, busy as bare-assed bees, in a by-the-hour room at the Temple Hotel.

I've always felt memories had tangible weight. They're what the dead leave you to carry. At that moment the space between us seemed filled with Claire, as if she'd only stepped from the room, not this world. Virginia Wagner and I exchanged a brief, guilty glance, conspirators recognizing each other for the first time. She dragged on the cigarette, then crushed the butt between the porcelain swan's wings. Exhaling, she said: "If I'd known making off with those photos was going to get her killed . . ."

"You didn't kill her," I said with a sigh. It sounded every bit as convincing as all the times I'd said it to myself.

"If I'd left that stuff in the safe, Claire would still be alive." She grabbed up the pack of Old Golds, eager for another. I poured more tea, just to do something.

"So when Claire was killed, you decided to go into hiding. In Alameda?"

Her eyes flashed with suspicion. I waited for her to place the cigarettes back on the table, then pointed to the matchbook.

"Quick work," she said. "You a detective, too?"

"Listen, Miss Wagner. I'm sorry about what happened. More than you might know. But if it's any consolation, I don't think you need to worry about Burney trying to kill you."

"Are they going to lock him up?"

"Definitely. Now that there's a witness, he doesn't stand a chance."

Her fingers grazed her throat and stayed there, as if checking for a pulse.

"When you were working for Sanders, did you ever meet a guy named Larry Daws? He's a fighter, did occasional jobs for Burney."

"Doesn't ring a bell. But I didn't get involved with the fight stuff. I don't have much appreciation for boxing."

"Daws is going to testify that he saw Burney hit Claire and kill her, but I'd give even or better odds it happened the other way around."

She mulled that over, swallowing tea and chasing it with smoke.

"I'm with you," she finally said. "Mr. San— *Burney* couldn't have killed her just by hitting her. Unless it was with a two-by-four. This Daws is selling him out."

She rose from the ottoman and went to the window, absorbing the cool night air as the curtains billowed around her. After a moment, she cranked the window to a slender crack. She returned and, with the fresh cigarette poised between her fingers, picked up the folder and handed it to me.

"This was with the stuff I took from the safe. Tell me if it means anything to you."

I set aside the tea, undid the ribbon, and pulled a sheaf of official-looking documents from the cardboard file. Embossed on the top sheet of stationery was a logo and "Mount Davidson Trust." I was as deft with financial matters as I was with needlepoint. I only skimmed, gleaning the basics: legal paperwork for some kind of holding company. Some of the pages displayed an inventory of assets—land parcels, mines, timber groves, oil wells—a diversified and lucrative assortment. Also included was a long list of names and addresses, under the heading "Investors." Several of them I recognized, from regular ads in ring programs, various union newsletters, passing acquaintances. Virgil Dardi was among the names, I noted.

"Go past all that," Virginia said. "Near the end there's a sheet that has both of them on it: Sanders and Threllkyl. Look at that."

It was a rider to the voluminous trust, a single-page document dated June 28, 1948, superseding all previous agreements and granting Burnell Sanders a 50 percent interest in the Mount Davidson Trust. It bore a notary's seal I couldn't make out. The pages fell back flat, and I reexamined the cover sheet. Threllkyl was among a scant roster of officers, as chief executive. Beneath him was Jerome Califro, chief counsel. Burney Sanders was nowhere to be found.

"How did you know Threllkyl?" she asked flatly.

"I didn't."

"But you're the one who brought him up," she said. "Today, on the streetcar."

I certainly wasn't about to admit that I'd learned of him only days ago, through the bars of the County Jail. That would boil her percolating paranoia. A carefully crafted half-truth was called for: "I used to hear Burney talk about his connection with this uptown lawyer named Threllkyl. When I saw his obit the other day . . . I wondered if you knew him—or that he'd died."

She assessed my answer. As far as lies go, it was quick and not very convincing. But it was all I had to keep the show going.

"So what do you make of all this?" she asked, skirting any doubts she may have had.

"I'm no expert," I replied. "But I think it makes Burney a millionaire."

"If it's legitimate. It could be a bunco scheme, don't you think?"

What I thought was that if Burney were a millionaire, he'd have been able to Get Jake without barking up my tree. I kept that opinion private.

I tucked the bundle back into the folder, and returned it to the table.

"I really can't tell you whether that's legitimate or not, Miss Wagner. I'm not a lawyer."

"To be completely honest, Mr. Nichols—that's one of the reasons I asked you here. To see if you knew an attorney who might be able to help me."

"Help you what?"

"If this is the only copy of the Mount Davidson Trust, don't you think it might be worth quite a bit to the concerned parties?"

"It might also be a fraud. You suggested that yourself. You could be considered an accessory."

"Exactly why I need an attorney, or at least somebody who can make heads or tails of this, to tell me if it's real."

"What's that got to do with me?"

"Because I have no intention of sticking my neck out and getting it chopped off. Not that I'd turn down a finder's fee for helping get these documents back in the proper hands."

"To offset your loss on the garage."

"You make it sound like I'm playing an angle. Let me put it plainly, Mr. Nichols: If this is a bunco operation, I'll turn the papers over to the authorities. If they're legitimate, I'll give them to their rightful owners. Either way, there'll be questions about how they ended up with me. I'd just as soon not say, for obvious reasons."

"Point taken."

She placed the file across her lap and began to carefully retie the ribbon. "Do you know someone you can trust, who can tell me what this is all about? You'd be doing me a favor." She issued me a look that carried freight. "Actually, you'd be returning me the favor."

Virginia Wagner had skillfully worked me into a corner. But she had no idea of the damage she could do. Burney Sanders believed that the file perched on his former secretary's thighs, like a gift to herself, was his only shot at salvation. I had no clue why. But I assumed a savvy shyster might discover something in the Mount Davidson Trust that could derail the DA's murder case against Sanders. I needed to stay on top of that file, make sure this woman didn't do anything rash with it. I opted for a strategy familiar to boxers everywhere—particularly those who find themselves over-matched: I climbed on my bicycle and stalled.

"There was a chief counsel listed in those trust papers, right? Maybe we should start with him. Wouldn't he be able to explain things easily enough?"

Disappointment clouded her bright eyes and tugged the corners of her mouth. She'd probably expected me to reach into my hat and pull out Jake Ehrlich.

"I want somebody I can trust," she said. "What if this chief counsel is in on it?"

"And what if there's no *it* to be in on?" I scooped up my hat, indicating our seminar had drawn to a close. "Here's my suggestion: You locate the lawyer who helped draft this thing, and I'll go see him. Go with me or not, it's your call. If you've never met this guy, you can pretend to be one of the disgruntled investors. That'd keep Virginia Wagner out of it."

To signify this was a take-it-or-leave-it offer, I stood up. Virginia remained seated. She bent forward, clutching herself, as if she'd been hit with cramps. "There's one other favor I need to ask," she mumbled.

I waited. Thirty silent seconds later, I put on my hat.

Finally: "I need to borrow some money. I'm late on the rent, and since I haven't been working I've . . . fallen a little behind."

Was this whole complicated setup a ruse to touch me for a few bucks? If so, I should have felt relief, not anger. I felt neither. The hurt on Virginia Wagner's face, the watery embarrassment in her eyes, was too genuine. If rent money was all she was after, she would have dropped the kimono a while ago.

I peeled a ten from my roll and handed it over. Her stealing those photos from Sanders was worth a hell of a lot more than a lousy sawbuck, despite how things turned out.

"I'll get you that lawyer's address," she said in a breathy rush, ushering me back down the hallway, through her little city of words. "I'll pay this back as soon as I can. That's a promise."

9

Two days later I vaguely mentioned an appointment to Fuzzy, and knocked off early. I ambled from the *Inquirer* over to 235 Montgomery, holding an envelope that had been delivered to the office earlier in the day. Inside were photographic reproductions, pertinent pages from the Mount Davidson Trust, each emblazoned with a bordered red-ink stamp: COPY. Not cheap to produce, especially for somebody behind on her rent. Virginia Wagner, understandably, wasn't going to cut loose the originals. I didn't want to be responsible for them anyway.

Clipped to the pages was a handwritten note, informing me that Jerome Califro had an office in the Russ Building. I'd been nothing but a snot-nosed kid, hugging a lamppost above the celebratory crowd, the day the tallest building in town—all thirty-one stories—opened for business. Erection of massive stone skyscrapers impressed the hell out of me in 1927, when I was still a boy, still capable of awe. I eagerly soaked up all the hoo-haw about how the architect based it on the Chicago Tribune Tower, and how the guy it was named after, Christian Russ, a jeweler from New York, bought the parcel of land in 1847 for thirty-seven bucks and change. The jewelry store soon became an assay office and Russ prospered mightily from the financial frenzy spurred by the Gold Rush, amassing affluence and influence. The kind that leads to one day having a building named for you.

As I was absorbed in its shadow twenty-one years later, 235 Montgomery resembled nothing so much as a Gothic cathedral. I'd once thought that the ornate aeries above street level were reserved for the statues of saints of Wall Street West. But in the wake of the depression, and another War to End All Wars, it was clear the Russ Building was no Sistine Chapel. The kind of high finance practiced on Montgomery Street didn't make saints of anybody.

Soon after the liveried operator brought the elevator to a stop on the twenty-fourth floor, I discovered that Jerome Califro, Attorney-at-

Law, was no longer one of the bees in this hive of industry. A downcast fellow locking up an import-export outfit across from Califro's office indicated there'd been "no clients in that broom closet" for more than two months. He'd heard the space was available, but had no idea what had become of the previous tenant.

Descending to the ground floor, I considered various methods for tracking down the elusive attorney, starting with cabbies who routinely shaped up curbside. Maybe one had occasionally driven Califro home. Crossing the lobby, I looked up in time to spot the row of telephone booths. Common sense seized me.

Jerome was the only Califro in the directory.

The starstruck cabbie was so busy recounting his amateur welter-weight career he got lost in a maze of streets twisting around the east side of Twin Peaks. Even on the ball he might have missed Argent Alley. It was a cul-de-sac, an eight-lot stretch of shoehorned residences that terminated abruptly in a short, sheer cliff. Directly below was the road we'd climbed, the last bend of Market Street.

The end of Argent Alley, however, was anything but dead. The dramatic view drew a whistle from my driver as he threw the brake. Remaining sunlight washed golden over a panorama stretching from the northern edge of downtown along the finger piers to the south. Oakland and the eastern hillsides were hazy in the distance, beyond the blue expanse of bay. Even the Mission glowed like a scattering of gems. Meanwhile, a blanket of fog was rolling over the crags above, about to enfold the city and tuck it in for the night. I inhaled the vista, pleased with the detour. I was eager to pay off this small debt, return to my routine business, and bury the last six months.

"Keep it running," I told the hack. "I won't be long."

The Califro residence was the last on the block, a single-story stucco cottage with a pitched slate roof. No driveway, no garage. The guy obviously preferred the picturesque to the practical. A burgeoning garden threatened to spill over the picket fence that surrounded the property. Some flowers, like the gently nodding gladiolus, craned their stalks to take in the view.

The buzzer did nothing. Rapping on the red front door, I finally rousted the lady of the house, a fleshy blonde crowding fifty. Artfully drawn brows arched inquisitively above her wary eyes.

"I'm looking for Jerome Califro," I said, smiling.

"He's not expecting anyone." The words were blunt and didn't seem to refer solely to *my* visit.

I brandished the envelope, as if it were a passport:. "Small unfinished legal matter to tidy up—won't take a minute."

Her eyes narrowed beneath the artifical brows. "He's unavailable," she said, shifting an ample hip against the door. Maybe she pegged me as a process server, looking to slap a subpoena.

"Need some information, that's all," I said. Offered what I hoped was a winning wink. She only went about five-five, but stem to stern she was a formidable chunk. I wasn't about to get my foot mashed in the ·door, certainly not for the sake of the Mount Davidson Trust, whatever it was. I was only a five-minute cab ride from home, where I could mix a cocktail, call Virginia Wagner, and claim with sincerity, "I tried."

"Del, is something wrong?" The muffled male voice came from a distance. "Is there someone at the door? Adele? What is it?"

Her broad shoulders sagged. I took the cue.

"One or two questions. Promise," I said, laying my hand on the door frame.

When Adele glanced at me again, her eyes were unguarded, weary. Her hip relaxed and she retreated to take the measure of me, gauging my fortitude. "You *sure* this is important?" she asked. There was a dry Southern rustle to her speech now.

I edged past the red door and into the foyer. The place was neat as a pin and stark, with no personal pictures or effects. Up close, Adele smelled of witch hazel and talcum powder.

"He's in his study," she said, with resignation. Fatigue had suddenly overtaken her sturdy facade. "This way."

She led me to a dim hallway at the rear of the house. A pair of paneled pocket doors were cracked about a foot, a narrow band of light thrown across the corridor.

"Dear, you have a visitor," she announced, before shoving the doors wide with a theatrical flourish.

Jerome Califro was sitting crossed-legged in a cracked brown leather throne, presiding over his personal devastation. A cyclone had been through the six-foot-square cubbyhole. Boxes upon boxes haphazardly stacked, loose files and stray papers on every surface—so much clutter that at first I didn't even notice the randomly stuffed shelves that reached floor to ceiling on both sides of the "study." Three of us couldn't fit in there and still draw breath. Adele, in the door frame, folded her arms beneath her substantial bosom and fixed her gaze on the floor.

The barrister was blotto. A near-empty bottle of Lord Calvert crowned the ludicrously littered rolltop desk, the only item in the wreckage he could lay hands on easily. The day was almost done, but Califro hadn't changed out of his pajamas, rumpled yellow flannels decorated with cactus and bucking broncos. He tried to tamp tobacco into the bowl of a well-chewed pipe. Wild West sleepwear caught most of it. He squinted my way, trying to determine which of the three to address.

"Do I know you, sir?" He coughed. For probably the hundredth time that day, he chose to cut the phlegm with a gargle of whiskey. The barbed-wire veins defacing his nose, the ravines in his forehead and cheeks, the saddlebags beneath his sunken eyes—it all branded him a long-gone gas hound. The thin mustache was not unlike mine, but its crooked line betrayed an unsteady hand with the razor.

One whiff of the man's state, and I opted for deception.

"Name's George Smith," I said, not bothering to shake. "I've got a couple of questions about the Mount Davidson Trust. Representing one of the investors." Though Adele stirred behind me, mention of the trust didn't rattle its chief counsel. Satisfied his bowl was sufficiently full, Califro snapped two matches trying to light it. I obliged him with the steadier flame of my lighter, despite the fact he hadn't offered me a drink. I don't care how big a lush you are, etiquette dictates you propose a pop to a houseguest.

Once he'd wreathed his head in smoke, Califro said: "Have you ever considered, Mr. Smith, how we as a *spee*-sheez are governed 'sclusively by bi'logical imperative?" The Calvert had caused some diction problems.

"How's that?"

"The common misassumsion is that our society is civ'lized. It's not—not at all. Far from it. We pre-zoom the laws of man promgulate our progress, but that's just a convenient lie we've concocted to delude ourselves. Salve to smooth over the barbaric truth. Prop'gation of the *spee*-sheez, don't you see? The simple prim'tive purpose of human existence. That's it. There's your answer, your Holy Grail. In a nutshell."

I glanced at Adele. Her expression: *You asked for it.*

"It is the function of the human," he blathered on, "to reproduce more of *his* kind. To ultimately outnumber and shove into oblivion the *others*. No matter if it happens through war or peace. Nazis? Just impatient. Germans get that way. Don't you see? Have you read *One World*? Willkie's manifesto? Don't you see? Even espout—es*pous*ing brotherhood, he comes to the same conclusion—a world in which we'll 'ventually s'cumb to the 'group brain.' No more in'viduals. Natural order *will* be achieved, don't you see? Once we are all toiling as loyally as ants in a conoly. *One* world. *One* mind—in*dust*rious, unquestioning, *invinbicle*. Don't you agree?"

"Sure."

I slid the trust documents from the envelope and held them in front of his face. "Tell me about the Mount Davidson Trust."

He smacked his lips, thirsty from his big soliloquy. He tipped a few fingers of the Lord's potion and slurped. His whiskey rictus twisted into an ugly smile.

"There's confirmation of my theory right there," he said. "Queen of the conoly—Astrid Threllkyl. A textbook example of how the drive to dominate eclipses all lesser motives and condiserations."

"Who's Astrid Threllkyl?" I practically moaned. I was beginning to regret that Mrs. Califro—if that's who she was—*hadn't* smashed my foot in the door.

Blitzed as he was, Califro appraised me warily, overly oiled gears starting to mesh. "Don't you know the Threllkyls?"

"I do not. I'm sure they're a swell bunch of people. What I want to know is whether these papers are on the level."

The shiny marbles in his sunken sockets swerved toward Adele, looking for a clue. I recognized *that* look—evidence they were husband and wife. When he didn't answer, I pressed:

"As the chief counsel—that's your name there, right?—I assume you have a copy of this around here somewhere." I disparagingly assayed the premises. "Maybe you can just tell me, off the top of your head, whether your version includes *this* page."

I displayed the rider, signed by Threllkyl and Sanders, that would, in theory at least, make Burney one wealthy bastard. Califro rattled more phlegm around his lungs, then rummaged on the desk.

"My glasses," he said weakly.

"In your pocket," Adele told him. Coldly.

He slipped on a pince-nez and pretended to read. It was a sorry charade, since we all realized, despite his relative coherence, he couldn't recognize even his own name.

"I'll simplify," I said. "It states that half the trust gets put in the name of Burnell Sanders. Did you endorse that? Recognize the notary seal?"

He removed the glasses and tried to draw courtroom composure into his gaunt, emaciated frame. "I'm afraid, Mr. Smith, that I would have to reference my copy of the trust to confirm the valifidy of that addemdum. Were I to reveal confidential information . . . Well, the partners in the trust, especially Mr. Threllkyl, wouldn't take that lying down."

"He takes everything lying down," I said.

Califro looked confused, so I added, "He's dead."

With that, Adele bolted from the room, leaving Califro gaping at the space she'd vacated. Two more folks who, like Virginia, didn't religiously read the obits. Since they didn't recognize Sanders's name, I figured they didn't read the papers at all.

In a heartbeat Adele was back, equipped with her own highball glass. Her husband watched, slack-jawed, as she served herself a healthy dose from his bottle.

"Salute!" she chimed, and they drained the booze in unison. It felt like the Feast of All Saints in the Califro bungalow.

"They'll immediately liquidate all the assets and disperse the money into untraceable accounts," Califro nattered to his wife, as if I'd vanished in a puff of smoke.

"You telling me this is legit?" I barked. "All the assets in here are for real and not some flimflam?"

"I have twelve thousand dollars of my own money in that trust," said Mrs. Califro, clutching my arm. "There are some very real properties and holdings in there, but I'm worried that most of them have been forfeited and may no longer have any value. Or that they're being hidden from legitimate investors. Somebody should file a lawsuit and get the whole thing out in the open."

Suddenly I looked like a lifeline. She was sizing me up as a possible stand-in for her sodden spouse, at least on the legal front.

"I'm no lawyer," I said. "I'm just representing a friend. Had some dough tied up in this thing—like you."

"Who's that?" croaked Califro, behind another cloud of aromatic smoke.

"Nobody you know, I'm sure. But what about Burnell Sanders—know him?"

Califro's ruined mug crunched in concentration. "Name sounds familiar," he said. "Did he work with Dex?"

"You gotta figure—he's the one supposed to get half. But you never dealt with him directly?"

"No. Only with Dex."

"Yet here you are, toasting Threllkyl's demise. Why's that? If you don't mind my asking."

Evidently they did, judging by the silence.

"I want to help you," the lawyer slurred. "I want to help myself." He looked toward his wife, shame-faced. "First I'll have to assemble the pertinent records."

"That could take some time," I said, again gesturing to the mountains of detritus.

"We had a break-in a while back," Adele said. "So we moved a lot of our records elsewhere, for safekeeping."

"The ranch," Califro said, with a grave nod. "We'll have to retrieve them. Perhaps later in the week. I can give you a call when everything's in order."

I was about to pull a business card from my suit pocket, but it occurred to me that not a single one read GEORGE SMITH.

"Don't bother," I said. "I'll call *you*."

The taxi was waiting in the dusk, and the driver picked right up where he'd left off, the third round of the 1926 Golden Gloves welter-weight finals. None of it registered. Heading off the Peaks, I studied the Mount Davidson paperwork in the fading twilight, wishing I'd never gone through that red door.

10

As I entered the house, I spotted Ida through the glass-paned French doors separating the foyer and dining room. She had the kid propped up beneath a framed poster from last year's testimonial banquet. She'd painstakingly lettered "Future Champ" on a square of oak tag and stuck it in the frame, right above his head.

"Good timing," she said. "I thought I could get this picture by myself and surprise you, but he's squirming all over. Give me a hand."

Shucking my overcoat onto a chair, I came to her rescue. As she futzed with the camera, I pinned the baby with one hand while pouring myself some bourbon from a nearby set of cut-crystal decanters. Dinner simmered invitingly, aromatically, on the stove, just beyond the swinging doors leading to the kitchen. Next to the baby was a pair of miniature boxing gloves, a gift from Ernie Flores, a former amateur who'd learned his leatherwork from the master, Sol Levinson.

"You were thinking he'd wear these?"

"Can you get them on him?" she asked, clamping a pack of film in the Polaroid camera I'd given her this past Christmas, when they first came out. She loved that contraption. There were more pictures of her sisters scattered around this house than I ever needed to see.

Stuffing the baby's tiny hands into souvenir boxing gloves was as easy as putting a rubber on a monkey. "How 'bout if he just holds 'em?" I proposed, giving up.

"Okay, get back," she said. "Sit him under the sign, then move away real quick."

The kid gurgled, swinging the gloves around. The first flash-blast pretty much paralyzed him. He blinked goofily, the gloves nestled in his diapered lap.

A loud mechanical whir, then the camera spat out its tongue of film. "Perfect," Ida said, snapping another. As the boy was transfixed, or blinded, she shot a few extras. I hoped I wouldn't be shelling out for eye doctors.

As he hazily observed the kooks around him, I studied the soft, pudgy face of six-month-old William Vincent Nichols. Didn't much resemble his mother. Of course, he looked nothing at all like the guy in the poster above his head. Jack Downey had done a nice drawing of me; the fraternity had scrawled their regards all around it. A big swallow of bourbon was required as I pondered all the skeptical appraisals to come, once this kid started making public appearances with a "father" who looked nothing like him.

"Honey! Catch him before he falls!"

I set down the drink and scooped up the baby. He shoved a doughy mitt against my cheek, chortling happily. Leaning his head back, Vincent examined my mug, as I had studied his. He rubbed my five o'clock shadow curiously. Ida crowded us, eagerly pulling at the triangular flap on the photo. A whiff of pungent chemicals arose as she peeled off the backing. "This stuff stinks," she said, wrinkling her nose. "But I kind of like it."

We huddled, awaiting development. If a real photographer had seen us, he might have gotten a portrait—miracle of miracles—that would pass for a normal middle-class American family. From indistinct blobs, an image of the "Future Champ" emerged. The kid looked happy enough. Ida waved the picture dry, beaming. She seemed as proud of taking a decent snapshot as she was of producing its flesh-and-blood subject.

"It was really important for you to have a kid, wasn't it?" I asked. I stared again at the boy's face, trying to imagine a sodden old bugger like that lawyer, Califro, ever looking this unformed, this *new*.

Ida looked flummoxed, like I'd questioned the necessity of breathing. "What would be the point of it all otherwise?" she said.

The befuddlement in her eyes was quickly replaced by a hopeful gleam. "What's on your mind?" she asked slyly, shooting me a glance. "Are you thinking what I'm thinking?"

"Doubtful," I grumbled, handing over the child and retrieving my drink. *Let's see how this one turns out first*, I thought.

What I said was "Something smells good. Let's eat."

I had Virginia meet me after-hours at the Russ Building. With no scurrying minions in the vaulted corridors, no doors swinging open and closed, no ceaselessly yo-yo-ing elevators, the place was eerily quiet. A professional purgatory. Waiting on the twenty-fourth floor, I couldn't make out the end of either corridor. North and south wings receded into gloom, then vanished into blackness.

Suddenly she was beside me, arriving without a sound. None of the lifts had opened, or even chimed. She was wearing the same black cape and toque ensemble from the streetcar. Beneath the hat, a hairdo freshly set in perfect waves. One final drag, then she stubbed the cigarette into the raked white sand of a bronze ashtray.

"What'd you find out?" Virginia asked, exhaling.

"The office is down this way," I replied, gripping her elbow. She slipped her arm through mine and huddled closer. We headed into the south wing, briefly moving through shafts of blue-gray cast by the lone window in the hallway. Only my footsteps echoed. She wasn't wearing shoes, or nylons.

"You'll catch cold," I lectured.

"I'll be fine," she whispered, lips near my ear.

We approached the door. There was a dim glow visible behind the pebbled glass. A desk lamp maybe. Then it was gone.

Virginia slipped. She clutched me to keep from falling.

"Something's on the floor," she gasped. "It's on my feet."

I crouched, squinting, sensing darkness and warmth spreading across the stone, seeping from beneath the office door.

"What is it?" she whispered, stepping away from the widening pool.

"I don't know," I said. "I can't see."

But I knew.

"We have to clean it up," she said, all at once on the verge of tears. "We can't leave it there."

Then she was gone. Hints of Virginia's small footprints were barely visible in the murkiness. Just enough to follow. She walked on the balls of her bare feet, trying not to slip again.

I found her facing a half-open door stenciled JANITOR.

"I don't want to go in," she moaned fearfully.

Stepping past her, I felt inside for a light switch. It was damp, cramped. *Maybe there's a pull chain*, I thought, coming up empty on the walls. Virginia took shallow, nervous breaths. My hand groped in the darkness. There were vague shapes inside the closet.

"Is that you?" A woman's voice. Not Virginia's. Toward the rear. Muffled.

My hand recoiled, like I'd stuck it in a socket. My heart hammered.

"Do you hear that?" Virginia asked. I couldn't answer. "It's the elevator," she added, terrified. "Somebody's coming."

I tried to back out of the room, which had turned hot, sweltering hot. Something pushed against my back, trapping me.

The light came on. In the blinding glare, a woman's hand grasped the chain hanging from a bare overhead bulb. She'd reached through paint-spattered canvas tarpaulins, hung haphazardly on hooks. Through a gap in the folds of fabric I saw her face.

It was Claire.

Alive.

The pupils of her wide eyes shone wetly and her crimson lips curled with the faintest trace of recognition. I reached for her, stumbling over wash buckets, shoving aside mop handles. She released the chain and sank backward, enveloped in the tarps. It took forever to work past the rough folds. She was propped against the back wall, rigid, wearing the blue-and-white polka-dot dress she'd had on at our luncheon interview. My shadow shrouded her face, still so beautiful.

Death hasn't done a thing to you, I wanted to say.

"Get me out," she pleaded. Perspiration beaded her brow. It was hellishly hot in there.

"Hurry," Virginia wailed, somewhere behind me.

Claire's dress was shorn at the waist, exposing everything below. A dark thatch glistened between her hips. My face ignited. I averted my eyes, ashamed, wanting but not wanting to see the garters and the length of her stockinged legs, pressed tightly together. It was wrong to see her like this. Guilt knotted my chest.

I looked.

Her feet were jammed into a filthy galvanized bucket, encased in rock-hard cement. Blood dribbled down her legs, leaking from her core. It started streaming. She gazed at me wordlessly, imploring, mouth agape.

The elevator bell broke the silence. Footsteps tattooed granite.

"They're coming," Virginia gasped.

* * *

"No offense, hon—but you look like hell." Ida brushed my hand as she set the steaming coffee in front of me.

"Bad night," I groaned. "Must have been something I ate."

"That I cooked? We ate the same thing."

"No, I mean yesterday. Before I got home. I'm trying to remember what I had for lunch."

Ida palmed my clammy forehead. "Maybe you should call in sick. Rest for a day."

I'd never taken a sick day in my career. A bad dream wasn't about to snap the streak. Adjusting my features, I stood up.

"I won't be home for dinner," I said, gulping lukewarm java. "There's a fight in Oakland. Don't wait up."

11

"What brings you to this side of the Bay, Nich?"

Woody Montague was the only guy—the *only* one—who called me Nich.

"I was hoping you could explain this to me," I said, placing the copies from the Mount Davidson Trust on Montague's shipshape desk. Tidy stacks of documents decorated the billiard-green blotter, each file topped with neatly handwritten notes. Before I could explain the subject, he changed it.

"Your buddy Bernal is pretty lucky," he said, folding his gangliness into a squealing swivel chair.

Between nuthouse dreams, work, the fights, Burney Sanders, Virginia Wagner—I'd neglected to check in again at the hospital with Tony Bernal. Maybe I didn't want his wife reading me the rest of the riot act.

"How's that?" I inquired, taking a seat across from Woody.

"He's got *me* working for him now." Montague laced his fingers behind his head and gave a satisfied smile.

"He doing okay?"

"They're not sure if he's going to walk again. And—as I predicted—the Major Liquor Company is playing tough. Denies any wrongdoing in the accident. Their attorneys insist the company will fight any injury claim."

Scoping Montague's modest office, I saw not one relic from his award-winning reportorial career. No plaques, no certificates, no grip 'n' grins. A family photo on the desktop, and maps tacked to the paneled walls: San Francisco, the greater East Bay, California. Two windows, flanking a filing cabinet, opened onto a particularly charmless stretch of San Pablo Avenue. With his smarts, Montague could have operated out of a Nob Hill penthouse. Instead, he seemed to scarcely be scraping by. He'd gone after Tony's accident like a hungry hyena.

"You never struck me as an ambulance chaser, Woody," I said. Sometimes I fail to censor—or edit—myself, and my words sting more than intended. Montague looked mildly offended. Then he laughed, tossing off his bulky specs and rubbing his eyes.

"I'm a bullshit chaser."

"Woodrow, watch the language. The kids are home from school." Susan Montague, Woodrow's wife, entered through a rear door, sorting mail. Woody's office was a converted corner storefront. The Montagues occupied the adjacent residence. A yammering gaggle of youngsters was coming up the driveway between the two buildings, a barking dog heralding their arrival.

Mrs. Montague was a delicate woman in her early thirties, dark hair pulled back severely from a soft-featured face. Woody reminded Susan who I was, but his wife was watching her kids as they clomped up the back stairs next door, bellowing for Mom and Dad. She called out to them from the porch, instructing where to find snacks and drinks, how to share properly, where to dispose of the evidence. Woody massaged his burred head and listened. Her voice seemed to soothe him, like Mozart affects some folks. Susan apologized for the interruption, then went on making order of the daily post.

"Dardi is a cancer," Montague said, rolling his chair up to the desk, picking right up where he'd left off. "It sickens me what he gets away with. That truck was off route. I've checked. Meanwhile, Dardi carries no insurance. It's amazing he's even licensed, let alone that he's got a blank check in the city. The arrogance is . . . unconscionable. But then, he's got Samish behind him."

"I figured Dardi for finished after that thing a few years ago."

"The 'Lost Five Hundred,'" Woody recalled, snickering bitterly. "What a boondoggle that was!"

Virgil Dardi stirred up a shit storm in 1945 when he blew into town with a slick and snappy sales crew. Employing lots of polished patter and deep discounts, they scored almost a million bucks in contracts with about five hundred tavern owners and liquor stores. The reps were pros, separating dupes from their dough upfront.

No deliveries were ever made.

"What finally happened with all that?" I asked.

"Nothing! The 'Lost Five Hundred' raised hell with the DA's

office, but Dardi was never even indicted. About two hundred grand got bounced back to the barkeeps. I could never track down who brokered that. Dardi got off clean and eight hundred thou to the good. Only thing different this time: He's changed the name of the company. New reps are out there commiserating with the same saloon owners, crying in their beer over the losses! Saying they'll cut a deal to help get 'em back on their feet! They don't even suspect it's Dardi again. Phenomenal!"

"Could make a hell of an exposé for the *Inquirer.*" I nudged him. "Your comeback piece."

Montague shifted his gaze to the window, focusing on something a thousand yards past the sparse traffic. Headlights drifted by in the avenue's deepening dusk. Susan's ears flushed. She'd obviously heard the Dardi diatribe more than once. "Woody's had trouble turning up witnesses," she said. "No one will say anything against that man. They're intimidated by his connections. I imagine the *Inquirer* would be, too. That's one reason Woody left the paper. A few too many stories spiked—from up top." Susan's voice had a fine grit. Despite her demure demeanor, I pegged her as tough.

"Let's not go into all that, Susan," Montague said, slipping his glasses back on. "I need for my work to matter, Nich," he said to me, starting to answer a question that had baffled many former colleagues. "I quit the paper because even though I was constantly kicking up dust, when it settled, everything was still the same. I prefer making a difference. So I chose a more . . . street-level approach."

"Why move across the Bay?" I asked. To most people, Oakland was the weak sister, servants' quarters for the City by the Bay. Especially since the war, with the huge numbers of Negroes who relocated from down South, drawn by shipyard work.

"Let's just say I needed some fresh air."

"My husband," Mrs. Montague said, "has perpetually been the target of smear campaigns by people in San Francisco who resent his dedication to justice."

"Jesus Christ, Susan—you sound like the narrator of a bad movie."

"And *you* promised you'd stop using the Lord's name in vain."

"Around the kids," Woody said, grinning. "And the kids are over there." He hoisted himself, taking several stacks of paperwork from the desk and depositing them in the file cabinet. "Nich, I simply believe in the truth. Maybe that's all I believe in. If people know the truth, most times they'll do the right thing. You can't make informed decisions based on lies, and our system produces plenty of those. Especially in certain parts of San Francisco. So . . . it's easier for me to work from here."

It was evident the Montagues were in the midst of their own drama. I didn't need to join them. Leaning forward, I flipped pages taken from the Mount Davidson Trust.

"Give me your take on the truth of this, if you would. You can make sense of these weasel-words. Me—I know from two guys slugging each other."

He riffled through the sheets, his tongue curling up to trace the line of his upper lip. Concentrating, absorbing. Susan perched on the sill of a window overlooking the driveway, and the kitchen next door. Monitoring the kids, but not wanting to leave: Her interest in Montague's business seemed keen. When Woody had scanned it all, including the rider, he reached for a folded newspaper at the edge of the desk.

Snapping the pages open, then quartering it, Montague handed over that morning's *Chronicle*. "You see this?" he asked.

A small item, buried in the mix on page eight:

MURDER TRIAL LOOMS

The San Francisco District Attorney's office reported yesterday that it expects its case against boxing promoter Burnell Sanders to go before Judge Harlan White within two weeks. Sanders is charged with first-degree murder in the death of Claire Escalante, wife of local heavyweight boxer Hack Escalante. According to Deputy DA William Corey, Mrs. Escalante's killing resulted from her involvement in an extortion scheme operated by Sanders. Sources at the Hall of Justice indicate that the DA's office is moving up several criminal prosecutions about which it "feels strongly" in hope of clearing the cases before the holidays.

"Is that your connection? This Sanders fellow?" Woody asked, again fingering the trust documents.

"In a roundabout way, yeah."

Goddamn it, this guy was *good*. He should have been digging dirt for a major daily.

"You an investor?"

"No. Trying to help one out."

"Not Sanders?"

"Not Sanders. What's your opinion of this?"

"Who's defending him?"

"No idea."

"If this thing is legit, he could hire Ehrlich. That's enough to make me suspicious. Does the DA know about this?"

"Why?"

"Simple: A dead body in proximity to this much cash? Dollars to doughnuts, you'll find a connection. Con job or not, *cherchez l'argent*. Did Sanders give these to you? It'd be interesting if he was getting screwed out of his money because of the murder rap." He glanced at his wife: "I wonder about precedent on that." Then back to me: "How involved are you in the case? Is he guilty so far as you know?"

I got the miserable, empty feeling I'd cut my own throat by having Woody sniff these papers.

"Honey, Mr. Nichols wasn't asking you to take this on," Susan said, stepping away from the window. "He only wanted your opinion."

I smiled at her, although I felt like giving her a hug.

"Yeah, stay loose, Woody," I said, with a fake laugh. "All I need is some advice as to whether this is real or a fraud. What should I do? That's all I'm trying to decide."

"I'd put an ad in the paper. Tell anyone with a connection to the . . . Mount Davidson Trust to contact you. Find out what their stories are."

"There's a battalion of them," I said.

He brightened considerably: "Call 'em up. There could be a class-action suit if these folks have been swindled."

"No time for that."

"Hire someone to track them down. Then steer 'em to me."

Susan had heard enough: "Woody, you can't handle anything more. You're already working five cases."

"I could pull Jeff Monroe in on it. If there's something there."

I stood up. It was the only thing I could do to stem the tide. "Woody, I've got to say again—I stopped by for some friendly counsel. I'm not a client."

"Let me know if Sanders needs legal help. It might be important to hear what he has to say about this. In the meantime, if you feel like a short vacation with the missus, take a drive up north. Check out some of the places listed here. Like this Cold Springs Resort—see what's actually there. No substitute for hard evidence."

"Good idea," I said, looking at my watch. "You know, I lost track of time. I gotta get over to the Auditorium."

I reached for the documents. Woody planted a palm on them.

"Leave these with me, Nich. I'll find out what's what. Take me a couple of days is all."

"Wouldn't feel right leaving those, Woody. They don't belong to me."

"They're copies," he reminded me, pointing to the bright red stamp on the top sheet. "They won't leave this office. How could there be a problem?"

Montague's confidence was wearing me down. Nobody else I knew, or trusted, could decipher this deal any faster. Woody'd have the whole thing sorted out before gasbag lawyer Jerome Califro shook off the DTs and unearthed his car keys for that trip to the "ranch." Montague relished complication. Unlike me.

"I have to play this one close to the vest, Woody," I stalled. "So I know you'll be discreet. I can't get tied up in it. Remember, I'm just fronting for a friend."

Montague inscribed a notepad, tore the sheet off, and set it on top of the trust documents. "Information only," he agreed.

"This isn't pro bono, either." I aimed that more at Susan, to defuse the objections she'd raise as soon as I left. Her husband had ignored all the cues she'd been broadcasting; she wanted to collate the documents, hand them back to me, and usher my ass elsewhere.

"Well, Nich—if I took money from you, then you'd be a client, right? Yet you just told me you weren't."

"Right."

I was navigating this whole thing like I'd been blindfolded and dropped in the woods.

"I'll call you when I've got something," he said, grinning.

I offered my good-byes, left the papers, and caught a cab to the fights.

12

"What did you tell your wife?" Virginia wanted to know as we neared the toll plaza on the city side of the Golden Gate Bridge. I gave her the four bits that would pay our admission to Marin County, along with a sidelong, circumspect glance.

"Ever been married?" I asked.

"Never."

She dropped the quarters from her white-gloved fingers into the meaty palm of the toll taker. Traffic heading out of town was fairly light that foggy Monday morning. The weather wasn't good enough for her to put down the ragtop.

"Once you *are* married, I'll give you the complete list of alibis. It'll be my wedding present."

"So I'll know when he's lying to me?" She upshifted, joining the flow of cars merging onto the bridge.

"You might use a few yourself," I said.

Black sunglasses turned my way. A red scarf, knotted beneath her chin, protected the hairdresser's work. A blue coupe tried to muscle into our lane. She ignored it, even as its driver laid on the horn. "Are you insinuating that I'm the cheating kind?"

"You'd have to be the marrying kind first. It was an innocent crack. Forget it."

She barreled down the left lane, skirting the oncoming southbound traffic. "Luckily for you, I like smart alecks," she said. Commuters whizzed by in the opposite direction, not more than an arm's length away. "I myself, being a cynic dwelling among the thin-skinned, appreciate your acerbic style."

"Did I just get reviewed?" I asked, slipping hands into my overcoat pockets to keep from clutching the dashboard.

"English major." She plunged into the next lane. Can't claim she was a bad driver; will testify that she was a scary one. Surprising, considering the majesty of the machine she drove.

"It's a forty-two Buick Roadmaster convertible coupe, straight-eight," she'd proudly explained when she picked me up outside the Fantasia Bakery. "Cad got it cheap. Belonged to a guy who died in the war. So I guess I did get something out of my time with that loser."

Miraculously, we made it down the Waldo Grade and into Marin intact, despite: nearly sideswiping a station wagon packed with hollering Brownies, getting trapped for several suspenseful seconds in an exit-only parade, and coming way too close to rear-ending a cattle carrier. Virginia seemed surprised to find it suddenly looming in front of us, although you could smell manure from a quarter mile back. When you don't drive, it's tough to criticize somebody else's skill behind the wheel. So I bit my tongue. Several times.

"Why are we stopping?" She was taking an off-ramp that veered from the highway into central San Rafael.

"I need a cigarette," she declared. "I don't smoke in the car."

"Why not?" The ashtray, like the rest of the vehicle, inside and out, was immaculate.

"This honey is all I've got to my name," Virginia explained, affectionately patting the dash. "I don't want to stink up the upholstery."

We eased to a stop on a side street. Leaning against the right front fender, she fired up. I stayed in the car, window rolled down. Virginia either craved nicotine badly or simply needed a break from her own reckless driving.

"You've got kids, don't you?" she asked out of nowhere.

"One," I replied.

"Got a picture?"

That was a new one. Wouldn't be the last time I'd get it, either. I showed upturned palms.

"Like being a father?" She tapped ash into the gutter. The cigarette had a ways to burn. We'd be a few minutes yet. *What the hell*, I figured.

"Technically, I'm not a father," I said, squinting up at her. Sun had started burning through the overcast.

"What are you selling now, smart aleck?"

"It's not my kid."

A deep drag helped her mull that over, then: "Some other guy's?"

"He's elsewhere," I confirmed, anticipating her next query.

"So that thing you had with Claire," she said, blindsiding me, "—you were settling a score with your wife?"

Turning it over, I concocted several smart-alecky rejoinders. We didn't need a cold front to cloud the day, so I stowed the stinging ripostes. I'd invited her on this goose chase, knowing it meant hours in the car with each other. But I was surprised she'd cut so deep, so fast. To my surprise, I found myself answering her honestly.

"I got even with the other guy, not my wife."

"What do you mean?" She looked skeptical.

"I had him beaten senseless and run out of town on a rail."

"You're kidding."

"I'm not. The past six months I've made a habit of shattering commandments left and right. Know what it's gotten me? A nice raise, offers from New York and Chicago outfits to syndicate my column, and a gilt-edged certificate of appreciation from the city's Board of Supervisors for 'significant contributions to the social, economic, and cultural development of San Francisco.'"

"Guess you didn't get even," she said, smirking. "You came out ahead."

"I only keep score in boxing. What'd Claire tell you about me?"

"Nothing much. I didn't pry. She said you were a good story-teller."

My expression must have been quizzical, because she quickly added, "She meant it in a good way." Virginia flicked the butt down. It hissed on the damp asphalt. Inspecting for ashes on her belted beige coat, she said, "You're not going to tell *me* any stories, are you?"

It was hard to draw a bead on this gal. She was a moving target. A fast-moving one, at that.

"Everybody tells stories," I replied, shooting from the lip. "Including you."

Route 121, snaking through the yellow hills of Napa County, was desolate compared with the 101, and narrower. I estimated the prospect of vehicular calamity had been considerably diminished. An hour of alternating switchbacks and straightaways brought us, woozy and famished, into downtown Nowhere.

We stopped at a Texaco and took on gas and a two-pound bag of cherries Virginia bought at a fruit stand next door to the filling station. I asked directions to Cold Springs Resort three times before getting more specifics than "Ain't nothing up there no more."

Armed with a vague verbal map, we headed into the foothills, the remainder of the trip a winding climb up a poorly maintained, sun-dappled logging road cut through towering pines and redwoods. I spent much of the drive spitting cherry pits out the window.

"Even one gets on my car," Virginia warned, "and you'll be walking home."

We were fortunate to find the place, considering there were no signs anywhere promoting the bucolic bounty awaiting travelers to Cold Springs. Virginia groused about dust and gravel ruining the waxed finish on the car's "Sequoia Cream" paint job. We topped a rise. There stood the lodge and a string of cabins, nestled in a wooded glen overlooking Napa Valley. Evidence that *something* listed in the Mount Davidson Trust was real.

Built with local timber, the spread had a rough-hewn frontier facade straight off a California Redwood Empire tourist brochure. A rustic getaway, far from the hectic pace of urban life. We cruised past a sign the elements had warped and worn, paint long since chipped away. It offered no clue as to when the resort was established. We pulled up in front of the lodge, but nobody came running to welcome us. Talk about a rustic getaway—*everyone* had gotten away.

Virginia peered through the dust cloud kicked up by the tires. "There you go. It exists," she sighed, disappointed; by sorrowful surroundings, or the residue settling on the Roadmaster's once shiny hood, I couldn't tell.

"Let's check it out," I proposed.

We hadn't gone five feet before we stopped in our tracks, staring at each other. Despite no evidence of life anywhere, the air was filled with more than fresh pine scent.

"What *is* that?"

"Opera," Virginia replied. "In Italian."

The mellifluous tones of a top-tier tenor emanated from somewhere behind the lodge. We couldn't resist trading grins, followed by another incredulous inspection of the seemingly abandoned premises.

"What the hell?" I asked, striding to the entrance. Virginia followed, cautiously maneuvering her open-toed pumps across the driveway's uneven stones.

The door wasn't locked.

Inside was everything you'd expect in re-created Western decor, from the burnished plank floor to the wagon wheel chandelier to the head of the six-point buck mounted over the wide stone hearth. Picture windows opened onto an orchard and a garden, with neatly tended rows of vegetables protected by chicken wire. Stretching toward the hillside behind the resort was a tall stand of corn. Somewhere, the country Caruso continued his serenade.

The lobby was deserted—except for a bucket and mop in front of the fireplace, around which the freshly washed floor shone. Wet footprints disappeared down the corridor, where I spied a sliver of daylight before the door closed.

Virginia looked toward me from across the lobby. The tenor's tune abruptly stopped. "What's going on?" she said.

We waited. Behind the front desk I lifted the receiver from a wall phone and got a dial tone. Apparently, these digs had living occupants.

"Oh, my God!" Virginia gasped. Her high heels skittered to the desk. She banged into it like she'd been shot from a cannon.

Looking past her, I saw figures creep around the edges of the huge windows. Colored guys, all of them, none appearing more than twenty years of age. Some wore work shirts, others were bare-chested. Their dark, muscled bodies were shiny with perspiration. They peered through the plate glass, squinting at us like we were goldfish in a tank. They didn't seem particularly hospitable.

"Let's get out of here," Virginia said, tugging my overcoat sleeve.

We'd nearly reached the door when its frame was filled by a burly man, black as coal. He wore an Oakland Oaks baseball cap and a bandanna tied around a neck thick as my thigh. A denim shirt barely contained his immense shoulders and chest. Virginia released my arm and slid the purse off her shoulder, fumbling with the clasp.

Suddenly the man's cold countenance cracked into a thousand-watt smile. "Man here look a lot like *Mr. Boxing!*" he sang out.

He stepped forward, paler palm outstretched, features coming into focus.

"Nightbird Jones," I said, exhaling slowly. We clasped hands.

Virginia dropped the purse. It clanked loudly on the floor.

"What in the world you doin' up here?" he asked, laughing. His relief seemed as great as mine.

"I could ask the same thing." I shook my head, still recovering.

Jones offered a hand to Virginia, now clutching the purse to her chest. "You and the missus looking to get away for a little while?"

Mistaken identity had nothing to do with how long it took Virginia to accept his gesture. In those interminable seconds, Jones sized her up, and marked her down on the debit side of his personal ledger.

"Naw, this is a friend of mine," I explained to the still-dubious Jones, who'd politely doffed his cap in a lady's presence. "Virginia Wagner. Virginia, meet Cecil 'Nightbird' Jones. Among the most colorful characters in the fight game. And the source of that singing we heard."

Sticking out an open-handed left lead, à la Jack Johnson, and clasping his cap to his chest, Nightbird issued a spontaneous, sonorous aria. Ridiculously beautiful, even if I didn't understand a word of it.

"A little Puccini for y'all," he announced, aware of the dumbfounded look on Virginia's face.

He'd picked up the gift as a kid on the show circuit with his parents, entertainers in Negro vaudeville. They drilled classic songs into him, so as to feature the boy in their act. Tiny colored kid belting out opera—brought down houses. At twenty, same kid couldn't get served a cup of coffee with all the Puccini in the world. That's when he laced 'em up. I'd profiled 'Bird a few times in the *Inquirer.*

"When Nightbird was fighting," I informed Virginia, "he'd serenade the crowd before and after a bout."

"That way should you lose—they still throw you a little sump'in." The big man smiled.

"I don't recall you losing too many," I said, boosting him. He'd been out of the ring for years. Longer than I recalled. When he'd pulled off the ball cap, he revealed a failing crop of kinky gray hair.

"That's considerate of you, Mr. Nichols. I always 'preciated the things you wrote about me." His humility shortly turned to concern: "You're not up here 'specting to write sump'in, are you?"

Several of the shades who'd been peeking in the window entered the lobby and warily assembled behind Jones. They didn't have to do much to generate a threat. Virginia stiffened at the mere sight of them. Her discomfort was again duly noted by Nightbird.

"What exactly are *you* doing in Napa?" I counterpunched.

"Fo' the last year I been runnin' this here resort as a boys' camp," he replied. "Know how they got Boys Town and so on? Well, not *every* boy's welcome in Boys Town, if you know what I mean. I was lookin' to set up a spot where boys who's gettin' the short end of the stick can learn things—keep themselves away from the short end of the night-stick, while they're at it."

He ushered us to the window, his gap-footed gait reminding me that Nightbird Jones was bow-legged as a man could be without a horse under him. Virginia stuck to me like white on rice. "See, we got our farm out here," Jones said, pointing proudly at the flourishing crops. "City boys learnin' to grow and harvest their own food. Got a big chicken coop out back. Wood shop in the barn. Mr. Sanders gave us a' old printing press, so the boys can make up their own handbills, tellin' 'bout what we runnin' here. Help spread the word down in the city, over in Oakland."

The juvenile janitor who'd Paul Revere'd earlier sauntered back to his bucket, a white undershirt draped around his neck like a stole. He manipulated the mop while boldly giving Virginia the once-over.

"Get your shirt back on, Earl," Nightbird ordered. We strolled away.

Virginia studied the floor as the dusky campers circulated.

"How many boys you taken in?" I asked.

"'Bout thirty now. All I can handle by myse'f. Hoping to get a couple other guys come help me out. Ones that's most likely to volunteer, though, they preach the Gospel too regular for my taste. I just want these boys fit to get a job, stay out of jail. They don't got to join no choir to do that."

"How'd you come to pick this place?" Virginia haltingly inquired.

"Mr. Sanders worked it out for us," Jones said, prompting an exchange of glances between me and Virginia. "Said he was tight wit' the owner, that we could caretake till they decided what they gonna do wit' it. Reopen, sell it. Whichever."

"Generous," I muttered. "You hear about his problems?"

"Mr. Sanders? Ain't seen him in a while. What sort of problems?"

"On-trial-for-murder problems. He killed Hack Escalante's wife."

"God*damn*. I can't b'lieve that!"

"Guess you're out of touch, this far off," I suggested, causing a quick shift in Nightbird's demeanor.

"Mr. Nichols, was you lookin' to get a story here? 'Cuz if you was, I'm gonna hafta talk you outta that. Las' thing I need is for folks down there round Napa to know that there a whole camp of colored boys a few miles up the mountain, know what I mean? We keep to ourselves, don't bother nobody, and that's how I want it to stay. Whatever else he mighta done, Mr. Sanders made all this happen—and I ain't never gonna have no better setup. But I don't need no publicity, see what I'm saying? That's why you didn't see nothing when you drove up. Keep the car out back, you understand? People who *need* to know we up here, they know. Take care of that ourselves."

"Don't sweat it, Nightbird," I assured him. "Strictly under my hat."

"When you made the deal to come here," Virginia said, "did you speak with anyone besides Mr. Sanders?"

Jones thoughtfully considered the question. He shook his head: "No, ma'am, never did."

"Ever meet a man named Threllkyl?" I asked. "Dexter Threllkyl?"

"The original owner or some such, I recall."

I nodded. "Ever see him? Talk with him?"

"Naw. Only know the name 'cuz Chaz, used to be caretaker here, mentioned him a couple times. Tol' me those folks ain't seen Cold Springs in years. Come up lots 'fore the war, he said."

"Chaz still around?"

"Died fo', five months ago. Nice fella. Older than some these red-woods."

"Get the feeling Threllkyl knew what was happening up here?"

"Cain't rightly say. That sump'in I oughta be worried 'bout?"

"I doubt it. He's no longer with us."

"Sorry to hear it," Nightbird said, with proper deference. Funny how only a stranger showed regret for Threllkyl's demise. Funny, too, how Jones didn't see it as his place to quiz *us*, considering how we dropped in out of nowhere. One-way interrogations must have been routine to Nightbird, and lots of guys his skin tone.

"I surely hope you'll stay and share supper with us," Jones said. "Since I make the best red beans and rice outside Louisiana. Fried chicken, too. And you *know* it don't get no fresher."

Virginia tried gamely to compose a cordial expression, but nerves undermined any hope of that. "We don't want to impose," she demurred.

"Livin' like this," Nightbird went on, "I don't get much news from the circuit. Sure would enjoy getting caught up, courtesy of *Mr. Boxing* hisself."

I clapped him on the shoulder. "How can we say no?"

White as a sheet, shrinking into her wool coat, Virginia clearly felt like a lamb circled by wolves. Either fear or prejudice was blinding her to the fact that we'd uncovered the first concrete connection linking Sanders, Threllkyl, and a tangible asset of the Mount Davidson Trust. Rudely blowing out of there seemed like a bad play on several fronts.

Nightbird flashed a gleaming smile. "Once you get a bellyful of my beans and rice, you might never *want* to leave," he said. Jones turned away from Virginia and slipped me a wink. "You decide to stay, we got plenty of rooms."

"Well, Claire had it right—you can certainly tell stories," Virginia attested, adjusting the rearview mirror. "Christ almighty, can you sling it!"

"I'll assume you mean that in a *good* way."

"I'll say this—I've learned all I need to know in one lifetime about the manly art of self-defense."

The road was pitch-black beyond the arc of our headlights. The yellow line streaked from the darkness and dashed beneath the Buick. Nightbird Jones's hospitality had eaten three hours off the clock, and Virginia drove as if trying to get back every minute. As for me, the rich and salty Southern-fried repast inspired belt-loosening cogitation.

"Okay, let's think this thing through," I began, hoping we could arrive at a plausible explanation by the time we reached the city. "If Sanders was a legitimate partner in these business deals with Threllkyl, what was the blackmail dodge about? How did his dirty-picture racket fit in?"

"You're asking me?" Virginia's confounded expression was tinted green by the glowing dashboard dials. "You had a more intimate involvement in that end of it."

She was still steamed. I hoped a calm, measured assessment might cool her off.

"Here's what I think: Sanders's role was to lure in gullible investors. Their money got filtered through bogus businesses and into some-body's bank account. Most likely Threllkyl's. Maybe it was all a high-stakes shell game. Could be they saved the blackmail for dupes who got uppity. Insurance against them going to the cops. What do you think?"

"I think we're being followed, is what I think."

Two white globes were visible about a hundred yards back. Virginia stomped on the gas, which propelled my pulse rate even faster than the car.

"Who the hell would be trailing us?" I wheezed.

"Who else?" she snapped. "You were having such a great time at the plantation I guess you never noticed that I was getting *undressed* back there!"

I anchored my right hand against the dashboard, not caring if I seemed scared shitless. I'd rubbed shoulders with hundreds of surly ghetto heroes with bad intentions and dangerous fists. None fright-ened me as much as this flighty white dame with the lead foot and wild imagination. If I'd still had my mother's rosary beads, they'd have been getting a workout.

"Take it easy!" I barked. "You can't even see the road!"

She hunkered over the wheel, jaw grimly set. The speedometer glided higher, but we couldn't shake the hounding headlights. For more than ten miles the roaring of the engine—surging down straight-aways, ebbing on curves—was the only sound in the night. Last thing I'd ever hear, I was convinced. What would Ida think when the High-way Patrol showed up, saying they'd found her husband in a wreck on a remote county road, his body crushed into a bloody knot with some strange woman?

Coming around a bend, we saw civilization ahead. Virginia gunned it. Within seconds we'd reached the Dew Drop Inn, a roadhouse that would have passed for the Wild West, if you ignored the garish neon. Virginia sent the roadster skidding across the yellow line, tires crunching and spraying gravel. She jerked to a stop inches from an old hitching rail, killing the motor and lights.

Back down the moonlit road, headlights swept out of the curve and came on fast.

Virginia yanked open her purse and fished for a split second. Out came the automatic, clutched in her fist.

"*Jesus Christ*," I pleaded. "Let's just go inside."

"Too late," she gruffly whispered.

Our pursuers traced the same arc into the gravel lot. In the wash of light, Virginia raised her blue metal guardian. The other speedster eased up to the rail about ten feet away, lamps extinguished. It was a long two-tone Cadillac, fully detailed. Virginia rolled down her window hurriedly, the better to blast away.

The driver's door of the Caddy opened, popping on a dome light.

A teenaged blonde hastily fluffed her bangs and checked her lipstick in the side mirror. Her well-mannered date came around to open the passenger door of his daddy's luxurious land yacht. As the girl stepped out daintily, the boy turned our way.

"You were gettin' along pretty good," he said, a grin spread across his eager face. "We're mighty hungry, too."

Virginia heaved a huge sigh and rested the gun on her thigh, watching the couple enter. Swing music drifted out as they went in. After a moment, she examined the pistol.

"Something else ol' Cad left behind?" I asked.

"I bought it myself," she said, admiring it in the half-light. "In Alameda. From Big Al, the Sportsman's Pal. It's a nine-millimeter Baretta. Takes thirty-eight-caliber ammo. Made in Italy. You know how it works?"

"Don't look at me, Annie Oakley."

13

Woody Montague rang next morning and told me to meet him that afternoon at the Bank Exchange bar. He'd uncovered some dope on the Mount Davidson Trust and was excited to hear I'd taken his advice and staked out Cold Springs Resort.

The Bank Exchange was at Montgomery and Washington, northeast corner of Monkey Block, a charmless four-story structure occupying the whole square block. There are more spectacular landmarks in the city, but Monkey Block holds an esteemed place in local lore, mainly on account of its indomitability. Erected in 1853, it had as its foundation a gigantic raft of redwood logs, intended to resist quakes and prevent a rising water table from swamping what was then the biggest building west of the Mississippi. Its legend grew in 1906, when the Block defiantly survived the fire that devoured most of downtown. It became a haven for artists and writers like Frank Norris, Ambrose Bierce, and Mark Twain. Currently, an ever-expanding tribe of bohemians rule the roost, sauntering around in ratty sweaters and berets, posturing with fat sketchbooks and skinny foreign cigarettes. They easily outnumber Monkey Block's remaining lawyers and accountants. Once a year, like clockwork, some demented developer announces plans to raze the whole block for a parking garage, or a hotel, or a real office building. Every year, Monkey Block prevails. It always will.

Seemed odd that Woody wanted to meet in a saloon, seeing as he was an unwavering straight arrow. Couldn't recall whiskey tainting his lips, ever. And hooch, truthfully, is what put the Bank Exchange, Poppa Coppa's, and all of Monkey Block on the map. I was reminded of this as I passed the plaque that the Clampers, a loony bunch of amateur historians and hard-drinking yahoos, had posted on the bar's brick facade: "Here in the Bank Exchange 1853–1918 Duncan Nicol invented and served Pisco Punch. *Benefactor Humani Generis*. Dedicated by E Clampus Vitus 29 January 1938."

Nicol concocted his mystical cocktail from Peruvian brandy spiced with secret liqueurs. They say he was bequeathed the recipe by a dying stranger. (When Nicol himself kicked off years later, the formula went with him.) He'd conduct his alchemy in the solitary confinement of the bar's cellar. A dumbwaiter then hoisted great bottles of the elixir up to his harried barkeeps. Pisco Punch belonged to Duncan Nicol exclusively, but it became renowned at watering holes worldwide. The tavern keeper's biggest breakthrough, however, was inviting women into a cordoned section of the bar. There, they could sample for themselves his laudable libation. Providing the gals with comfortable booths and table service, Nicol created the city's first cocktail lounge. Clearly, he deserved a monument, not just a bronze plaque.

Woodrow Montague was stationed at the rail, towering above the late lunch hour assembly of lubricious lawyers, brokers, and bankers. He sipped what regrettably looked like iced tea and flashed me a toothy grin.

"That fight in Oakland last week sounded like a barn burner," Woody said, clasping my shoulder. "Your account suggested you didn't agree with the decision."

"Turner did more work inside. Could have gone either way." I signaled to the publican for a short draft.

"You blew out so fast that night," he said, "you didn't get to meet my kids." He produced a billfold and drew out several candids of his children. Two boys and a girl; bright-eyed, good-looking youngsters. He attached names and vital statistics and predicted careers. When I'd had enough, I fished in my jacket pocket.

"Here's mine," I offered. "Vincent. Six months old." I handed over one of the Polaroids Ida'd shot of the Future Champ. Stuck it in my wallet only that morning.

The crack investigative reporter examined the photo, grinning. "Chip off the ol' block, huh?" I displayed a false smirk and repocketed the picture. The first sip of cold beer was refreshing.

"So you actually saw Cold Springs Resort with your own eyes," Woody said, sparing us further familial chitchat. My nod brightened his expression. "Well, that puts a new wrinkle on things, 'cause I found plenty of nothing behind most of the assets listed in the Mount Davidson Trust. Unless they're incorporated out of state, these enterprises seem to be nothing but smoke and mirrors."

I trotted out my post-Napa theory, suggesting the trust was a blue-sky racket created to bilk gullible investors. Having reported on scams of every variety, he didn't discount it.

"There was one seemingly legitimate concern among those I checked," Montague said. "Something called Great Western Mining and Drilling. If you read the trust provisions closely, you'll see a rider stipulates division of *certain* assets of the trust, not *all* assets. The ones like this mining and drilling outfit, and Cold Springs Resort—the stuff Burnell Sanders was supposed to get half of—I'm willing to bet all *those* are real."

"Where should I go from here?" I asked.

"With me—over to the DA's office. I sent copies of the papers over there the other day, once I'd decided a lot of this was bogus. They agreed to give me fifteen minutes today, if you can believe it." He checked his watch, while I scanned the crowd for a spot to lose my breakfast. "I'm headed over there in a few minutes," he said. "Tag along—we'll see what they make of it."

"Woody, I specifically told you to keep a low profile." I banged my beer glass down on the bar. "—Now here you go firing copies off to the DA."

Montague inspected me like I was a traitor to the Fourth Estate. "Let me get this straight," he said firmly. "—On the cuff and with no tail-chasing, I funnel your flimflam straight to the DA—and you're *complaining*? Hell, you couldn't have gotten better service if you were William Randolph Hearst."

"Not saying I don't appreciate it. But do me a favor: Leave Sanders out of it, okay?"

After a moment, and a dark look, he muttered, "Yeah, yeah, sure." Delivered with the same tone he'd use to reassure someone begging, *Don't quote me on that.*

We strode past the entrance to County Jail No. 1 on our way to the Hall of Justice. The morning's clear blue sky was being invaded by threatening clouds moving in fast off the Pacific.

"I covered one of my first stories for the *Inquirer* here," Woody said, aiming his chin at the jail's street entrance. He was trying to liven up my suddenly sour mood. "It was about how the prisoners in the top-floor cells got a free peep show whenever artists' models posed nude on the roof of Monkey Block. Silly shit, but that's what they give you when you're starting out."

As he bantered, Burney Sanders was eight stories up, stewing in a cell, waiting to be fed into the gears of the justice system. I couldn't shake the feeling that even behind bars, Sanders was pulling the strings that kept me entangled in his sordid fortunes.

When we crested Kearny, I glanced south, where the Russ Building loomed over other downtown towers. Phantoms from that bloody dream still lingered in the back of my mind, days later. A headshrinker didn't have to tell me what it meant—that I'd been unable to protect Claire when it mattered.

Now, it was Virginia Wagner at risk. I didn't want to let her down. Whatever the DA had to say about the Mount Davidson Trust, I'd be able to give her a firsthand account. If Woody started digging where he shouldn't, I'd be there to rein him in. I had no real role in these unfolding events, I reassured myself. I was no more accountable than a reporter was for the news he uncovered.

Despite the misgivings, I accompanied Montague into the Hall of Justice. Didn't have a choice, really. Whatever I was mixed up in—*a story? a favor?*—was about to take on a life of its own, beyond my purview. That rankled me.

"I'll go along for the ride," I told Montague.

Quick-stepping up the granite stairway, we negotiated the hall's first-floor bustle of cops, lawyers, witnesses, bondsmen. Ascending more steps to less clamorous corridors, we bypassed in-session courtrooms before arriving at the offices of the District Attorney. Montague had an appointment, but we were still left to cool our heels on a bench outside Pat Brown's sanctum.

Shortly, the personification of my worst case scenario—Deputy District Attorney William Corey—emerged from Brown's office to greet us. He was jacketless, his tweed trousers hitched up by braces, his fat tie loosened just enough to free up a protuberant Adam's apple. The manufactured amiability that annoyed me that night at the fights was still intact.

"Surprised to see *you* here," Corey told me, holding open the door to his office while extending the mackerel at the end of his cuff.

"Didn't expect to be here," I replied, catching then releasing his hand. "Keeping Woodrow company."

As a Pat Brown foot soldier, Corey didn't rate an anteroom or a secretary. We single-filed into an austere office, bare beige walls above mahogany wainscoting. The only plus was the view of Telegraph Hill through the venetian blinds. Woody sat opposite Corey, in a government-issue ass-breaker that seemed too fragile for his frame. I perched on a straight-back in the corner, between the flag and the coatrack. I tried my best to disappear.

Once situated behind his desk, Corey slid a slim sheaf of papers from a manila envelope. The office was so small that even where I sat I could read the handwritten address: "Edmund G. Brown, S.F. District Attorney, Hall of Justice." The dreaded Mount Davidson Trust was spreading like a cancer.

"We only had time for a cursory examination of these papers," Corey began, with more than a hint of weary disdain. "But my first impression tells me it's some sort of bunco scheme. We couldn't determine any validity to the holdings listed here." His blasé speech sounded practiced.

Montague glanced my way, perhaps hoping I'd jump in, confirm the reality of Cold Springs Resort. Instead, I tugged loose my handkerchief and blew my nose. Through the window, I watched dark clouds scuttle in off the Bay.

"Appears to me," said Montague, turning back to the deputy DA, "that the late Dexter Threllkyl was involved in soliciting investors for various phony enterprises. Some returns may have been used to buy actual assets under other names. But I'm convinced these innocent investors won't see any of the benefits to which they're entitled—unless the DA's office takes action."

"Are you representing any of these 'innocent investors'?" Corey wanted to know.

"At the moment, no," Montague said. He made a steeple of his long, tapered fingers. "I'm here merely as a concerned citizen."

Corey sniffed at the "concerned citizen" line, then cast a jaundiced eye my way: "You're not a client of Mr. Montague's?" I dangled an ankle in response. I may have pursed my lips. I said nothing. Outside, clouds massed over Coit Tower.

"Mr. Nichols is a friend," Montague said. "Not a client."

"This all you got?" Corey asked. "Without a full copy of this trust there's not a lot we can do. Photocopies of a few papers? We'd need the originals. You have them?"

"If the city is interested in pursuing this, I'll marshal the supporting material."

"Let's have it all first," Corey said. "Our office is backed up with big-ticket crimes. Any leg-up you can give might get this off the back burner."

Montague chuckled. "Million-dollar bunco rackets don't rate the front burner?"

"With all due respect, Mr. Montague"—Corey fanned the pages, accentuating their skimpiness—"this is lightweight."

Montague extended his elongated limbs as the deputy DA tucked the papers back in the envelope. Woody placidly withdrew a single folded sheet from his jacket, leaned over Corey's desk, and smoothed the page out on the brown blotter. My heart skipped, recognizing the histrionic style of a veteran reporter dropping heavy evidence on an unwitting subject.

"Would you call *this* lightweight?"

He showed the goddamned rider. With Burney Sanders's name on it.

Corey studied it for several moments, jaw muscles working silently, while I considered methods of murdering Montague and escaping from the Hall of Justice.

"Don't know what this is all about," Corey said, resting his palms on the document. "But I can assure you one thing. It is the priority of this office to convict Burnell Sanders of murder. His purported involvement in some other penny-ante scheme—it will not be allowed to impede the prosecution."

He gave us both what he imagined was an intimidating glower. Outside, it would have earned a bantamweight bleeder like Corey a swift backhand. In the Hall, pumped up on Pat Brown's juice, he delivered a fairly convincing threat.

It was not, however, sufficient to detour Woody Montague: "Counselor," he addressed Corey, the words iced with sarcasm, "you have no idea whether this helps or hurts your case. Or what connection it might even have. If any. I'd suggest a little investigative work might be in order."

"Our case is strong enough," said the deputy DA.

Woody rubbed the bristles on the back of his head, then shot his cuffs. Maybe he was reliving the final days of his newspaper career, when editors wouldn't let him follow white-hot leads. Maybe his "crusader for justice" principles were being degraded.

The charcoal-gray clouds, rolling southeast, passed over the Hall. Daylight dimmed, as distinctly as if someone had shut the blinds.

"How'd this get into *your* hands?" the deputy DA cross-examined Montague. Before Woody could answer, Corey fired another salvo at me: "Did Sanders fill you in on this when you talked to him last week? Tell you where to find it?"

Montague peered over his shoulder at me, eyes baffled behind thick lenses. Corey picked up on Woody's perplexity. Any sharp attorney would.

"No," I said. "He didn't say anything about it." My chair felt uncomfortably like a witness stand.

"Then where'd this come from?" Corey stabbed at the envelope.

I shrugged, feigning ignorance. Raindrops began pinging off the windows.

"What difference does it make?" Woody protested, trying to regroup. "Threllkyl's name is all over the damn thing. You want to get to the bottom of it, that's where you start."

"Appreciate the advice, but I'm asking where these copies came from."

"By way of an anonymous tip," I said.

That didn't please the deputy District Attorney. He dismissed me with a glare and returned his attention to Montague.

"Were you aware that Mr. Nichols could be called as a witness against Sanders?" Corey inquired. "And that he has been previously cautioned about potential conflict of interest in the case? Frankly, I'm surprised to see him here today. Particularly in connection to this." He held up the envelope and the rider and dropped both into a desk drawer.

"I was not informed of that," Woody said, with a little cough. "But then, that's not the sole reason I'm here. There's also the matter of my ongoing investigation of Virgil Dardi and the Major Liquor Company."

"Ah, I should have known," Corey muttered, his jaded grimace a parody of a seen-it-all beat cop. "You just won't give up on that, will you?"

"One of his drivers nearly killed a man last week," Montague said, "and Dardi is trying to duck the claim. As you may or may not know, his company—which has trucks running pell-mell all over this town—doesn't carry insurance. Reason enough to run him in."

Corey's patience was evaporating fast: "What's your pitch, Montague?"

"I want to see the DA's dossier on Dardi—I suspect it contains ample evidence of his history of illegal activity in San Francisco. This being an elected office, those files are a matter of public record."

"That's been settled," Corey said. "A dead issue." His words dropped like ice cubes in a highball glass. Enmity shrouded the room as quickly and completely as had the cloud cover.

"Yet Dardi's back in business," Montague jabbed. "Why does the District Attorney have a hands-off policy for this crook?" Moments like that, it was as if he were back on the job, buttonholing a shifty subject.

The deputy District Attorney stood up: meeting adjourned.

"Mr. Montague," he said. "Years as a reporter have you seeing conspiracies where none exist."

Woody unfolded from his chair like a fireman's ladder. Seemed his head might crack the ceiling. "Maybe that's because I'm used to seeing this office produce 'witnesses' where none exist," he said, staring down the diminutive deputy. The mercury had shot all the way to the top of Woody's thermometer.

"Keep in touch," Corey said. He came around his desk and flipped on the overhead light, which gave us all a sickly yellowish pallor. He swung wide the door, issuing us into the hollow echoes of the corridor.

* * *

"What the fuck was *that* about?" I yelled at Montague through hammering rain. "We went in there upstanding, *concerned citizens*. Next thing I know, I'm gonna have to referee!"

We dashed past all the neon Bail Bonds signage on Kearny. I got winded keeping pace with Woody's loping gait. He slid to a halt, peering at me from under a soggy morning edition of the *Chronicle* he'd cadged in lieu of a hat. "You neglected to tell me that you had a personal connection to this murder trial—what's *that* about?"

I pulled him under the awning of the Silver Stable saloon. Hail lashed the taut fabric, forcing us to shout. "I'm not *connected* to it. I provided some information that helped the cops nail Sanders. That's all."

Montague shook his head, melancholy, scattering raindrops from his scalp. He doffed spectacles and swabbed at them with his tie. "You should have let me know you were tied up in it."

"I *told* you not to mention Sanders," I said. "I told you flat out. Then you had to pull that grandstanding stunt!"

"They need to know somebody's watching," Montague said, sliding the glasses back on and drilling me with a pained look. "Nich, you got a chance to see for yourself what I've been dealing with for years. That office operates on its own agenda; it has carte blanche to persecute or protect whomever it wants, for whatever reason. I've been a turd in their punch bowl for years, you might as well know. Pat Brown has a wiretap on my office phone, out of courtesy. It's standard procedure for the DA's office, when people aren't on their side."

"Goddamnit, they had no reason to keep tabs on *me*. Until *now*. Christ, Corey would more than likely have given us a fair shake on the trust until you got crazy over that truck accident thing."

"Nich, they're not going to dig into the trust, no matter how Sanders is mixed up in it. They want him to go down. Simple as that. Be careful how they try to use you. Because believe me, they'll stop at nothing. Like this thing with your pal, Bernal. Last week I couldn't locate a single reliable witness to the accident. But soon as I did? Dardi's lawyers—out of the blue—come up with a guy who claims to have seen the whole incident, and will say under oath that Bernal was at fault. We go to court, I guarantee the DA will support this guy's perjury, hook, line and sinker. It happens all the time."

"I was a block away when that wreck happened, you know. There weren't a lot of witnesses around."

"You wouldn't have missed this guy. He's huge. His name's Emmanuel Gold—and my guys say he's building quite a résumé as a 'reliable witness.'"

14

A few nights later my wife and I were witnesses to a culinary car wreck. I'd tactlessly wrangled an invitation out of Manny Gold to dine at his St. Francis Wood manse, payback for greasing the skids with the promotions manager at the *Inquirer*.

"Ten thousand pocket guards," Gold crowed to Ida. "That's not to be taken lightly. It's a foot in the door of this city's leading newspaper, and likely just the first taste of what will be a long, fruitful relationship with Mr. Hearst."

Only Manny could convert a handout from some flunky into a gilt-edged pass to San Simeon. That required imagination—and as I'd learned from Woody Montague, Gold's was vivid.

"I owe it all to your husband," Manny proclaimed, Mr. Magnanimous. Ida was using a fork to excavate edible morsels from the gustatory catastrophe on her plate. Realizing Manny was speaking to her, she paused and delivered a demure smile. "That's such good news," she replied, generically.

Manny presided at the head of the table, mammoth torso swathed in a crimson smoking jacket, accented with black velvet cuffs and lapels. A gold ascot featuring a dizzying pattern of whorls was almost tucked inside his starched size-twenty collar. Hoisting a goblet of red wine, whose bottom he'd examined several times already, our florid host proposed yet another toast: "To my good friend—and in this case, benefactor—the finest sporting scribe not only in this city or state . . ."

Manny enacted the effusive emcee awhile longer, which allowed me to sit humbly with hands folded, avoiding the sodden vegetables in watery butter sauce and slab of meat so petrified I could have been gnawing pumice. Masons could set bricks with those mashed potatoes.

I felt bad for Ida. She'd eagerly anticipated, first off, a night out, but specifically a long-delayed reunion with Pacific Heights purebred Peggy Winokur Gold. Originally, the plan included the women impressing each other with their children, but that didn't pan out. Manny unsubtly suggested a sitter, specific reasons unstated. Ida enlisted her sister Paula to watch our towheaded tyke and gamely decided to make the best of it.

As we'd gotten dressed, Ida recounted all the clever cooking tips she'd learned from Peggy over the years, especially for holiday fêtes. The Golds were known to lay out a gala groaning board. All of Manny's associates, square and shifty, enjoyed uproarious hours of hot toddies and savory hors d'oeuvres. Some years had passed since the last Yuletide extravaganza. In the interim, it wasn't only Peggy's soufflés that had fallen.

"At the post office today," she started in, apropos of nothing, "an older woman was behind me. She kept asking over my shoulder if this was the stamp window. Just for buying stamps. Then she shouted at the clerk. While he was trying to count out my change. And I told her over my shoulder, you know, politely, casually, that she shouldn't be bothering the clerk. Not when he had a customer already. She got mad. She thought it was taking me too long, having my change counted. I could tell she was giving me dirty looks. I felt them. Felt them in the back of my head."

Peggy sat opposite her husband, at the far end of a table long enough to serve as the boarding platform at West Portal station. Manny had the chance to make things more intimate by removing a few leaves, but I suspected his intention was to relegate Peggy to Outer Slobovia.

"I was trying to tell the clerk that I thought mail service had become unsatisfactory," Peggy droned on, "because we've gotten other people's mail. In our box so many times, and then the clerk said: 'You'll have to do something about that.' The woman behind me was still there, and she said: 'This isn't the complaint window.' I got *so* mad. That bitch. I thought I might turn around and choke her. I hate people like that. People who just get so . . . *close.*"

Ida displayed a brittle smile, but her eyes were mortified.

"Service at most agencies is brutal these days," I said; conversational camouflage.

We'd been at the Golds' over two hours and had yet to board Peggy's train of thought. Departures were frequent, destinations indecipherable.

Peggy Winokur once was a fixture in the Society section of the *Inquirer*, chairing charity fashion shows, glamorizing Salvation Army donation drives. I couldn't recall, though, the last time I'd seen her wide, toothy kisser in the paper, or a mention of her in Rosalie Marchmont's column, which slavishly recorded the antics of the city's pelf-drunk elite. The specimen at the dinner table may have been a prize filly in her youth, but she'd gone gaunt and leathery. A green silk tunic hung from shoulders stiff and narrow as a coat hanger.

"I was hoping to see Daniel tonight," Ida remarked. For the twelfth time. "It's been so long. He must be a big boy now."

"Almost nine," Manny said, trying to distract my wife.

"Such a handful," Peggy moaned. "I'm glad he was tired. He wanted to go to bed. Poor boy gets wound up. And then . . . he falls apart. Like his mother." A flag went up in Peggy's mind, her train detouring again: "Psychologists think they're mind changers. Witch doctors. I just told him, 'Why should I exploit myself or my family to answer your questions? You agreed to prescribe for me. I'm not your doctor. Who's paying who? You want to know these things—*why*? I'm glad for eight minutes to talk. But is it really worth the privacy that's gone? Or the pills? Or the dollars? How do I *feel*? I can ask that myself.'"

Beneath the table, Ida gave me a kick. Manny compulsively rotated a band of gold the size of a napkin ring on his finger. He observed his wife with weary eyes.

Ida mercifully brought the miserable meal to a close, excusing herself to use the ladies' room. Manny encouraged his wife to clear the table, which she managed amid a running diatribe directed at no one in particular. Gold shunted me into the living room, where embers glowed in the huge fireplace. From a cabinet, he produced a humidor.

"You know Teddy Salazar?" he asked. "Shitheel stiffed me on a deal. Squeezed these out of him, though. A decent smoke." He clipped a cigar and handed it over.

The room, framed by a procession of elegant French doors, let out to a front lawn on which the 49ers could have scrimmaged. Through scores of beveled panes I observed St. Francis Woods' broad streets and tended hedges, illuminated by antique streetlamps. Flaring up my stogie, I spotted a big galvanized tub in the corner, positioned to catch drippings from a soggy stretch of ceiling.

"Goddamn rains," Manny sighed, puffing like a locomotive. I had a feeling the water damage had gone unattended through several stormy spells.

"Thanks for dinner," I said.

"Thanks for pretending to eat it. I got stuck, I'll admit. She can't cook anymore. Or do much of anything, for that matter. Tried to help, but I can't boil water." He took two port glasses and a bottle from a liquor cart. "Don't know what I'm going to do, William. Look at her. Something's obviously wrong. She's had a dozen tests, doctors, psychologists, every goddamn thing. Nobody can put a name on it. A week or a month goes by, she'll be like everybody remembers her. Then out of the blue—it's as if the world's coming to an end. Goes wild if she's not . . . controlled."

The mantel was crowded with framed photos of Peggy in her halcyon days, always the center of attention, even in the shots with her newborn. No Manny, though. He must have been behind the camera, smitten.

"What happened?"

"Damned if I know. Hard to believe, looking at her, she's only thirty-six years old. I still love her, William. But I don't know how long I can keep riding this roller-coaster. It's not easy. That's why I had you over, partially. Needed someone to see for themselves. I needed you to know."

"Can you put her somewhere?"

His eyes flared, like he might bust the bottle over my head for suggesting such a thing. But the fire died quickly.

"Those places are expensive. I could be paying out another fifty years. Even if I wanted to, I don't know that I could afford it. Let me be honest. I'm having a bad run these days. Flat on my ass thanks to some of the lousy deals I've worked lately. Screwed six ways from Sunday."

"Still got this place. Worse comes to worst . . ."

"Lucky not to get a double hernia carrying this mortgage."

"You've got plenty of leverage, Manny."

"Leverage?" he scoffed. "I can't leverage a goddamn dime off a lunch counter."

"Her family won't help?"

He nearly snapped his cigar in half. "Fucking goy bastards! Rather see her rot than lift a finger. Once she hooked up with the big Jew, they disowned her. If she divorced me—*then* maybe they'd pitch in. You can't possibly know what it's like, my friend. I stole their prize. A dirty Yid from the Fillmore! Think I'd give them the satisfaction of crawling back, begging? They'd want me arrested for ruining their precious baby. Anyway, I'd kill myself before letting them see me squirm."

I sipped some port and kept my mouth shut.

"God damn it," Manny said, cracking a smile even though he looked ready to bawl. "Broad showed a lot of guts marrying me. She was something, back then."

Despite feeling like a two-ton prick, I had to get to it now, before I drowned in all this pathos.

"Heard from a friend you saw that accident at Third and Howard, the one Dardi's truck was mixed up in."

He rotated the cigar between his lips, moist eyes gleaming warily. No reply.

"Supposed to testify, in fact. That the other driver was at fault."

"He was," Manny declared. "And, yeah, I saw the whole thing."

"Manny, the wreck was a minute or two after you left me in front of the Hearst Building. You were walking toward Sutter to get your car. How the hell do you end up at Third and Howard? It's half a mile away."

"It's five blocks. I drove. What's the big deal?"

"Guy in the other car was a friend of mine. Tony Bernal. Works at the *Inquirer*. He was on his way to pick me up."

Gold plucked the cigar from his downturned lips. No surprise in his eyes, only dejection, exhaustion.

"If that isn't a damn shame," he said. He poured another dose of port and downed it in a gulp.

"I was there, too, Manny. Right after it happened. Didn't see *you* anywhere."

"What are you saying?"

"That I didn't see you. There were cops on the scene who barely got anything in the way of eyewitness accounts."

"I was in my car, coming down New Montgomery," he said, tracing the route in the air with his huge mitt. "Turned onto Howard. Wasn't even a half block back when I saw a green coupe turn into Third. Right in front of the truck. *Bang!* Just like that. The way it always happens."

"Why didn't you stop? You could've helped, least told the cops what you saw."

"I'd been away all day. Getting those pocket guards printed up. Had to make it home." He nodded toward the other room, as if that was explanation enough. Maybe it was.

"Why Howard?" I was compelled to ask. "Why not take Mission? Everybody else does."

"So you're the driving expert now?" he said. "Of all people. And you feel you can question my honesty, in my own house? That's what you're doing, isn't it? You don't believe I was *there*? For fuck's sake, my old pal gangs up on the Jew now, too?"

"Ease off, Manny. Tony Bernal's a buddy of mine. I'd hate to see him get screwed over. Already, he might not walk again."

"And who doesn't have problems? What I saw is what I saw, and I'm just doing what any good citizen's s'posed to. Providing the truth."

To the highest bidder, I was tempted to add. But I couldn't. Manny's story, though far-fetched, was plausible.

"Hard to swallow, how things work out sometimes," I said, draining my glass.

"Ain't it though," he sighed, doing the same.

Peggy gave an embarrassing waterworks farewell at the door. It left us drained and mute as Ida piloted our sedan along winding, tree-lined streets, downhill to Portola Drive.

"When I went to the bathroom," she eventually said, "I found all kinds of prescriptions in the medicine cabinet."

"What were you looking in there for?"

"Are you serious? Peggy's loony. Maybe it's because she's all pilled up."

"Ida, leave well enough alone."

"So sorry, I can't. And I didn't."

I glanced over at her. Another shoe was set to drop.

"As I came out, I heard what sounded like crying, so I went that way. The door was closed at the end of the hall, but there were these big sobs on the other side. So I went in. Daniel was in bed, under the covers, crying, sweating like he had a fever. I sat down to say hello, to sit with him a minute and calm him down. But he looked up at me and his *eyes*—he was terrified. Heaving and panting. He didn't move. Then I pulled back the sheets"—Ida was beginning to weep herself—"and saw that he was *tied* to the bed."

We sat silently, waiting to make a left, headlights floating past.

"I didn't know what to do," she sobbed. "What *can* you do? I went back out and talked to Peggy, acting like nothing had happened, but I wanted to call the police or something. I still want to. What should we do?"

"Not our problem," I grunted. "We don't know enough about what's going on in their home to get involved."

"We can't just leave that poor boy at her mercy. She's not a fit mother. We have to do something."

"My father used to have an expression," I said, gazing unblinking into the oncoming lights. "One I never really understood until recently. Practically every day—after he'd talked to my mother, or a friend, or read something in the paper—he'd give this bitter little laugh, and he'd say, 'No good deed ever goes unpunished.'"

I couldn't see a damn thing. My glasses were fogged with fine yellow dust. Condensation caked the residue into a muddy film. Only when a bead of sweat trickled from under my hat and splashed the lenses could I see anything at all.

Landscape was barren, save for the yawning mouth of a cave before me, situated between two hillocks dotted with scrub. White sky. Yellow land. Wind roared and stung my ears. I desperately wanted to wipe my glasses. No chance. Because my hands gripped a thick rope, which I was pulling for all I was worth. It led straight into the cave, and whatever was on the other end had this tug-of-war at a standstill.

"What are we pulling?" I asked, sensing others behind me on the rope.

"Who the hell knows," came a sandpaper laugh over my right shoulder. "But you better not let go."

Burney Sanders's voice.

Then *he* released the rope, and the pull from the other end jerked me forward. My feet banged against something solid. I glanced down: My heels were wedged against a cross-tie. A railroad track led into the cave. Mine shaft?

Sanders walked into view, barely distinguishable from the terrain in a dust-encrusted suit and tie. The brim of his salt-rimmed hat flapped furiously. Bending down, he hoisted a dangerous-looking piece of equipment, heavy enough to wobble his legs.

There was another unmistakable voice—Manny Gold's: "And what's the drill for?"

"For you, you fat fuck," Sanders said. "Start pulling your weight, or I'm gonna yank your thumb outta your ass and shove this in there instead."

"Enough bullshit," Gold said. "Nobody's ever helped me—what do I need this for?"

Now Manny let go. I lurched forward, stumbling to my knees, still clutching the rope. I tugged hard as I could, but whatever was at the other end drew me inexorably toward the mouth of the tunnel. Sanders stood there, implacably coercing a cord on the drill. It sputtered, but wouldn't come to life. Manny walked up the hillside and peered into the dark opening.

"What's in there?" I grunted, twisting rope around my arms, struggling for any purchase. I couldn't stand up, afraid I'd lose my balance altogether.

"Nothing," Manny hollered faintly, into the wind. "Nothing at all."

That made Sanders laugh like hell.

I must have been awake for half an hour, staring into the darkness, before I made the connection. Maybe I was talking to myself, as much as dreaming.

Leaving Ida asleep in the sack, I felt my way down the pitch-black corridor to the back bedroom I used as an office. The luminous dial on my desk clock read one-thirty. I clicked on the lamp next to the azalea. I'd given the plant to Claire, but dug it out of her garden after she'd died. I hunkered down on the floor. Opening the bottom drawer, I rooted through numerous accordion wallets filled with poorly organized financial records.

Fifteen minutes later, I found what I was after: a share certificate dated 1940, emblazoned "Red Dog Mines," recorded in Stanislaus County.

Not wanting to wake Ida or the baby, I shut our bedroom door and gingerly made my way downstairs, to the desk in the foyer. By then, my eyes had adjusted. I didn't need a light to dial the phone.

Third ring, she picked up: "Who the hell is this?" Appropriate, given the hour.

"Virginia, it's Billy. I need you to do me a favor. Right now."

"Are you all right?" I envisioned her sitting up in bed, rearranging the covers.

"I'll survive. Sorry to call so late. Can you check the Davidson papers real quick? See if there's a listing among the assets for something called Red Dog Mines."

"Wouldn't that be in the copies I gave you?"

"Just check, Ginny. Please."

Last thing she needed to know was I didn't even *have* those copies anymore. I heard her slide free of the covers and pad out of the bedroom, grousing mildly. She was more organized than me. It took her only a couple of minutes.

"Red Dog Mines. One of four so-called explorations. The trust holds loans on the mortgages of all four, under the heading 'Resources.' What's it all about?"

"This is getting out of hand," I whispered. "Starting to scare me."

"Tell me what's going on."

"If I could, I would. Talk to you later. Thanks."

I thought about being civil and waiting until morning. But my finger used muscle memory, ratcheting the number. The phone was scooped up before the first ring ended.

"Matthew, is that you?" she breathed into the speaker. "Where are you?"

"Peggy—it's Billy Nichols. I need to talk to Manny."

"Are you someplace I can see you?"

What a pathetic mess. I felt sorry for Peggy, for her husband, for her kid, and for nearly everybody I could think of at the moment. Manny wrestled the phone from her, and he wasn't discreet about it. Everybody's rope has an end.

"Who's this?" Manny barked. I wondered if he slept at all anymore. Or if he double-dosed her once in a while to get some relief.

"It's Billy," I said. "Who's Matthew?"

"Her brother. What gives? It's practically morning. No food poisoning, I hope."

"Maybe this brother can help out with her."

"He's dead."

"Sorry. *Christ.* Manny, I was wondering what you've got planned tomorrow."

"I'm taking Daniel to Playland-at-the-Beach. I promised him."

"What time? 'Cause I'm gonna meet you there. Remember that wedding present you gave me and Ida? I've got some questions about that."

15

I rode the streetcar to Ocean Beach with about twenty rambunctious lads, all making the Saturday excursion as honored guests of the rival *San Francisco News*. Contest winners, they were—newsboys who'd signed up fresh subscribers. I scouted out the ace achievers and tried to lure them over to the *Inquirer*.

"Playland's for kids," I told them, as their chaperone was busy counting out transfers. "We're giving our newsies all-expenses-paid trips to Sally Stanford's crib."

"Already been there," crowed one little wisenheimer.

As last stops went, it was tough to beat Playland-at-the-Beach. The streetcar turnaround swiveled in the crosshatched shadows of the gigantic, rickety Big Dipper roller-coaster, which had hurtled screaming San Francisco kids through the misty sea air for decades. The sprawling ten-acre amusement park was at the north end of the Great Highway, a ribbon of asphalt that paralleled the pounding Pacific. The road climbed to the Cliff House, now only a sawed-off stepchild of the spectacular Bavarian confection that glowered over Seal Rock in the late 1800s.

Like most city kids, I had my first trip to Playland on a birthday, my eighth. Mother rounded up some of my pals and shepherded us across town. It required multiple transfers. Back then, the outer Sunset and Richmond districts were shacks and sand. To a bunch of Butchertown boys, it felt like camel-riding the Sahara.

We swarmed all over Playland, which seemed to ramble on forever. I was a terror on any ride that stayed horizontal, but the precarious latticework scaffolding of the hugely popular Shoot the Chutes attraction looked to my already suspicious eyes like a jerry-rigged trap, ripe for collapse. While the other kids crammed in line, I clung to my mother, my cohorts jeering as I sniveled. All the way home I pleaded with my mother: *Don't tell Father I was afraid.*

My second trip to Playland, I was eighteen—big man in the making. I'd scoped out the Skyliner ride as the perfect distraction to steal a smooch from dishy Maura Whitecart, a former schoolmate trying to catch on at the *Inquirer* as a linotype operator. Riding the Skyliner, however, you got more than your money's worth, when the wind gusted off the whitecaps and lashed the little two-seat welded-metal planes and the skinny cables from which they swung. Turbulence nearly launched my lunch into Maura's lap. I've never flown again, with or without cables. Never got that kiss from Maura, either.

Manny Gold waited, as agreed, in the main hall. Steamed-up windows vibrated, echoing the cacophony of squealing children. Standing stone-still in his commodious topcoat and broad-brimmed hat, Manny could have passed for an attraction. I thought some kid might run up and slip a token in him. Looming above Gold on the wall was a trio of lacquered papier-mâché faces: One laughed, one wept, and the largest one in the middle, with waxed mustache and Valentino pomade, smiled down and with a rattling, recorded chortle welcomed you to Playland.

"You're late," Manny griped.

"Five minutes. Had to take the streetcar."

"He's getting cranky," Manny went on. He gestured toward the Whirling Wheel, a circular parquet floor spinning at the bottom of a banked ring. It swished kids around like they were being fried in a skillet. "I've left him on that goddamn thing four straight rides, waiting for you to show. He's about to toss his cookies."

"Pull him off," I said. "Put him on something else. We'll talk."

Gold gathered in his son, fragile as a bird in his father's massive embrace. The boy wore a bulky blue cardigan, buttoned up. His cheeks flushed blotchy pink and perspiration glued dark curls to his glazed, pale forehead. Daniel seemed a delicate boy. Took after his mother, obviously.

"Having fun?" Manny asked him. He gently smoothed his son's hair with a hammy palm. Daniel's eyes spun, exhilarated or delirious.

"Can we ride the Big Dipper next?" Dad looked dubious.

"Danny, this is a friend of mine. Mr. Nichols. He's a famous writer." A hint he should behave.

We traded tiny waves. The kid slipped from his father's arms like a cat squirming loose. "Big Dipper!" he shrieked, tugging the old man's sleeve. "Big Dipper!"

Playland was lots more fun than being tied to a bed.

The boy was less than enthused, however, when his father plunked him down on one of the ornate wooden horses in the merry-go-round. Manny tried to step off as the carousel began revolving, but Daniel grabbed him, rooting his father to the spot. Manny grinned down as he passed, showing upturned palms. I grabbed a horse's hoof and hoisted myself aboard. We were quite a sight, Manny and me: stolid figures in overcoats and fedoras, in a whirl of blinking lights, bobbing ponies, calliope music. A couple of Hoover's men, trailing underage Reds.

"What's your connection to Dexter Threllkyl?" I asked Manny, beside a gracefully dipping swan.

"You know Dex?" He looked confounded.

"Long story, Manny. Give me the straight dope. Then I'll get out of your hair. Let you enjoy the rest of the day. Deal?"

"I met him in . . . thirty-nine, I guess—right after he came back from D.C. Introduced by Peggy's family. He did some work for them, I heard. Never really clear on that."

"I thought he was an attorney."

"That's what it said on his card. You could tell he was into lots of things. An operator."

"Takes one to know one."

"It's all a hustle, William. Top to the bottom. And every level in between. The Threllkyl family came off strictly upper crust, 'to the manner born' and all that. His wife always went around with her nose in the air, acting like their shit didn't stink. But I knew better."

"How's that?"

"Threllkyl wasn't any blueblood. Born an Okie. But smart and shifty enough to pass."

"Where'd you fit in?"

"Since I had connections around town, Dex thought I could help him line up investors, folks looking for easy money. Sorts of people he wouldn't ordinarily meet in his circles."

"What kind of investments?"

"Property speculation and such."

"Like what you gave me and Ida as a wedding present?" I sneered. "One hundred shares in 'Red Dog Mines.' Ida figured that'd put a kid through college one day."

"Only thing worse than buying too fast is selling too soon," Manny said, shrugging his huge shoulders and chest.

"Cut the crap, Manny. It's all a racket, isn't it? A big con job. What was Threllkyl's dodge? For real. He can't do anything to you now."

"I'm no fool. I could see what he was cooking up. Selling suckers worthless deeds and shares in bogus corporations. Not that he'd admit to it. Cattle-grazing acreage, mining claims, timberland, inland oil drilling, insurance outfits—you name it. His game was hooking investors. Like trout. He loved it, he was good at it. To keep it going, though, he had to draw from the bottom of the deck, if you read me."

Manny rubbed his son's head as the horses slowed from gallop to canter.

"I guess that's why he used guys like me," he added.

As soon as he had dismounted, Danny hightailed for the Big Dipper. There was a long line already, including a group of girls mustered single-file by a stout sister, decked out in full regalia: capacious white coronet, outsized dangling crucifix, brutal black shoes, the whole nine yards of habit. A pair of younger postulants helped her tend the flock. Yapping around them, like a pack of puppies, were the newsboys. Their chaperone had vanished. Probably bound and gagged behind the Chutes. One of the bootjacks gave me the lowdown: the quail were on a field trip from St. Joe's Orphanage. Manny, Danny, and I stood to the side, watching the pint-sized sinners slip past Sister Battle-Ax to worm their way into seats with the lonesome lasses.

"He'll have to go up with an adult, or one of these other kids," the attendant declared, catching my attention. "He's too small to ride by himself."

Daniel's eyes implored his old man.

"The line's too long," Manny said. "We'll wait'll it thins out."

Watching the train fill up, I diagnosed the real issue: Manny couldn't fit. The cars weren't designed for asses the size of Alcatraz.

The kid started bawling. Manny edged him to the side and hunkered down for a parental powwow. It took about five minutes of cajoling to shut off the faucets. I can only imagine what he had to promise.

So this is what I have to look forward to, I thought.

"I know what you'll get a kick out of," Manny said, leading the kid away from the Big Dipper. But as we approached the fun house, we saw signs: CLOSED FOR RECONSTRUCTION. Weeks earlier, two corpses were discovered in there, a man and a woman, the mirrors all shot to hell. The dailies cashed in: lots of photos with dotted-line diagrams. Reopened, it'd be more popular than ever.

Gold marched his sullen son over to the slides. Dutifully, Danny trudged to the top as if ascending the gallows.

"How were Threllkyl and Burney Sanders connected?" I nudged Manny, trying to regain the thread.

"I introduced 'em," he explained. "Threllkyl goes through finders like shit through a goose. *Went* through 'em, I should say. He wore me out, I'll tell you. Dex was dirtier than I thought, and I wanted to play it straight now that I was married to Peggy."

"This was when?"

"Years ago."

"He was running these cons during the war?"

"I don't know. I cut him loose, I told you. But after the war, he came looking for me again. All geared up for another go. I gave him the okeydoke. Burney Sanders seemed like the kind of guy who'd work with an operator like Dex. So I put them together and I sort of back-doored it."

Some bucktoothed eager beaver was trying to cut in front of Danny at the top of the slide. Manny bellowed: "Hey! Howdy Doody! He's ahead of you—back off!"

"What do you know about the Mount Davidson Trust?" I asked, trying my best Woody Montague impression.

"Not a damn thing. What is it?"

"Whole mishmash of Threllkyl's assets, I guess. Some real, some phony. Red Dog Mines is in there."

Gold looked away, red-faced.

"I shouldn't ask my broker to buy more, huh?"

"When I gave you that I didn't know what Threllkyl was all about," Manny maintained. His eyes fixed on Danny, descending the wavy slide. "I wouldn't have. You know that."

By then, I had no idea what I knew.

"Listen," Manny said, turning back to me and stuffing his hands in the pockets of his overcoat. "This is what I finally figured: In Washington, Threllkyl had ten years of easy-does-it government jobs. Department of the Interior. Bureau of Land Management. That's how he knew where all these federal parcels were. He'd lie and claim they were private property and give a big spiel about how he had inside dope on development plans. Then he'd take the investors' deposits and go buy something legit that the marks could never trace. Most of the paper he circulated was forged. Hell, I wouldn't be surprised if his death certificate was, too."

"*What?* You can't be serious."

"Actually, I am. Heard stories that he faked his death before—in twenty-nine. Things got hot, he had creditors up his ass. Took a powder back East until things cooled off."

"Gimme a break. You can't pretend you're dead then show up ten years later."

"Long as nobody puts the finger on you—why not?"

My jaw must have been down around my chest, 'cause Manny took a look at me and started backtracking: "I'm not saying he's not dead, you understand. But if he turns up again—different name, different place—don't be surprised."

"Had enough for one day?" Manny tugged the sweater tighter around his son. The kid looked crestfallen; he knew the fun was coming to an end. Dad tried a bribe: "Don't you want an It's-It?"

"C'mon," I told the sulking kid, tapping his shoulder. "Let's ride the Big Dipper."

Manny looked at me like I'd turned water into wine.

The clanking antique drew us slowly up the rails. Scaffolding groaned under the strain, a truly awful sound. Danny gripped the side bar with all his might. The cars had no front: All the better, I surmised, to expose the terror as the goddamn thing jerked around. All that was holding us in was a flimsy belt, with a buckle I wouldn't trust on my trousers.

Reaching the ride's apex, we were treated to a perfect view: endless ocean to the west, coastline stretching south, dense greenery of Golden Gate Park to the east, bordered on both sides by rolling avenues of tract houses. Downtown disappeared in a distant fog. Stunned by this magical perspective—top of the world—Danny looked up at me, awestruck. I had to crack a smile.

So this is what I have to look forward to, I thought.

It would have been nice to have a moment to enjoy the vista. Next thing we knew, we were plunging downward and kids were screaming, full voice, like the ground was going to open and drop us into hell. I tugged down my hat until it hurt. The brim flapped up, pinned by the wind. I must have looked like Leo Gorcey. We flew into a sharp curve and I thought we were both going to go sailing onto the Great Highway. Danny let go of the freezing metal rail and grabbed my arm instead. I relinquished my death grip on the car and held his hand. The kid was rigid with fright.

Nudging up his sleeve, I took note of the pinkish indentation encircling his wrist.

Then my lid blew off. Goddamn twenty-five-dollar beaver-felt Knox. As we careened into another banked turn, I saw the wind take it away, flipping it this way and that, taunting me. We lurched hard to the left, then into another stomach-churning drop, and I never saw that hat again.

Danny wobbled off the platform and into his father's waiting arms. "Can I go again?" he wheezed, breathless. Manny cut loose a happy cackle. Proud, I supposed, that his kid had not only survived, but was ready for more punishment.

"Where's your hat?" Manny asked me, as he hefted his son onto his shoulder.

"Don't ask." Cold air needled my scalp. Hatless was as bad as trouserless, far as I was concerned. "I was hoping you saw it fly off, thought maybe you'd picked it up."

Manny suddenly looked glum.

"That was *yours*?" he asked, wincing. "Guy picked a hat up—right over there. Put it on and walked away, like it was his. If I'da known . . ."

"No good deed," I grumbled to myself, checking to see if all my other parts were still attached.

"No need to worry," Manny said, throwing an arm around my shoulder. "I got a haberdasher—he's gonna fix you right up. Least I can do for our Uncle William. Right, Danny?"

16

I filed my final Golden Gloves advance piece Monday morning, trusting Fuzzy could find a slot for it somewhere in the wall-to-wall coverage of Saturday's Big Game. The Bears had squeaked past the Indians, 7–6, in a contest that drew eighty thousand to Memorial Stadium on the Berkeley campus. Sunday Sports featured slavish accounts, with several full pages devoted to stop-action, sequential photos of the two touchdowns, and the critical missed extra point. Dotted-line diagrams tracking the various trajectories of players and ball looped and twisted all over the spreads. Monday's early editions reprised the whole shebang.

I'd be fortunate to squeeze in a two-column squib, previewing the Gloves' opening night.

The whole department maintained a vigil that morning, waiting to hear if the narrow win would earn Cal the nod over Oregon as Pac-10 representative in the Rose Bowl. If the Bears were picked, Sports would fly into a frenzy, coverage spilling over from page one. I strolled nonchalantly off the floor, telling Fuzzy I had a lunch date. He treated me to a baleful gaze, with the fully furrowed brow. I assured him I'd be back within the hour, ready to help carry the load.

An "M" car deposited me at Market and Hyde. I legged it to the Civic Center, heading west on Grove past the Auditorium, where my two-week amateur tournament would jump off the following night. Across the plaza, beyond bluntly pruned, denuded plane trees, loomed City Hall—where the pros battled daily. I crossed Polk and entered the Department of Public Health, three stories of lifeless limestone sulking in the shadow of the Hall's grandiose copper dome.

Its interior was a combination of cold gray granite and burnished blond wood, exuding the requisite air of numbing municipal solidity. The only reminder of old-time San Francisco was provided by alabaster lanterns in trident sconces, swept upward on waves of brass filigree. On this gray day, the lamps burned. Halfway down a corridor off the lobby was a window stenciled BIRTH AND DEATH CERTIFICATES. A young woman with bright, enthusiastic eyes stood behind the glass, civil servant's disease evidently still in the developmental stage.

"I'd like to review a death certificate," I told her, in my blandest, most officious tone. "For one Dexter Threllkyl." I spelled the surname on a slip of paper and passed it over. "Would have been recently filed."

"Are you a family member?" she asked. "If not, I'll need to know the purpose of your request."

Shoving the tail of my overcoat aside, I hauled out my wallet. No easy feat. It was bursting with cards, receipts, clippings, detritus. When not cloaked by a jacket, it looked like I suffered from goiter of the right ass cheek. I plucked a creased *Inquirer* press credential from the mash. First time it'd been used for something other than a weigh-in.

"Fact-checking for the paper," I explained.

Returning moments later, she pushed a small square document across the counter: confirmation of the Mystery Man's demise. Recorded on October 27, date of expiration October 25. Myocardial infarction—heart attack—given as the cause.

It looked legit to me, right down to the embossed Health Department stamp. A single detail, though, tickled my reporter's instincts, such as they were.

Age at death: 84.

I reconsulted the wallet. I'd clipped Threllkyl's death notice, just in case, and stuffed it in with the rest of the flotsam I toted around in my folding leather file cabinet. The clerk huffed when I started excavating scraps and rummaging through them.

Bingo. The type was agate, but right then it read like a screamer headline:

THRELLKYL, Dexter—Age 63, returned home to rest . . .

Woody Montague preyed on my mind as I hit the street. Many a time he'd felt the adrenaline surge that was coursing through me at that moment. He'd probably have some sage advice on how to follow up on this intriguing discrepancy. Without thinking it through too clearly—a specialty of mine—I ducked into a corner phone booth and placed a station-to-station call to Montague's Oakland office. Maybe I wanted to impress him with my intrepid investigative skill.

No answer.

I retraced my steps down Grove, pausing to check out placards touting the tournament. With the *Inquirer* sponsoring it, there was plenty of bally for my exclusive coverage. I barely absorbed any of it. This twenty-one-year age difference had me keyed up, like I'd stumbled across a gold nugget while panning in the silt. And what's the first thing an amateur, or an imbecile, does?

Clattering into another phone booth at Market and Hyde, I dialed Ginny Wagner. Had to tell *somebody*.

"Who is this?" she snapped, short of breath.

"Billy. Jesus, you sound wound up. What's going on?"

"I've got to get out of here." Betty Boop sounded hoarse and harried. "Someone followed me this morning—exactly what I was afraid of. See? It's *not* safe. Sanders has his people after me."

"Hold it, hold it, hold it," I stalled, trying to sound reassuring. "What makes you so sure this guy was trailing you?"

"He waited outside the store I was in. For twenty minutes. I ducked into a lunch counter, and he hung around across the street, watching. When a cab pulled up, I ran and jumped in. I lost him, but I'm sure he knows where I live! Billy, I'm afraid to stay here!" She sounded fit to be tied.

Instinct told me to dash over to Pine Street and soothe her. I resisted the urge, not only because I was on Fuzzy Reasnor's clock. "Lock the door and don't go anywhere. Read a book. Get somebody to stay with you if you're nervous."

She gulped a few deep breaths. "Can you come over?"

My breath steamed up the booth's glass walls. No reminders needed of how my last indiscretion ended. Remorse was part of me now, in my blood. It's what I lived, what I dreamed. "Ginny, I can't. I've got to work. But we have to talk."

"Better make it quick, or I'll be gone. I'm getting out of here. I should have known better than to ever come back."

"Might not be Sanders."

I could barely hear throaty rasps on the other end of the line.

"Who would it be then?"

"Something else is happening. I'm still not sure what. It probably has to do with those papers—but not necessarily with Sanders. I don't have the whole picture. Yet."

"This isn't reassuring me, you know. Assuming you care."

"Sorry. We'll have a talk. I dug up some things about the trust."

"Is it on the level?"

"Some yes, some no. You'll have to make a decision, what to do with that file."

"Can you meet me tomorrow?"

"The Golden Gloves is opening," I said. Bouts started at 7 P.M., but I usually spent the afternoon sizing up as many new kids as I could, evaluating the best prospects. Fitting Ginny in wouldn't be easy.

"I may not stick around much longer," she said. "I may not *be* around much longer."

"Okay, one o'clock. At your place." It was only a stone's throw from the Civic.

"I'll already be on Irving, near the park," she said. "Make it Stow Lake. By the boathouse. Half past one."

She rang off before I could haggle.

In the doorway, Ida watched warily as I had the operator connect me with the Montagues' residence. Earlier calls to Woody's office had gone unanswered. Again, the damn ringer bleated in my ear endlessly. I cradled the phone when it became clear that something was bothering my wife.

"Can I talk to you for a minute, hon?" she cooed too sweetly, tripping all my alarms.

"Certainly," I replied, hiding all misgivings.

I gathered up my cocktail, along with the four-star Final I'd brought home, and stepped past her into our breakfast nook. Evenings, we took dinner in the smaller room off the kitchen. Vincent presided in his high chair, waiting to be served.

"What's on your mind?" I asked, sitting down and flattening the news section.

"I don't want to start World War Three," she began. Always a promising gambit. "But you haven't been holding up your end of the bargain. I felt it was time to point that out."

"Meaning what?"

"For one, you promised me that you were going to be a father to this boy."

Incredulous, I looked away from the paper and gazed out the window into darkness. In the game of Never Leave Well Enough Alone, my wife had a rare gift.

"You don't come home on time," she went on. "You're out till all hours some nights, and when you do show up you seem barely int—"

"Home *on time*? So you're setting my work schedule now? You've checked this with the promoters, have you? With Fuzzy Reasnor?"

"There aren't fights on all the nights you're rolling in at ten or eleven o'clock," she declared. Her artificial sweetness had dissolved. When the bell rang, we seldom wasted time feinting and feeling each other out.

"I can't believe you," I said, with a choked laugh. "That you'd have the gall to question me—after I let you back in this house."

Yanking the broadsheet upright provided a shield against her frigid glare. I scanned the page, trying to distract myself, not lose control. More stories about the never-ending dockworkers' strike; increased tension in China; two spectators who dropped dead of heart failure during the Big Game.

I inhaled bourbon, cracking an ice cube furiously between my teeth.

"This isn't about us," she continued. "A *father* should be at home regular hours. A *father* ought to show interest in his child. A *father* should help out now and then. A *father*—"

"Jesus Christ! Now I need to hear a 'shirking my duty' speech from *you*? Wake up, Ida—count your blessings and don't push your luck. He's not my kid. If I wanted to be a bastard—a bastard within his rights—I could have tossed you *and* the kid out in the street." I almost ripped a page turning it, then slapped it flat.

"Don't you dare talk to me that way! Who do you think you are? So special you can parade around town, day or night, leaving a wife and baby at home? Always out charging your batteries, making sure everybody knows what a big—"

"Shut the hell up!"

I wasn't really yelling at Ida. Truthfully, I'd barely registered her gripes. It was the blurb on page six that brought me up short, a shot in the gut:

ACE REPORTER
IN CAR WRECK

Award-winning journalist Woodrow Montague, formerly of the *Inquirer* staff, is listed in critical condition at San Francisco General Hospital, following an automobile accident south of the city.

The Highway Patrol discovered a sedan crashed at the bottom of a ravine in Brisbane at approximately 8:30 A.M. this morning. The vehicle had apparently plunged from an access road leading to Bayshore Highway.

A rescue crew worked frantically for more than thirty minutes to free the driver, the car's only occupant. After being rushed to the emergency room at S.F. General, the injured party was identified as the one-time *Inquirer* reporter, in recent years an East Bay attorney.

Sources at the hospital said that Montague has not regained consciousness, and could lapse into coma. No witnesses to the accident, which the Highway Patrol is investigating, have come forward. Anyone with information is urged . . .

17

For the second time in as many weeks I shifted my sorry ass from a brisk morning chill into the overheated, dispiriting confines of S.F. General. Two friends, two weeks, two car wrecks. Was it their connection to me that put both Tony Bernal and Woody Montague in the wrong place at the wrong time? Felt that way to me. If there'd been a procedure for cutting pangs of guilt off the heart, I'd have gone straight to Admissions and signed up for surgery.

Loping across the lobby, toward Critical Care, I passed a bank of telephone booths, uninhabited and gloomy. Except the last one: Susan Montague was shut inside, harsh overhead light beating on her drawn face and slumped shoulders, like she was taking the third degree. Through the gap in the glass doors leaked a forceful, feminine voice, demanding and defiant, at odds with her wilted posture:

"That's absurd," she snapped. "There's absolutely no reason it needs to be moved right away. It is not *on* the road. It is most definitely *off* the road. No, not blocking anything. The owner of the vehicle, that's who. I'm sorry, you will *not* tow it—not until we have had the scene and the car thoroughly inspected. *No!* It doesn't matter to me one bit if the police have already been there. Do not touch that car until *I* say so. If you do, you will be sued—simple as that. Am I clear? Say yes, if you understand me. Fine—tell the men from the city that I'll sue them as well."

She thrust the phone onto the hook. I stepped back, anticipating an angry, clattering exit. Instead, Mrs. Montague remained seated, drawing deep, restorative breaths. When she glanced up, it took her only a split second to ID me. She opened the folding panels. Once the inner lamp clicked off, her features softened considerably.

"How is he?" I asked.

"In a coma," Susan stated flatly. "His jaw was shattered and will have to be reconstructed. Thankfully, it wasn't his skull." She consulted the watch on her slender wrist. "He's back in surgery. One lung collapsed during the night. He may come out of it yet, but there's no guarantee he'll be the same person."

Cold recitation of essential facts, a skill she must have picked up from her husband. Steely resolve wasn't transferable, however. That was built in. Susan Montague seemed tougher than many sentimental old goats in the fight game. Certainly stronger than me. I stared at the toe of my shoe and made vague *tsk*ing noises that were meant to be philosophical, or at any rate sympathetic.

"At least he's not dead," she declared. Her firm assessment of the situation's upside. Blunt and devoid of false hope, it still managed to sound optimistic.

I nodded toward the telephone: "What was that all about?"

"Trying to get the towing company not to move the car before we have somebody check it out. In case it wasn't an accident."

"That's how you see it?"

Susan stood, which didn't much alter our height difference. A brown-and-white-checked car coat enveloped her petite figure. Cuffed trousers peeked out below the hem. Delicate hands stretched and worried a pair of brown leather gloves, her only visible display of anxiety.

"I don't jump to conclusions, Mr. Nichols," she said softly. "Something I learned from Woody. But that doesn't make me naïve. He's been involved in numerous cases with people who might have an ax to grind."

"What was he doing in South San Francisco?"

"I couldn't say."

"Pardon me," I said, elbowing her gently aside and stepping into the booth she'd vacated. Leaving the door open, I snatched up the phone and dialed "O." The receiver was still warm and slightly damp. Some of the Montagues' determination had rubbed off on me, I guess.

"Let me have the number and address of the Major Liquor Company," I told the operator. Susan watched me, twisting the gloves. "That a city address? Uh-huh. Okay. Thanks."

Her brown eyes assessed me, differently than before.

"Major Liquor Company's in Brisbane," I reported.

She nodded. "Although that doesn't prove anything."

"I'm not making assumptions either." I held up my palms. "But I'm working toward one. I was with Woody the other day. We stopped by the DA's office. He got into a beef with the deputy DA over Virgil Dardi and the Major Liquor Company. Woody tell you any of this?"

"I'm aware of the dispute," she sighed. "It's nothing new."

With the fistful of gloves, Susan traced a loopy pattern in the stale air, like a bird stunned by buckshot. Her gaze drifted toward the entry-way to Critical Care. She abruptly opened her handbag, thrust the gloves inside, and snapped it shut.

"He wanted to see the truck," she reasoned. "The one in that recent accident. He had the license number. It's just Woody's style to sneak out there before the start of their work day."

"He told you all that?"

"No. But he asked where our camera was before he left. I'd used it to take some pictures of the kids."

Asking after the children seemed the polite thing, but I couldn't manage it. Imagining them without a father was more than I cared to contemplate.

"Woody mentioned that the DA had a monitor on his phone," I said instead. "You know anything about that?"

"It's called a wiretap," she said, like a lawyer instructing a particularly dim client. "The authorities are in love with them. Helps keep track of suspected Reds. Unionists. Jews. You name it. The list gets longer by the day, I'm certain. People they think are a threat. Or those they don't particularly like."

"How do they manage it?"

"It's perfectly legal. At least so far."

"No, no—I mean how does one of those things, a wiretap, actually work?"

"All they need is access to the phone line. The wire itself. They hook into it, like you'd siphon water or electricity, then they route it wherever they want. The FBI's become quite proficient. They have 'listening posts' to eavesdrop on Commies or whomever."

"That's why there's one on your phone?"

Her brown eyes peered up into mine, sadly. "Our line's been tapped for a long while. Nothing to do with politics, I'm afraid. Although that could easily be used as an excuse. The DA enjoys keeping tabs on

Woody, that's all. Some of his clients are considered 'undesirables.'"
She smiled wanly. "Woody devised his own monitor for the monitor,
so he can tell when the tap is engaged."

We shared a gaze that made me feel we were on the same page. Her
expression, however, was distant and resigned, as though she knew this
page was merely prologue. The full life story, her face suggested, was
long, complex, and impenetrable.

"I'm going to check on him," she said quietly. "Did you want to
come?"

"Need to make a call first," I replied. "I'll catch up."

I sank into the booth and dialed home.

Ida's sister Paula answered. Gruffly, I told her to put my wife on.

"Have you seen anybody around the house lately?" I asked, soon as
Ida had the phone. "Service guy from the phone company maybe?
Anybody at all around back? It's important—think for a minute."

"I don't remember," she whimpered, clearly annoyed by my brusque
manner.

"Ida—it's important. Try."

"A meter reader was by the other day. I saw him through the window, going to the back of the house."

"When? What day? Forget the date—what day of the week?"

"Thursday? Before I went over to Phyl's. That's right. Definitely
Thursday."

"You're sure he was a meter reader? From the gas company?"

"That's what I imagined."

"Why? Was he wearing a uniform?"

"He had a tool belt, you know. I don't know. I figured he came in to
read the meter. What's this all about? What's wrong?"

"You're certain of the day?"

"Thursday. Positive."

The eighteenth, I calculated.

"Okay," I said. "I'll see you later."

She was still talking when I banged down the hook, ending the call.
I kept banging. An operator's voice piped up in my ear.

"Get me Pacific Gas & Electric Company," I barked. "Service department."

It took a while to get patched through to Installations and Repairs. When the dispatcher came on, I gave my name and address. "I think one of your guys left some tools outside my house the other day," I improvised. "Thursday, the eighteenth. He probably came back looking for them, but my wife took 'em in so they wouldn't get rained on. We've still got 'em over here."

He reconfirmed the address.

"Must be somebody else's gear. No service calls to your address that day."

"Maybe he was a meter reader."

"Nope. That neighborhood's on a different schedule."

I hung up, then got the operator back. This time I was connected to Bell Telephone's offices. I ran the same routine.

With similar results.

A nurse tried to bar me from Critical Care, protesting that only family members were allowed on the ward. A heavyweight orderly was summoned to detail the rules more persuasively. It wasn't that I was eager to survey the damage done to Woody Montague, or to stand silent vigil while his life hung in the balance.

Frankly, I didn't want my last image of his valiant wife to be her tiny figure at the end of the corridor, slumped against a wall, shuddering with sobs she could no longer contain.

18

Stow Lake was deserted that cold November afternoon, unless you counted the flotillas of ducks and swans idly gliding over the lake's moss-green surface, or the squadrons of pigeons and seagulls pecking the ground for scraps or perched in random formation on the boat-house roof. Spring and summer, waterfowl shared the place with human hordes, who chartered canoes and paddleboats for cruises around Strawberry Hill, the verdant man-made island that rose from the center of the lake. Footpaths snaking through its spreading fir trees made it an ideal spot for trysts. Good for first kisses and teary breakups. Lovebirds of the unfeathered variety usually huddled on benches all around the shoreline. But off-season, even "Armstrong heaters" weren't enough to ward off the chill.

Much of my childhood was strangled by respiratory ailments, so my mother occasionally took me out of school for fog-drenched circuits around Stow Lake. A doctor, God bless him, suggested the damp air might be good for my congested lungs. The place was so peaceful and picturesque that I learned in short order how to fake a croupy cough. Regarding my mother's bid for sainthood, I realized soon enough she enjoyed plying the placid, tree-lined canals as much as I did.

The boathouse was a broad cabinlike structure with red-and-white shutters, housing rental offices and a concession stand. The ticket booth had closed for the winter weeks ago, but the snack bar remained open, manned by a hardy soul in a logger's jacket and railroad worker's cap. Unless he spoke Gull, he must have been starved for conversation. So I propped an elbow on the counter, ordered a coffee, and let him gab while I waited for Ginny.

Naturally, he went on and on about the Big Game, wondering whether I'd heard the latest on Cal's up-in-the-air Rose Bowl bid. Not my chosen topic, considering the ass-chewing I'd gotten from Fuzzy after returning from the hospital that morning. The department was caught shorthanded when word came over the wire that the Bears were Rose Bowl–bound, so Reasnor was livid when I came back late.

"You had all yesterday to dummy up stories in advance," I said.

Fuzz blew his stack, then sentenced me to several silly phone interviews gathering the Bears' reaction. I banged a piece out by noon and announced that I was leaving early for the Civic. Big Game mania was history, I told my boss. It was time for the Gloves to get some play. Fuzzy's a pro, and a true pal, but I still worried he might stab me with his copy spike. I grabbed a taxi to the park.

As the concessionaire prattled on, I casually scanned the footpath that encircled the lake. Things brightened as sun struggled through the day's gray canopy. A flash of red appeared between willows on the eastern shore, and I recognized Virginia Wagner's distinctive high-heeled stride. Something worth watching, coming or going. Again, she modeled a cap and cape combo, this ensemble a fiery scarlet. Needless to say, she had a book clutched to her bosom.

"Fire up a couple of dogs, while you're at it," I told the counterman, interrupting his recap of immortal gridiron feats. "I'll take a refill on the coffee, too. And pour a fresh one." Courtesy couldn't hurt, both for Ginny and this lonesome, cooped-up cook. To be honest, I was relieved Ginny had made it. I didn't want to visit her in a hospital bed, next to Bernal and Montague. Or on a slab in the morgue.

"By the way," I informed the guy, suddenly filled with camaraderie, "Cal's going to the Rose Bowl." The news turned him into one giddy, frankfurter-frying fool.

When I swiveled back toward the lake, Virginia had vanished.

She'd been no more than fifty yards distant, approaching at a brisk pace. It was impossible to miss that blazing, billowing cape.

Pushing away from the counter, I startled a flock of gulls gathered around my feet. They scattered, squawking, and in seconds the stillness gave way to screeches and squeals and flapping wings. I trotted past the pier at water's edge, eyes darting every which way for a glimpse of crimson. Rounding the curve of the shore, I had an uninterrupted view of the trail where I'd seen Ginny.

No trace of her.

Striding on, I spooked a paddling of mallards that emerged from the reeds. Nowhere she could have gone, except the lake, or a grove of eucalpytus trees on the other side of the narrow road surrounding it. Hustling across the road, I found myself at the crest of a steep hill, carpeted completely in glistening green ivy. It sloped down into a ravine. No trail anywhere among the towering eucalyptus shooting skyward. Fallen limbs littered the ground, crisscrossing between trees, ivy insidiously creeping up the smooth, slender trunks.

Far below, snagged on a branch among dense shadows, was Ginny's red cape.

A single incautious step onto the slope and the sodden hillside gave way. I fell in a heap, then slid down the slimy ivy until my foot was snared in a tangle of vines. I fought my way upright. *Somebody snatched her,* my brain shouted. It was the only explanation. *Does he have a gun? What will I do then?* I negotiated the clinging vegetation as quickly and quietly as I could, trying to ignore the awful options and dreadful visions.

Near the cape I found a red shoe, streaked with mud. I shoved it in my overcoat pocket.

Peering between trees in the deepest, dankest part of the grove, I spotted Ginny. At least part of her. Mostly I saw the rear of a broad-shouldered man in brown suit and hat, shoving her against the massive trunk of a redwood, rough bark hiking up her gray skirt. Stockinged legs flailed, lifted off the ground. He had her by the throat. Hearing no screams, I figured his other hand was clamped on her mouth. Or she'd been gagged.

No time for plans or second thoughts. I headed straight for the guy. With any luck, I'd get a choke hold on him before he heard me coming.

I got about ten feet closer when that notion fizzled. His muscles tensed, then he threw a glance over his shoulder.

"Let her go!" I yelled, moving toward him. Famous last words.

He turned, but didn't loosen his grip on Ginny. Her eyes were wide with terror. He'd stuffed a handkerchief in her mouth. I intended to barrel right into him, but a few steps shy of impact, I pulled up short.

I recognized the guy.

Larry Daws. Down-on-his-luck light heavyweight. Former stooge of Burney Sanders. The primary witness against him.

In the space of several heartbeats, the fighter's hard, ruddy face ran through a range of convolutions: vicious to confounded to deferential. He stepped back cautiously, affecting innocence while still using his reach to pin Virginia's shoulder, the way he'd employ a jab to keep an opponent pinned on the ropes.

"Hey there, Mr. Nichols," he greeted me, groveling absurdly in the presence of *Mr. Boxing*. "Don't get the wrong idea—you just caught me making some time with my girl here."

His girl used the distraction to sink the pointy toe of her remaining shoe deep into Daws's testicles. His yowl cleared every bird from the dell.

Down went Daws.

As his features compressed into a rictus of pain, Ginny planted another bull's-eye between his splayed legs. He howled. Next thing I knew, Larry's lapels were in my grip. His cheeks turned blotchy. Sweat rose in a high tide.

"What the fuck are you pulling here?" I hollered, shaking Daws hard enough to dislodge his stingy-brimmed hat. "Who put you up to this?"

A miserable moan slithered from his throat. Midway, it turned into something you might hear prowling a junkyard. A fierce, feral growl, not even remotely human. Daws's squeezed-shut lids parted, revealing eyes that gleamed crazily. Spittle flecked his lips, drawn back to reveal stained, gritted teeth. He struggled to get up. I leaned on him, hoping to pitch him backward. Instead Daws hoisted me higher, like a six-foot sack of potatoes. His footing gave way, thankfully, and we collapsed to the ground.

Behind us, Ginny was on all fours, the gag spit out. She frantically scoured the ivy, and emerged clutching her purse. Seconds later, wobbly but upright, she had her artillery aimed.

"Are you crazy!" I shouted, desperately directing a knee into Daws's chest.

Ginny lurched forward, her dirt-smeared face set in a demented glower. As I grappled with Daws, still trying to bowl him over, she threw her arm in a sweeping, level arc. The gun in her fist cracked against the side of Daws's dome. He grunted. A thin plume of blood squirted from the fresh gash in his ear. He buckled, taking a knee. Subduing the savage bastard suddenly seemed conceivable. Releasing him, I sought better purchase in the slippery greenery.

Before I could make another move, Ginny crowded me aside and wielded the gun again. An uppercut this time. The butt smacked Daws square on the beak, breaking it. Loudly. Blood erupted from his nostrils, soaking the front of his suit.

Ginny struck a lopsided stance above her attacker, legs spread as far as the sheath skirt permitted. Daws was crumpled, but not entirely spent. With one hand he futilely sought to stanch the flow from his busted nose. He groped blindly with the other, a TKO clutching for the bottom rope.

"This son of a bitch killed Claire," Ginny panted. "It was him."

She aimed the gun at the top of Daws's bowed head.

I grabbed Ginny from behind in a bear hug; she struggled to break free; we toppled onto the bed of ivy. She was no easier to handle than Daws.

"You don't want to kill anybody," I chanted repeatedly, hoarsely, my teeth scraping her ear.

When she'd quit squirming, Daws was already off and running. He made a stumbling, broken-field exit east of the eucalyptus grove, where the ravine leveled out, and scrambled across a wide emerald pasture. Moved pretty good for a guy with his balls in his lungs.

We spent fifteen minutes regrouping, searching for Ginny's toque cap and freshly bought copy of *Intruder in the Dust*. We finally gave up, bequeathing both to the dense ivy, and climbed back up the hill. Nearing the boathouse, I spied a pair of hot dogs and two coffees on the counter, all saucered and blowed.

"You *knew* the guy," Ginny marveled, incredulous. Her heels clicked against the pavement, several steps behind. I'd returned her missing shoe.

"He's a boxer," I explained, my heartbeat still racing. "Larry Daws. The one tailing you yesterday, I take it."

"That was him," Ginny confirmed, skipping apace, trying to keep up in those pumps. "You all right?" she asked. "You're walking kind of funny."

"Fell on my satchel," I said. "I'll live."

"Plus you got mud all over the back of that beautiful overcoat," she moaned, slapping at my hindquarters. I broke stride and she bumped right into me.

"You've got it all over everything," I informed her. Fortunately, the recovered cape hid most of the damage, except splashes crusted on her shoes and ankles and calves. The fine line of her jaw, high cheekbones, pouty lips—all spattered with specks and streaks of soil. Noting my stare, she attempted to wipe the grime off with gloved fingers. Despite the gallant attempt to appear calm, her hands quivered.

"You're only making it worse," I said, plucking a scrap of ivy from her fouled-up hairdo. Hard to believe such sweet features belonged to a hellcat who'd just broken the nose of a veteran light heavyweight. And I'd swear to Christ, she would have sent that slug into Daws's skull if I hadn't pinned her down.

"I could go for a hot bath," she said, rummaging in her purse for the pack of Old Golds. "How about you?"

A little flirtation was permissible—perhaps even inevitable—seeing as we'd recently saved each other's lives. Tough to rise to the bait, though.

"I'll get you another copy of that book," I said. "Who was it by again?"

"It's all right. I didn't love it."

"Don't you want to know how it turns out?"

"Yeah, I guess. Thanks."

The counterman, seeing how badly shaken we were, immediately suggested "something more substantial" in the way of refreshment. He fetched his personal fifth and a pair of paper cups, while I recounted how I'd seen Ginny slip down the hillside, then gone tumbling after her.

The bogus explanation earned me an elbow in the ribs.

"Why fib?" Ginny griped, exhaling a stream of cigarette smoke. "Ask him for a phone so we can call the cops."

"Let it rest," I insisted. "They wouldn't do anything anyway."

Two Coca-Cola cups were set on the counter, into which our physician dispensed medicinal doses of Old Fitzgerald.

"Hundred proof," he prescribed. "Smooth you right out."

Ginny folded her arm over the crook of my elbow and squeezed.

She seemed mesmerized by the trickles of sour mash. I handed over her ration.

After sniffing it approvingly, she stalled the shot halfway to her trembling lips.

"I can't," she decided, replacing it on the counter. "I . . . have a problem. With this stuff."

Virginia Wagner was full of surprises today.

"Don't let me stop you," she sighed heavily, sliding the bourbon in front of me.

"Get us some fresh ones," I requested, gesturing to the stagnant cups of cold coffee. 'We'll skip the food."

"Make mine a ginger ale," Ginny corrected, wiping grit from beneath an eye. "My stomach could use some settling. That handkerchief was *used*."

Rude or not, I saluted our host and gunned both shots. Once Ginny had the ginger ale, I steered her from the boathouse to a wharf rimming the lake's edge. Pigeons tracked us hopefully.

"What good will it do, pressing charges against Daws?" I demanded, rhetorically. She searched my face for hints of rational behavior, as I masked my subterfuge with a wry grin. "It won't stick. He hadn't done anything—yet—except drag you down in that gulley. In fact," I added, broadening the false smile, "you'd better hope Daws doesn't lodge a complaint against *you*."

Suspicion flickered as she gazed over the lip of the cup, sipping soda, pondering this unexpected counsel. Virginia had to trust me, had to believe I could somehow handle the situation without getting the law involved. Orchestrating this shell game was loathsome, but I needed more time to piece the whole mess together—and avoid jeopardizing the murder case against Sanders. Bringing cops down on Daws right now would louse up everything.

"It's like when we went to that resort," Ginny said. Drawing on the last of her cigarette, she eyed me as if revising her initial appraisal. "These guys all *know* you," she realized. "I'd have been sunk if this Daws character wasn't a boxer." She tossed her curls, shaking loose something distantly akin to a laugh. "Can you beat that? The only reason we escaped was because Sanders hired a professional fighter to do his dirty work. Somebody only you"—she poked me in the chest—"would know on sight, or be able to finger for the cops. But you don't want to turn him in. Am I missing something here?"

"Yeah. Sanders didn't hire him. This is what I tried to tell you yesterday."

"What are you saying? Of course he did. Who else? Sanders must blame me for everything that's happened to him." She ground out the butt with the toe of her shoe.

"Daws was sicced on you by somebody who wants those trust papers."

"Yeah!—Sanders! You said yourself they made him a millionaire."

"Sanders is about to go on trial for Claire's murder," I reminded her. "And Larry Daws is the prosecution's chief witness." That froze her. "It's his testimony that's going to send Sanders to San Quentin. You really believe they'd still be in cahoots?"

"He was about to kill me," Ginny maintained, touching her throat. Discolored reminders of Daws's vise grip were still showing. "Once he'd raped me."

"He only wanted to put a scare into you—so you'd cough up that file."

She didn't buy that reasoning. "Wouldn't he have said something along those lines?"

"Didn't have time—which you should be thankful for."

For a few moments she squinted into the patterns of light shimmering on the water, now that the sun had broken through. A gull splashed into the lake and sank its head below the surface, fishing.

Virginia turned back to me. "Nobody was supposed to know I have that stuff," she recalled coldly. "You were going to find out what everything was worth but leave me out of it, remember? So who the hell knows I'm mixed up in this?"

"The District Attorney."

Ginny pitched the cup to the ground, soda and all. "You expect me to believe the *DA* paid this pug to strong-arm me?"

"The *deputy* DA, if that's any easier to swallow." I picked up the cup, if only to duck the look she was giving me. When I stood upright, I stared into liquid eyes, wounded by betrayal.

"You told them about me?" Her voice was brittle. She'd been sold out by smooth-talking cads more than once, I assumed.

"No, Ginny," I said, crushing the cup and flinging it into a nearby ash can. "I didn't say a word about you."

"Oh, *okay*—then how would the *deputy* DA know I have the trust papers?"

"Give me a ride," I proposed, taking her arm. "We'll see if I've got an answer to that."

19

Virginia carefully curbed the Roadmaster in the cramped confines of Argent Alley. Considering her frayed nerves, it was miraculous we'd navigated Cole Valley and threaded the serpentine lanes below Twin Peaks without incident. Across the alley, a porch light gleamed above the red door of Jerome Califro's house.

"You're sure this is how they found out about me?" asked Ginny, gloved hands still gripping the steering wheel, the engine idling.

"Only explanation that makes sense. There's a connection; has to be."

"Well, I'm not going in there."

"You don't need to. I'll only be a minute. Have a smoke. Enjoy the view."

"You really think confronting him's a good idea?"

"This sad sack is no Larry Daws. Don't worry."

An afternoon edition of the *News*, protecting the pristine upholstery, crackled as I clambered out. Soiled individuals weren't allowed in Ginny's car, so she'd manufactured emergency slipcovers.

Crossing the asphalt, I noticed two girls in a sedan parked farther up the block, barely visible behind the windshield's glare. My brief glance caused both to avert their eyes. Playing hooky on a Tuesday afternoon made them as nervous as Virginia.

Mrs. Califro answered the bell so rapidly she must have spotted me coming up the walk. But the arching of her brows immediately flattened; she evidently was expecting someone else. This time, I didn't await permission to cross the threshold.

"Man of the house available?" I inquired sarcastically, barging into their tidy powder blue foyer. Nearly being killed plays hell with the social graces.

"*Excuse me!* Jerry isn't home. I'll have to ask you to leave!"

I headed straight down the central corridor, figuring to see Califro lurch from his fetid office into the hallway, slopping Lord Calvert onto the carpet. The pocket doors, however, were sealed tight. Prying them open revealed only hopeless clutter, unchanged, shrouded in gloom.

"Where is he, Del?" I demanded. Caught between flabbergasted and fighting mad, she was shocked I'd remembered her name. "I need to talk to him," I insisted. "It's very important."

"He's gone out," she improvised.

I scoffed: "How? In an ambulance? That'd be the only way." I forged farther toward the rear of the house. "Where's he hiding?"

Del rode my heels, so close her mantle of bosom nudged my back. "You're intolerably rude," she carped, grappling with me as I entered a bedroom dimly visible through stale gray light. More boxes everywhere, linens in a swirl, garments scattered. Empty glasses and bottles on the nightstand. The residue of spent pipe tobacco choked the air. Drawn venetian blinds hung askew. Peering into the bowels of their privacy defused some of my belligerence. I wondered whether her devotion and tolerance extended to sack duty in this pit, or if she maintained a sanitary nest someplace else.

"I already told you, he's not here!" she shouted. "Now get out—before I call the cops!"

I hastily retraced my steps, distancing myself from her muttered curses. Crossing the foyer, I detoured into a short hallway opposite the living room. A strip of light showed beneath the farther of two closed doors. I grabbed its knob and pushed.

For a second all my bearings disappeared, as in a dream, where you find yourself elsewhere, instantly, impossibly.

This room was small, wallpaper decorated with pink and blue bunnies hopping through tufts of bright green grass. The reek of chemicals was more pungent than at S.F. General. No furnishings—except for the steel table, rigged with a pair of stirrups. A large ocular in a metal socket loomed over it, stark light blazing off the table's polished surface. The orb extended from a cantilevered arm, connected to an iron post on wheels. Atop a nearby counter, sinister tools were precisely arranged across a folded white towel. Beside that was an antiseptic bath, source of the noxious, nostril-stinging vapors. Glass cabinets housed a paltry assortment of medical supplies. The floor's glistening reflective tiles sloped subtly toward a drain at the operating room's center.

Moving became a major effort. It felt like I'd dropped into a tank at the aquarium. A tingling sensation spread across my shoulders and biceps.

Del Califro shoved past and made straight for her tools.

"Did you do Claire Escalante?" I asked numbly, words barely forming properly. Tiny stars burst before my eyes, effervescent, drifting and exploding.

She whirled, a scalpel brandished in her pallid fist. "I'm warning you. Go," she hissed.

The door frame slammed into a shoulder blade as I stumbled back. "Claire Escalante," I repeated. "Did she come here? Is this where she got it done?"

A muffled thud came from someplace outside the room.

"Just leave," Mrs. Califro commanded, stabbing the scalpel in my direction. Unsteadily, I edged away.

A door burst free down the hall, knob bruising plaster. Beyond the opening, a naked bulb dangled, high above a skinny set of stairs. Jerome Califro was splayed at the head of them, struggling to regain his footing. Flannel pajamas again. Leaping swordfish today, not bucking broncos. Below eyes blurred by pain, he exhibited a cadaverous grimace. His teeth were filmed with blood.

"Bit my goddamn tongue!" he swore, oblivious to me. "Del! I fell down and bit my goddamn tongue."

Pouncing, I grabbed his lapels and pulled him upright. The steps he'd failed to negotiate descended, steeply, to a cellar. Spinning Califro around, I used his gaunt frame as a shield against his wife's nasty little weapon.

"Del—what's happening?" Califro stammered as he was hustled past her. I manhandled his fragile bones, keeping them between me and his seething spouse. It was like shaking a marionette. Crashing into the living room, I pitched him onto a plushly stuffed davenport. An adjacent end table held a decorative lamp: green porcelain coolie doing a carefree dance. I grabbed its head and pulled, wrenching the cord from the wall. That scalpel wasn't getting anywhere near me.

Confusion clouded Califro's eyes; blood drizzled from the corners of his mouth. A cotton swordfish was crumpled in my other fist.

"Answer my questions," I said, "or I'll crack your fucking skull."

"Get out of our house," Mrs. Califro screeched from the archway, still clutching the blade at waist level.

"Go ahead. Call the cops. They'll be intrigued as hell by that unusual guest room." I aimed the lamp's base at her, suggesting she maintain some distance.

"Why are you doing this?" the limp attorney whimpered, wiping reddened lips on his sleeve. "Please don't break that lamp. It's part of a set."

"You tipped the DA's office to those trust papers I showed you."

"I don't know what you're talking about." He didn't seem, or smell, soused. But his limbs shook, severely, victim of the DTs.

Turning loose his pajamas, I slapped him across the face. Even open-handed, the sound reverberated, like a door slamming shut. He gave a high-pitched wail—his tongue must have burned like poison. Speckles of blood spotted his sleepwear. We all froze for a second, stunned.

"Don't you *dare* strike him!" Del said, a little late. But she made no move. I'd clearly become one dangerous, crazy bastard.

Califro's eyes welled with tears. Strands of pink saliva oozed down his chin. I'd never hit anybody before. Looking away from his imploring mug, I saw he'd lost one alligator-skin slipper, probably back on the stairs. The bare foot, waxen and translucent, was twisted against the carpet. A sorry state of affairs. His mortality seemed somehow summarized by the varicose veins and discolored toenails on that pitiful, exposed extremity.

I'd assaulted and battered a decaying, helpless drunk. *What was happening to me?*

"Are you from the police?" Califro mewed, sneaking a terrified glance at his wife. He had no recollection of our previous meeting, in this very house.

"I'm no cop," I replied, as I yanked out my display handkerchief and stuffed it in his palsied hand. I redirected the interrogation: "Tell me what I want to know," I urged the woman, "or I'll have the screws down on this place in no time."

"*I* contacted the District Attorney," she said.

That galvanized Jerome Califro, who ceased swabbing his bloodied mouth. We blurted "Why?" simultaneously.

"Something had to be done," she stated matter-of-factly. "I wanted my money back from that Mount Davidson disaster."

"Who'd you talk to? Corey?"

"Yes, he's the one."

"Gave him names, I suppose. Which ones?"

"Sanders. Yours. The woman."

"I never mentioned any woman."

"From the envelope you brought with you. The return address. I thought she might figure in it somehow." Beat *that*. Her husband couldn't see straight, but she had eyes like a goddamn hawk.

"Why go behind my back?" Califro complained. "I said I'd take care of it. I just needed time to get some things in order."

"Jerry," Mrs. Califro said, again pointing the scalpel my way, "have you ever met this man before?"

Without confidence, Califro sized me up. Nothing registered. His wife raised her eyebrows placidly at each of us, as if no further explanation of her motives was needed. Ever.

"I got tired of waiting." Adele wanted to put the scalpel someplace, but it stayed in her hand, just in case. I felt even more foolish, armed absurdly with a lamp. Our mutual outrage and fear had dissipated.

"You should never have called Bill," Califro said to his wife. "That wasn't a sensible idea."

"*Bill?*" I repeated. "You know Corey—the deputy DA?"

"I worked in the DA's office. Years ago. Matt Brady was still in charge." He inspected bloodstains on my handkerchief, as though they'd come from his professional wounds, which, I gathered, were numerous and deep.

"I thought the DA might help us," his wife said. "Maybe do a favor for one of their own. Considering the connection."

"One of their *own?*" Califro glanced up at me. Self-loathing had permanently eroded any dignity in his features. Not a pleasant thing to observe. "My wife is unclear on several things, Mr. . . . ?"

Shit—I couldn't remember the bogus name I'd used before. It had been simple, one I wouldn't forget. . . .

"Smith," Del said, letting me know I wasn't getting away with anything. "Mr. *George* Smith."

At least she'd swallowed my ruse whole and passed it on to Corey. Score one for my side.

"Yeah, right—Smith," I conceded, before prompting Califro: "What exactly is your wife not clear on?"

"That Bill Corey is Threllkyl's brother-in-law, for starters."

Del's slacked jaw mirrored mine. But Califro wasn't done:

"That's how I got the job. Dex Threllkyl wanted an illusion of legal propriety. Corey referred me to him, after Pat Brown swept out the DA's office and brought in all his own people. Joining the private sector, most of my time was soon spent assuring dozens of deceived investors—including my own wife—that everything was perfectly aboveboard with all the holdings that eventually comprised the Mount Davidson Trust. *Chief counsel*—crucial to the charade, you know."

"Jerome! What are you saying!"

"I didn't understand at first. I thought these were sound, risk-free investments. That's why I encouraged you to buy in. By the time I realized what was being done, it was too late."

And you've been drowning your regret and remorse ever since, I thought.

"You let them steal our money. You helped them." Her tone was more resigned than accusatory.

"The alternative, my dear, was unthinkable. They knew about this humble public service clinic you operate. If I didn't do as I was told, they'd have sent you straight to Tehachapi or Atascadero or somewhere. I'd have been jailed separately. No real choice, you see. They banked on that."

Del moved to the front door. Pulling aside pleated diaphanous curtains, she peered through a slender window. Maybe she envisioned squad cars, cops banging through her picturesque picket gate. Maybe she was trying to see farther than the cul-de-sac, all the way back to the first wrong turn.

"Gotten what you came for?" she asked. "If so, I'd like you to leave."

I set the lamp back and adjusted its shade. Califro and I exchanged abbreviated frowns. The handkerchief served as apology, so I said no more. I forced my feet into the foyer. Del Califro's spine was pressed to the door, as if it was propping her up. She was a vision of white, I belat-edly noticed: gleaming orthopedic shoes; pressed, bleached trousers and blouse; crisp, immaculate smock; thick waves of hair peroxided platinum.

"Claire Escalante," I quizzed her again. "Did she come here?"

"I have a short memory," she replied. "Which serves me well."

"You'd have remembered her. I'm sure of it."

"Are you the guy?"

Vague words, but they stung worse than if she'd slashed me with that scalpel. True enough, I was *the guy*. The guy who made love to Claire, ignoring laws against adultery; the guy who got her pregnant; the guy who shelled out money to "fix" things. Cash that went straight into the Califros' depleted bank account. Burney Sanders and Larry Daws had only delivered the coup de grâce, roughing Claire up after Del Califro had scraped the life out of her insides.

"She's dead, you know," I said.

"I read the papers."

There was plenty more to say, but I couldn't utter another word. She opened the door and motioned for me to exit, knowing full well that as I hit the street, I carried with me what was left of their future. More responsibility than I'd bargained for, brazenly invading their home on a tide of righteousness. The red door shut, a barely audible *snick* locking me out, locking them inside.

20

Ginny's roadster was gone. We'd endured a death-defying escape hardly an hour before. Now she'd brushed me off like a no-account barroom pickup.

Son of a *bitch*.

Scoping the street showed that the two girls were still in the sedan, silhouetted behind the foggy windshield. Reality smacked me cold—and provided inspiration.

I strode to the vehicle and rapped on its steamed-up glass until the driver lowered her window. I tugged out my wallet, flashing press credentials, quickly, into the terrified young face staring upward.

"SFPD," I barked. "Open your back door."

Panicking, she tried to turn the key and punch the starter. I clutched the steering wheel and glowered past her at the other girl. "No funny business or you'll both be in worse trouble," I commanded, flexing my newfound expertise at intimidating innocents. "Open up."

I slid onto the backseat, slamming the door. The air was as humid and close and full of anxiety as any locker room.

"Don't bother with any backchat," I snarled. "I know what you're here for. But I'm going to give you a break. We just might get you out of here before the place is raided. Turn this thing around. Get on Market and head downtown."

The freckled Irish redhead at the wheel was maybe a year out of high school, bundled in a hooded car coat and wearing knitted mittens. She had flawless skin and a charming upturned nose, and was a much better driver than Virginia Wagner. Her accomplice was a dark, sultry beauty with heavy-lidded, long-lashed brown eyes, lifted from a woman three times her age. Full lips trembled slightly as she turned, smartly, so as not to leave her back to me. She had a classic Grecian profile. Neither had hit twenty, and I inventoried their features, their hair, their complexions, as if they were potential mates. Always with the sexual Tale of the Tape, without fail.

"Whose car?" I grilled them as we turned onto Seventeenth Street and headed downhill.

"My mother's," said the redhead. "You won't have to call her, will you?"

"About which? The car or the other thing? Who had the appointment?"

The guilty glances and body language all pointed to pert little Colleen. We rolled a few more blocks in silence, until I envisioned her, on that metal table in the Califros' bungalow, feet trapped in those stirrups, scared to death. I couldn't get the image out of my head.

"How'd he talk you into it?" I spat, leaning back in the seat. "Which lie did he use? *You're the only girl I've ever felt this way about? You're the most beautiful thing I've ever seen?* Get used to 'em. You're both gonna hear 'em for the rest of your lives. Or at least until you get married. Then after a few years you're gonna be begging for a dose of that crap again. It's all bullshit, you know—whatever a guy tells you, whether he's fifteen or fifty, you better believe he's planning one thing—how he's gonna get you in bed. And if he isn't the kind to actually work at it, believe me, he's thinking about it. It's all we think about, really. Wish I knew why. Perpetuation of the species. That's what a . . . professor told me one time. Said it's what drives all human interaction. The need for people to reproduce themselves. So . . . see what you're up against? Like a tidal wave, people just keep coming, swarming over everything, each one with its own peculiar brain, convinced it's the center of everything. But smart as any one of them might be—and I don't care if it's fucking Albert Einstein—you can never figure out another person, no matter how hard you try. You can't know what they're thinking or what they're feeling, much less what they think about *you*. Doesn't matter if it's somebody you just met or whether you've been married to 'em for fifty years—makes no damn difference. Turn here. This mope who got you pregnant, you don't know him, and he sure as hell doesn't know you. What is he, some college boy? Fed you a line about how you'll be as close as two people can be? *You're the only one I could ever love. This night is perfect, more magical than any other.* What horseshit. Where is he now? Left you to rely on your friend here, right? Let me make something clear while you're still young enough to learn—if you've got a friend sticking by you, you're the luckiest person in the world. Hold on to that—'cause it might not last. You could end up falling for the same two-timing lowlife and try to scratch each other's eyes out. Step on it or you'll miss the Go. Maybe you're just saps like me. I don't know, maybe I asked for it. More than likely. But let me warn you about doing favors: No good deed goes unpunished. So keep your head down. You do the simplest little thing to help somebody, the next minute you're up to your ass in trouble and all these so-called friends are stabbing you in the back while you're looking around for a way out. Know what's good? A job. Do something productive with your life. It'll keep your mind off how we're all just spinning around trying to fuck each other up. Get in the left lane."

She made the turn and we traveled a few blocks in silence.

"Are you really a cop?" asked the beauty riding shotgun, her wide eyes examining me.

"I sure as shit feel like one."

Farther down Market we noticed flames lighting up the wide boulevard. Packs of people ran through the street, like fireflies swirling around bonfires. The girls were too scared to speak, so I muttered, "What the hell is going on?" for all of us. I leaned forward and directed Colleen to go left at Franklin, get us off Market. A bunch of wooden barricades had been piled up and torched. A mob of liquored-up louts in Cal sweatshirts were whooping and hollering and reeling about in ecstatic abandon.

I sank backward. "Don't worry," I said. "It's not the end of the world. They're just celebrating the Bears going to the Rose Bowl."

A few blocks later we pulled up in front of the Civic. I climbed out and wrestled the wallet free again, tapping on the passenger window until it rolled down. I peered in at the redhead, who was trying to disappear inside her coat. "Let me give you something for the lift," I said, forking over eighty bucks. Everything I had, minus carfare. "Promise me you won't go back there."

I added one of my cards. "Call me in a day or two. If you're gonna go through with it, use someplace safe. I'll check around for you. Okay?"

"Thank you, Mr. Nichols," she said, barely able to get the words out. Her friend gawked at me like I'd come down on one of those flying saucers everybody was talking about. She started to offer a handshake but thought better of it. Before anything stranger happened, they sped off.

Inside the Civic, hundreds of young men were preparing to test their mettle, to prove themselves by staring down their fear and coming out swinging. The crowds would chant and coins would rain down from the rafters and we'd all go home feeling good about ourselves.

Nobody would be cheering on that little redhead when she looked her worst nightmare in the face.

21

I revisited County Jail No. 1 the following afternoon, this time uninvited. Entering through Dunbar Alley, I passed a gang of feral cats
scavenging in the garbage for sips of sour milk. The stench from the
ground-floor kitchen suggested that feeding time was part of the punishment at the city's premier Gray Bar Hotel. The rank odors even
seeped into the elevator.

There must have been a pipeline to Corey's office, because after I
requested a face-to-face with Burney Sanders, the guards let my heels
cool for more than an hour outside the visitors' area. When only fifteen minutes remained for visitation, I started improvising.

I told the bull behind the desk that if I didn't get to see Sanders—a
full twenty-minute allotment—I'd have Jake Ehrlich down there in no
time flat, press corps right behind. He advised me to put a sock in it
and have a seat.

Instead, I snatched the receiver off the public phone bolted to the
wall and angrily spun numbers.

"Let me talk to Jake," I snapped.

"Jake who? This is the *Inquirer* sports department."

"Billy Nichols. It's urgent. Put him on."

"Billy? It's Fuzzy. What kind of damn fool stunt are you pulling?"

"Jake. Billy. Listen—I showed up to talk to him at County One, like
you said. But they're playing games over here, stalling me till it's too
late to see him. Uh-huh. I told them already. No, not yet . . ."

"I swear, you must be losing your marbles. How 'bout coming in
and doing some work?" He hung up.

I hoped like hell *this* phone wasn't tapped. The desk jockey was
already on the horn, pretending, poorly, that his call had nothing to do
with me. I took it up a notch, making sure the screw didn't miss a word:

"Yeah, sure, I can have a photographer from the *Inquirer* over here
in five minutes. Make a hell of a good picture. If you say so. Okay. I'll
give it one more go. They don't play ball, I'll ring you right back. Get
you into all the late editions."

The guard eyeballed me as I recradled the phone. He grinned inanely and waved me over, like he wanted to buy me a drink. I exploited my sudden advantage: "Jake says I ought to see my guy in private," I informed him. "Not the common area." I capped it off with a shrug, implying, *Don't blame me—you know how Jake gets.*

A paunchy flatfoot escorted me into a dank closet stenciled ATTORNEYS' ROOM and left me alone. First thing, I checked for wires and microphones in obvious locations. When Sanders was brought in, he saw me bent double, probing around under the table. As the guard backed out, quietly closing the door, Sanders applauded sarcastically.

"Now you're showing some smarts," he said approvingly, lowering his gaunt frame into the chair opposite me. He was even more emaciated than the last time I'd seen him, nothing like the diminutive dynamo I used to know. Nonetheless, he seemed surprisingly composed, considering he was standing trial for murder in a few days.

"You look beat," I said.

"I feel okay. Jesus looked beat too, when he took his bum rap."

Stir crazy, I suspected. Any other explanation for Burney Sanders comparing himself to the Son of God?

"You find Ginny?" he asked, pinpoints of hope in his sunken eyes. "She have the papers?"

I resisted the temptation to spew what I'd learned during the wild goose chase that Sanders had managed to set in motion. He wasn't my editor; I wasn't about to report to him. My goal now was to untangle this mess, while leaving Burney right where he belonged.

"It's obvious Corey's out to get you," I said, in a barely audible whisper, in case anybody was electronically eavesdropping. "He's Dexter Threllkyl's brother-in-law, if you didn't know."

Burney leaned forward and laid his arms on the table. A massive weight seemed to rise from his scrawny physique. He placed his palms flat, inhaled deeply, and let a brief beatific grin creep across his lips.

"He that shall endure till the end," Sanders intoned, "—the same shall be saved."

Bunking with a jailhouse preacher, I speculated. Burney's eyelids rose slowly. He searched my face for a reaction to his newfound piety.

I steamrolled: "How old was Threllkyl?"

"Sixty, maybe. Why? What's that got to do with anything?" He moved closer. "What about Ginny? She show you the trust stuff?"

"Threllkyl's obit gave his age as sixty-three. But the death certificate has him eighty-four. How you figure that?"

Sanders pondered for a minute, a broader smile eventually emerging.

"Could be the old man," he proposed, proud of his deduction. "Threllkyl's father—ancient Okie. He lived with 'em. Sharp old coot, but one foot in the grave. Had that lung thing, always gasping and wheezing."

"Emphysema?"

"Yeah. Had it bad."

"Manny Gold thinks it's another scam. Says Threllkyl could've faked his death and skipped out on the whole deal."

"How the hell did Manny get involved?"

"Didn't he fix you up with Threllkyl in the first place?"

"Jesus, you *are* a reporter. Where'd you come up with that?"

"Easy. Manny told me."

"Swell. Take everything that gasbag says with a two-ton grain of salt."

"Maybe. What about you, Burney? Should I buy whatever you're gonna sell me? Seeing as I'm the last one standing between you and San Quentin?"

"The good Lord pardons everyone that prepareth his heart to seek God."

"Shitcan it, Burney—stick to the facts. From the start."

Over the next ten minutes, Sanders laid out the entire scheme. I could have sung harmony. It was exactly as I'd pieced it together. Sanders scouted suckers for Threllkyl. No one saw a nickel's return. Shell corporations were registered to show negative profit. Skimmed-off cash was secretly purchasing legitimate, hidden assets.

Burney enhanced his account with bitter allegations about the Threllkyl family, evoked in distinctly un-Christian terms: "Lower than arrogant, stuck-up shitheels *born* to money. They'd kill their own if they had to, to stay high on the hog." An assessment one might apply to Sanders himself.

Finally, Burney sketched in crucial missing pieces, relating directly to the trust's rider, the single-page document that, on paper at least, made him a wealthy man.

"I'd earned Dex a mint, pulling in marks. So I figured I deserved a bigger cut. Plus Dex was feeling the heat; he wasn't stupid. I convinced him to throw something back, so the system would hold together. Like a faro bank in a carny scam: one winner to keep the suckers at the table. So he came up with this trust, and some genuine investments, to satisfy the noisier dupes. That's when I decided I deserved a partner's stake. I had more than just a kickback coming. See, he'd been running this three-ring bunco circus. Whenever someone threatened to blow the whistle, my job was to convince them otherwise."

"By trapping them in your dirty-picture racket."

Sullen silence was answer enough. As for the Mount Davidson Trust, I couldn't decide whether Sanders was on the level about a "partnership"with Threllkyl—or if the mastermind got fleeced by his own henchman. Either way, it was clear the Threllkyls had no intention of gifting Sanders with half the trust. I'd unwittingly done them a huge favor, producing circumstantial evidence tying Claire's murder to Burney. Now it was up to Corey, the family's bulldog, to run Sanders into a prison cell.

"Hell is never full; so the eyes of man are never satisfied." Like everybody who quoted Scripture, Sanders looked insufferably smug.

"Knock that shit off."

"I got greedy," Sanders admitted. "I'm only human. But I've changed. Like it says in Relevations 2:16—'Repent, or I'll come onto thee quickly.'"

"Needs work, Burney. How many investors had to be shut up with the blackmail?"

"Half dozen, thereabouts."

"You used Claire every time? To get 'em in those 'compromising positions'?"

"She was a pro."

"*I* wasn't an investor. Why go after me?"

"No, you screwed her for the hell of it. Fuck a guy's wife behind his back when he's off serving his country. Don't go getting all high and mighty with me."

Whoremongers and adulterers, God will judge, I recalled. One spicy remnant of catechism that stuck. Go by that, Burney and I were both due for sentencing.

"I'm only human," I finally muttered, miserably aware that I was echoing Burney.

"Since you know all this," he said, "that must mean you found Ginny—and the papers."

I studied Sanders, weighing his value in the overall scheme of things. His wife and kid might be better off without him. While he was jugged she might meet a man who had a goal in life *other* than putting the bite on everybody.

"Tell me you got those trust documents," Sanders pleaded. "*Please, God.*" He actually crossed himself.

"Never found her," I lied. "This Wagner broad might be on the lam for good."

"Damn it!" He smacked the table. "Those papers are my whole case."

"Get off the pipe, Burney. You got nothing, no matter what. So what if you had the trust deeds? Will a judge care? None of it has anything to do with Claire Escalante's death—which is what you're booked for, if you didn't notice."

"Don't be so sure. I got you into this because I hoped you'd be able to find Ginny. But the matter of fact is—I don't need you anymore. Not now."

"How you figure?"

"I got Jake. Ehrlich'll track her down. Once he gets a look at those papers, he'll hook me up with Threllkyl and blow this frame apart."

"You *must* be dreaming."

"Like hell."

In the dark hollows of his eyes, cinders of his hustler's fire glowed. "My wife went to see Ehrlich. He gave her ten minutes. When she told him Corey was part of the setup, he jumped all over it."

"You've *met* with Ehrlich?"

"Right here. Day before yesterday. My punk PD nearly pissed his pants when Jake talked about taking over my defense. Picture Corey's reaction. Florence, God love her, got Jake to hear me out. I told him we needed to find Ginny Wagner, because she had papers that would show how I was working with Threllkyl. He said if we can prove a connection between me and Threllkyl, then the fact that Threllkyl and Corey are related would get me a mistrial, easy. With that asshole Corey out of the way, I can get a fair shake. That's all I've asked, remember. After that—I'll put my faith in the Lord."

Sanders's holy roller routine was suddenly logical, in light of another entry on Ehrlich's lengthy curriculum vitae: Bible scholar. Jake could coach conversion faster than any man of the cloth, even if it only lasted till a verdict came down.

"What'd you tell Jake about me?" I asked.

"Nothing. *Yet.* Waiting to see if you'd show up with Ginny. But if you can't find her, what the fuck good are you? Maybe I should let Jake know you were banging Claire. That'd throw some reasonable doubt into the situation, huh? Nothing else, you gotta figure it might play hell with *Mr. Boxing*'s career."

"Let me be the first to tell you, Burney—you make a shitty Psalm-singer."

"Says you. Vengeance is mine, sayeth the Lord."

22

Outside the jail, I hailed a cab and rode it straight to Ginny's apartment. Had to reach her before Ehrlich. She was already paranoid. No telling what would happen if she discovered that in addition to being hunted by a hired thug from the DA's office, she was now a target of the most relentless criminal attorney in the Golden State.

Her only ally was a broke-dick sportswriter who'd lied to her from the opening bell about damn near everything. In her shoes, I wouldn't even pause to pack my bags. To hell with everybody else. I wasn't going to let Ginny Wagner sink any deeper in this mud. If one of us was to walk away unscathed, it would be her.

Not surprisingly, the buzzer went unanswered. She could have already fled to her previous hideout in Alameda. I loitered under the awning. A tenant exited the elevator and high-heeled across the lobby. Feinting like I'd just rung someone, I gave the leopard-coated matron hauling open the door my most deluxe, disarming smile. She returned one equally as winning, along with a *Thank you, dear man*, as I chivalrously held the door. Let's hope Larry Daws couldn't muster my bogus social charm.

Knocking on 506 got me nowhere. I felt pitifully small in the dim corridor, a rat that had scurried toward another inevitable dead end. But I worried more for Virginia Wagner, a slightly daffy but smart girl whose hide had been toughened from having every break bounce off her. Removing my hat, I pressed an ear against one of the door's ornate carved panels: faint voices, in rapid, urgent conversation. One participant was a woman, but I couldn't be sure it was Ginny. I rapped more loudly. It didn't disrupt the dialogue.

Then I heard the trademark sound of swelling organ music: It was only an afternoon broadcast melodrama. Little comfort. In my overheated brain, a muted radio behind a locked door at the far end of a gloomy corridor amounted to nothing but the worst.

Returning to the lobby, I searched the directory for the manager's apartment. I hurtled up to the first floor three steps at a time and banged on 103. There were grimy smudges around the door handle, always a swell indicator of first-class maintenance. Then I was staring at Tony Galento's uglier brother. He was substantial enough to fill the door frame, but not large enough to hide the filthy mess littering his digs. Evidence of a lonely, lifelong loser. His dubious eyes were doubly magnified by lenses thick as sidewalk glass.

"What's your story?" he inquired unpleasantly.

"I wonder if you'd check on a tenant. Up in 506."

"What's the problem?"

"I think something . . . may have happened. She doesn't answer."

"Maybe she's not home. Ever think of that?"

"We'd planned to meet here at four. Don't you have a passkey, so we can just make sure?"

"No chance, buddy. These are private residences. I'm not barging into somebody's apartment on account of you got stood up. So she found another boyfriend. Tough luck."

He started to shut the door, but I blocked it with my hand. "It's not like that—she could be hurt in there. Or worse. Can you go up and look around?" My normal strategy was to coerce the recalcitrant with glibness and grease, but this clown rated nothing more than a short right hand.

"Move back before I break your arm," he said. The enlarged eyes seemed to glower from every direction at once. He muscled toward me, blocking the gap between door and frame. I retreated, which put a crooked smile on his bovine face.

"She ain't in, that makes you feel any better," he said with a smirk. "Wagner, 506, right? Went out with a guy a little while ago. Seen 'em leave. So now you don't have to worry. Satisfied?"

"What'd this guy look like?"

"Taller than you. Dressed nicer than you. Better-looking than you. Other than that . . ." He reduced the door's gap to a thin sliver. "Knock again and see what happens," he suggested, before the slam.

Goddamn son of a bitch.

I punched the button for the elevator, many times, much too hard. Clanging my way out onto the fifth floor, I bolted down to 506. The door took a few more hits for good measure. I contemplated kicking it in. Behind me came the abrupt chunking and whirring sounds of the lift being recalled. I pulled out my notebook and scrawled:

Wed. 4:30 P.M.
Ginny—Call me. Urgent.
               BN

I tore off the sheet and slid it under the door.

While I waited for the elevator, my mind raced through possibilities, none good. The worst, one that made the bile rise, was that I was leaving Ginny dead on the floor in her apartment. If she'd gone out, like the super said, it couldn't have been with Daws—she'd have fought him tooth and nail, and taken half the building down with her. Maybe she, and the trust papers, had already been nabbed by Ehrlich and squired to his offices. True, Jake was better-dressed than me, but he definitely wasn't taller.

I tried to convince myself the super was just blowing smoke up my ass, trying to get under my skin.

Through the twin windows on the elevator's door the cage rose into view. Bulging, cartoon eyeballs were staring at me again. He shunted aside the accordion bars, and grabbed the front of my overcoat.

"I don't allow trespassers in the building bothering my tenants," the super said, pulling me into the elevator and shoving me against a hardwood wall. He punched the button for the lobby without looking. The bastard's bulk ate up most of the space, and air, in the cramped box.

"She really leave with somebody?" I asked. "Or you just yanking my chain?"

No answer. We hit bottom. Retracting the gate, he propelled me forward. Midway through the bum's rush, he broke the silence. "If I wanted to fuck with you," he grunted, "—you'd know. Take it on the arches."

I hit Pine Street with no clues as to my next move. A couple of hours remained until the Golden Gloves jumped off. I walked down to Polk, then headed toward the Civic. Detouring into the Daily Double for a cocktail, I hoped inspiration might float up from the bottom of the glass and introduce itself. Not that I would have recognized it. Not through the thundercloud of guilt and self-pity hovering over my bar stool. Tracing back through the tangle, I felt awful about Woody Montague and Tony Bernal—during the chaos of the past few days, I hadn't checked in with either. Their miserable circumstances couldn't be blamed on this Sanders debacle—they had nothing to do with it. I was the one responsible for putting them in the wrong place at the wrong time.

Likewise, at the heart of it, I'd been responsible for Claire's death.

Mercifully, Archie Lazore, a buddy of mine, passed by as I was contemplating another cocktail. I hailed him through the window, threw down a buck, and scooted outside.

"Archie! Going to the Gloves tonight?"

"Naturally."

"Your car nearby?"

"For what? We can walk from here easy."

"No, I need a lift. Out to Silver Avenue. We can get there and back, still make the first bout. As a favor."

The house was on the hill above Butchertown. A pink stucco two-story, both sides common-wall, garage underneath. Identical to all the others on the block, except the color. The precise address I gleaned from my little broken-back contact book. With no space on the street, Archie angled his coupe into the driveway and cut the engine.

"How long'll this take, Billy?"

He was antsy, even more so after I'd dictated an additional detour to Petrini's. I climbed out, hefting in my arms the sack holding a sixteen-pound turkey, biggest the butcher had. "Just a few. Sure you don't want to pay your respects?"

"I don't even know him. I can't stand this stuff. Poor guy laid out in bed, house all dark and quiet and shit. I'll wait here, that's all right with you."

Next door, a two-man team in overalls and caps wrestled with a metal gate, installing it across the arched entrance to the neighbor's house. The place beyond that was gated, too. About half the homes on the block were fortified with the latest in fashionable iron bar decor. Tony Bernal, however, still believed he lived in a safe neighborhood. I schlepped the bird through his unbarred archway and climbed speck-led stone steps, the scrape of my footsteps amplified in the tall, open-air passage.

Bill collectors got warmer receptions than what Mrs. Bernal gave me. She eyed the bulky package suspiciously, then scanned the stair-way. "Where's your driver?"

I moved inside, uninvited. "Here," I announced, the nape of my neck prickling. "A holiday turkey. Happy Thanksgiving." I offered the dead weight.

Her eyes were black, lifeless shoe buttons. She prodded the sack, but wouldn't accept it. One of her sons appeared around a corner and sidled closer to us, curious.

"What am I supposed to do with this?" his ungrateful mother wanted to know.

"Some people eat them, particularly this time of year. Cooked, of course. Good with cranberries, I hear." Why *not* be sarcastic? She couldn't hate me any worse.

"Who's at the door?" Tony's voice came from down the corridor to my right. He sounded pretty strong, which bolstered my spirits con-siderably.

"Paulie," Mrs. Bernal finally told her son, with a sigh of histrionic weariness. "Take this thing into the kitchen. See if you can make room in the icebox." The boy nodded to me and mouthed *Hello*, then duti-fully hoisted the turkey and transported it the few steps to the kitchen. This was a modest house. Every doorway was visible from where I stood. The three kids must have bunked in a single bedroom.

"How is he?" I inquired.

"See for yourself." She frowned, pointing down the hallway. I couldn't swivel away fast enough.

"Happy Thanksgiving," she parroted, sneering at my backside.

Tony was propped up in bed, reading the papers. Sections of four separate dailies were strewn about. Beneath the covers, his left leg was twice the size of the right, encased in a massive cast, hip to foot. A brief smile may have appeared on his gray, drawn features, but I didn't notice. I was distracted by the stitching on his forehead, tracking into parts of his skull where hair had been shaved away.

Stretching to the nightstand, he carefully set his cigarette in an ashtray packed with stubbed-out butts. He extended a weak hand, which I shook gingerly.

"Sorry it took me so long to check in." Too quick, not sincere enough.

"I knew the Gloves were starting up," he said, waving off the lame apology.

I doffed my hat, but stopped short before depositing it on the foot of the bed. "Go ahead," Tony said. "I'm not one for superstitions."

I perched the fedora on top of a nearby dresser.

Grinning wanly, Tony gestured to a chair beside the window. "Take a seat. Visit awhile." The drapes were parted enough to reveal fading streaks of daylight on homes across the street.

"What's with all the bars going up?" I wondered, moving around the bed. "Some sort of crime wave?"

"Yeah, one-man crime wave—a salesman. Lady got robbed the next block over by a colored guy. So a rep with one of these security companies goes door-to-door, telling everybody that the shines who've moved into Bayview are gonna come swarming up the hill, raping and robbing. You believe that?"

"He got half the neighborhood to believe it," I noted, stealing a glance out the window at Archie's car, directly below. His fingers drummed the steering wheel. He wouldn't stage a vanishing act, like Ginny had at Califros'. I hoped.

Fanning the tails of my overcoat, I parked on the bedside chair. Tony and I weren't alone: An orange tabby was resting against his plastered leg, giving me a disdainful gaze.

"He part of the recovery treatment?" I joked.

"Better'n those doctors," Tony said. His left hand reached down to idly scratch the cat's flank. It blinked slowly, only once, then spread the toes on a paw as big as a catcher's mitt. "His name's Keekat. On accounta how my oldest boy used to say 'kitty cat.' Eighteen years old, can you beat that?"

"Don't normally live that long, do they?" Keekat's head tilted back slightly, lids at half-mast. He seemed ambivalent toward me, or vaguely disapproving. I didn't take it personally; all humans probably rated the same. Reminded me of tamed lions I'd seen as a kid at Fleish-hacker. Dignified even in jail.

"He got hit by a car out front two years ago," Tony related. "We fig-ured he was a goner. Vet said to put him down, but the boys wouldn't let me. Now he's good as new. Walks lopsided 'cause his ass end is all kattywampus, but he gets around. Kills anything that gets in the base-ment."

"Tough customer."

"An inspiration, now. My hero."

Keekat craned his neck so Tony's fingertips could reach his cheek. Yellow eyes closed blissfully as fingers kept stroking his furry cheek.

"You hear about what happened to Montague?" Tony quietly inquired.

"Yeah, I did. What's the latest? Any improvement?"

"My wife talked to his yesterday. Not good. He's in way worse shape than me." Tony twisted awkwardly, trying to sit up. No reaction from the cat. Like a two-ton anchor, Bernal's leg didn't budge. I shifted my eyes from his painful grimaces to the papers jumbled all around him. From here on out, this might be Tony's place in the world. No longer *in* the circuit. It'd be reheated for him, on newsprint, while he lay there, an invalid. No more jitterbugging around a composing room, no more swaggering through nightclubs . . .

"Not to sound like a selfish prick," Tony went on, "but without Montague I'm up shit's creek. He was going after those booze peddlers for me *gratis*. Now his wife says she wants to take over the case. Can you b'lieve that? She's already got a brief together and everything. But I don't know if she knows her shit at all. Top of that, I learn they got some witness who'll claim it was *my* fault. Montague told me you were there when the wreck happened—that right?"

"Little bit after. Didn't actually see it. Don't you remember us talk-ing before the ambulance came?"

"All I remember was thinking I was gonna die. But other people were around. I saw 'em across the street right when I got hit. Some-body musta seen it, seen that bastard run the sign. 'Cause that's what he did—*that* part I remember."

All I could do was shake my head: rueful commiseration.

"Susan Montague says things might look different, you'd been a couple blocks closer," Tony mused. "Near enough to see the crash." He gave me a weighty stare before turning his attention back to the cat. It wasn't directly solicited perjury, but the suggestion lingered.

No use bringing up Manny Gold. Why make poor Tony agonize further over how deviously Virgil Dardi could manipulate a defense? Better I covertly lean on Manny, getting him to back off his story, whether it was bullshit or not. That'd be a far more useful Thanksgiving present than freshly plucked fowl. I just needed to figure out where my theoretical leverage was supposed to come from. One more goddamn headache I never asked for.

A change of subject was in order.

"What do the doctors say? You'll be okay?"

"Might not walk again—which case, we're pretty much ruined. Shoulda made one of the boys learn to set type."

I sat up straight and winced. We could have talked about guild benefits and all that, but my heart wasn't in it.

"We'll see how it goes," Tony continued, adopting the brave front. "They had this old boy written off, too." He rubbed behind the cat's ears. Neither of us could conjure up much else to say. Keekat began purring like an unmuffled motor.

"Handsome animal," I murmured.

"Too damn proud to quit."

Outside, Archie punched the horn, one abbreviated bleat.

"My ride." I stood, relieved. "The Gloves. Gotta go. Take care of yourself."

Jake Ehrlich was ringside that night, sitting directly across from me. Concentrating on the bouts wasn't easy. Every so often I'd glance across the bright expanse of the ring, through the slender shuffling legs of the young combatants, and Ehrlich's hooded gaze would meet mine. Looked just like a crocodile: eyes peering calmly, dangerously, over a canvas swamp.

23

Thanksgiving dinner with Ida's family was as well worn and comfortable as an old shoe—the one that rubs your heel raw. But once I'd mastered the routine, it was simply a matter of sticking to the fight plan and gutting out all fifteen rounds. This holiday, however, going the distance would be tougher.

It was the first full-blown gathering of the tribe since Vincent had been born. Ida's folks remained mum about the curious circumstances by which their daughter, after seven years of marriage, at last became a mother. They must have known it wasn't my seed that spawned their towheaded grandson. But in stoic Old World tradition, they refrained from comment. My father-in-law, Karl(heinz) Lindstrom, had a trademark response to practically every story he read in the paper: *This is anybody's business?* he'd demand, puffing his pipe in agitation whenever someone's personal misfortunes made headlines. Given that, his muteness regarding my fraudulent fatherhood was to be expected.

The sordid details of Ida's adventure had, on the other hand, been dissected by her sisters with the same compassion and understanding buzzards exhibit competing for carrion. This night, Paula, Mary, and Phyllis would serve up generous rations of smug smiles, sidelong glances, and none-too-subtle innuendoes, right alongside the candied yams and brandied carrots.

My strategy was to keep to the ropes and let 'em punch themselves out. If I steered clear of haymakers and kept my blood below the boiling point, it was even possible to enjoy the mean-spirited camaraderie of it all, provided the cutlery was used according to Emily Post, not Edgar Allan Poe.

The day before, Karl made his annual pilgrimage to a turkey farm near Half Moon Bay to personally pick the unfortunate fowl he'd serve to his own gobbling flock. My holiday duties didn't extend much further than dropping the occasional witticism, like pearl onions into a tureen of butter beans. That, and carve the turkey.

It must have burned Gil Rayburn and Jack Gallagher, my brothers-in-law, that I always was given the honor of slicing up and doling out Karl Lindstrom's ceremonial bird. Once I demurred, proposing, "Let Jack have a whack at it," but Karl snatched the carving utensils from Gallagher's hands and returned them to me. My supposed privilege always prompted undercurrents of tension among the sisters and their husbands. But old Karl couldn't be swayed from his notions of a manly pecking order. Until I dropped dead, or one of the other menfolk got elected mayor, *Mr. Boxing* would remain in charge of cutting up and dispensing the meat.

My father-in-law was a retired Pinkerton who over the years quit scouring the docks for Commies and anarchists only long enough to get his wife pregnant eight times. That only four Lindstrom children survived, all daughters, explained why I couldn't look at my mother-in-law, a hobbled, arthritic Irish brood mare named Irene, without feeling the weight of her world. Four times she'd carried a child on a bum hip, only to lose it through a miscarriage or stillbirth. Determination is admirable, to a point. Giving until it kills is something else. Not that the in-laws and I would ever discuss it.

"You believe that scene on Market the other day?" offered Gil, spearing a gherkin with a cellophaned toothpick. "I thought those Cal kids were gonna burn down the Palace!"

"Makes you wonder what'll happen next year," I speculated. "When the Bears *don't* get that invite."

Gallagher gave a laugh. He was always happy to talk sports, sports, and, for variety, more sports. Jack was a decent sort; worked for a sheet-metal fabricator. He and Phyllis had two kids, boy and girl, currently chasing each other up and down the stairs, screaming. "They must be playing house," Mary said, plugging her ears. "Taking after their parents," snickered Paula, always quick with a barb. The sisters all filed into the kitchen to help their mother. All except recently divorced Paula.

She'd split from her first husband after meeting a decorated fighter pilot. Guy had flown a P-47 Thunderbolt in the Pacific, been shot down, captured, fed nothing but blood sausage for months in a Jap POW camp. After all that, he got engaged to Paula Lindstrom. Still trying to prove how tough he was, I figured.

Paula lazed in a chair by the radio, feet up, flashing the kids nasty looks when they bumped into the four-inch stacked heels she dangled off the ottoman. Paula was a fireplug, with a hot-and-cold-running disposition. Things were lukewarm at the moment. Her betrothed was off getting briefed on the Red uprising in China. But her mood could change instantly. There was no predicting Paula.

Vincent, well behaved as usual, sat placidly in his high chair next to me. The kid was growing on me. Especially when he watched me with those guileless eyes. In the circuit I could get splattered with guile. The kid's face was a nice tonic waiting for me at home. And Ida was undoubtedly at her best with a child; I'd catch her gazing at him with something close to rapture on her face. As if there was nothing else in the world she needed to make her happy.

"Why'd they move the Golden Gloves up this year?" Gil asked. "I don't remember them ever being over Thanksgiving before."

"Didn't want a conflict with that Graziano fight at the end of the month," I explained. "Now, of course, everybody's sore because the kids don't get to be home with their families. And they decided to go dark tonight, which frosted the union guys, who wanted holiday pay. Can't win."

"Ain't that the truth."

Karl tottered out of the kitchen struggling beneath a platter bearing the golden bird. One aromatic whiff and nobody cared about anything else. Irene Lindstrom could cook. One true cause for celebration.

"Gilbert, would you do the honors?" Karl Lindstrom asked, giving Gil Rayburn the carving tools.

"Uh, let Billy do it," Gil stammered. "He always does a good job."

"So, we have it different for a change," the old man declared, placing the knife in Gil's hand. "This year, you prepare it for us."

The sisters, huddled behind their father, exchanged looks, like witnesses who'd just seen Lazarus arise.

I went downstairs to get something to drink about 11 P.M., after Ida had replayed The Carving Incident for the five hundreth time since we left her parents' house. Couldn't listen to it again. I wasn't upset with her. She just refused to let it rest, and I was close to saying something regrettable. I vetoed additional booze and went for a glass of milk instead.

When the phone rang, I motored out to the foyer. Didn't want the kid to wake up. This late it was probably one of the boys, looking for me to settle a barroom bet. An annoying occupational sideline, but one required of *Mr. Boxing*.

"Billy—it's Ginny."

"Where the hell'd you go?" I practically shouted, then brought it down a notch, trying to regain my composure. I carried the phone into the dining room, so my voice wouldn't carry. The cord extended just far enough. "You left me high and dry up there on Twin Peaks. What kind of stunt was that? After what we'd just been through?"

"I'm fine, thanks for asking. And how was *your* holiday?"

"Don't crack wise with me. I thought we were together on that thing, when you dropped me like a bad habit. I didn't appreciate it."

"I'll make it up to you."

"Anybody get hold of you from Jake Ehrlich's office?"

"The lawyer? No. Why?"

"Are you at your apartment?"

"No. I don't think it's safe. I'm staying at a hotel downtown."

"We need to get together."

"That's why I'm calling. Can you meet me tomorrow night? I've got something for you."

"I've got the Gloves."

Suddenly, I remembered the goddamn wiretap.

"Ginny, I can't talk anymore. Call me in the morning, at the office. Don't use this number anymore."

24

My Kind of Town
By Sam Francisco

District Attorney **"Pat" Brown** has fired off his Christmas wishes to Santa. Sources in the North Pole postal pipeline advise me he's asked for just one item: a clean slate. That's why legal elves are working overtime at the Hall of Justice, trying to tie ribbons on several major cases before the holidays.

We hate to shovel lumps of coal into Brown's stocking, but one entry on the slate—the murder trial of local boxing promoter **Burnell Sanders**—promises to be anything but an open-and-shut affair, as our DA's office has been advertising. You heard it first from your Mole-About-Town: None other than **Jake Ehrlich** will step into court to defend Sanders, only days before the trial is set to start.

Jake was mum when I grilled him—there's a shocker—but expect a formal announcement Monday, less than 48 hours prior to Hizzoner White's opening gavel. Sanders is charged with killing the wife of heavyweight **Hack Escalante.** Following his recent loss to champ **Chester Carter,** Escalante reportedly ditched town for sunnier southland scenery. Ehrlich better hope the widowed warrior stays there, and the DA doesn't yank him back for sympathy-inducing courtroom appearances.

Pressing the newspaper against the steering wheel, I inadvertently honked the horn. Bustlers along the slope of Powell Street glanced over, startled, but scurried on when they realized the bleat had emanated from the Cadillac stationed in front of Sears Fine Foods. For years, the pink Caddy has owned this curbside spot, providing a warm, plushly upholstered lobby to overflow customers waiting for tables. Food's only a notch above greasy spoon, but the joint pulls a brisk breakfast and lunch trade, courtesy of nearby hotels like the Drake, Manx, Cecil, and St. Francis.

The morning light was crystal-bright, the air frigid. The streets surrounding Union Square shone with eye-stinging clarity. It made the contents of "My Kind of Town" read that much sharper—and deadlier. I deliberately refolded *Sam Francisco*'s column within the morning edition. I was tempted to crush him into a ball and pitch him out the window, onto whining cable car tracks.

"Sam" was really Bob Pattison, a rogue reporter who came on the scene a couple of years back and promptly wangled a sweet deal as the loosest cannon on the *Inquirer* staff. He had an engaging way of breaking loose dirt and blowing it into eight or ten brazen column inches. Unlike, say, Woody Montague, Pattison had no qualms about building his stories on a swamp ground of hearsay and innuendo. To many Press Club colleagues, he was a pariah—primarily because his cannon was selectively loose. Everybody knew Hearst could train "Sam's" sights wherever he wanted, whenever he wanted.

Sam Francisco may have been nearing the end of his scandalmongering days. Rival sheets were chasing rumors that "Bob Pattison" was also an alias, for a serial check forger from back East whose paper-hanging had earned him a couple of prison jolts.

"My Kind of Town," all right.

Shoppers and tourists wove through intersections and swarmed sidewalks. It was officially the start of the yuletide shopping season, a traditional bust-out day for retailers. But store owners were antsy. Even though the months-old longshore strike had been settled yesterday, tons of merchandise were still stranded on the waterfront, waiting to be broken out and delivered.

Moored at the bottom of the hill, bulky as a cargo ship, was Manny Gold. When traffic stopped, he shoved off across Post, leaving twin streams of normal-sized humans in his wake. Throughout the short haul up Powell, Gold's labored breathing produced steamy gusts, swirling under his upturned hat brim.

Manny hiked the hill like every colossal heavyweight who'd climbed into a ring: grim as an undertaker, ashamed of his size, but completely convinced he couldn't be toppled. I felt sorry for outsized, ponderous fighters, who took nothing but mockery and abuse from rowdy crowds. Right now, I couldn't afford such sympathy. Toppling Manny Gold was just a preliminary bout on my card today. Harsh judgment, with no mercy, had to be passed on my old pal.

When he'd huffed halfway up Powell I got a surprise: Manny's son, Daniel, was clinging to the old man's dangling mitt. The boy had been camouflaged behind Gold's broad bow. A regrettable complication. Manny must have planned it this way, after mulling over why I'd called to wish him Happy Thanksgiving and arrange this breakfast meeting.

I tooted the horn before they reached the entrance of Sears. Bending to peer through the passenger window, Manny displayed a sour scowl. We exchanged beckoning gestures.

Recognizing his partner from the Big Dipper, Gold Junior attached himself to the Caddy like an iron shaving to a magnet. I leaned over and unlatched the long, heavy door. Putting Gold on the defensive was essential; luring him into the car was the first step.

"Nobody's lined up," Manny called in. "We can get a table right now."

"Get in for a minute, Manny. So we can talk."

"Is this your car?" squealed Daniel, pulling the handle. As it swung open, the door nearly knocked him ass-over-teakettle. His father tried to rein him in. Frail or no, Daniel shook loose and clambered onto the expansive stretch of snowy tuck-and-roll. "Are you taking us for a ride?" he asked. More a plea than a query.

"This isn't mine, Daniel. It stays parked here. Belongs to the restaurant."

"Let's talk inside," Gold insisted. "Over a stack of flapjacks." Daniel didn't rise to the bait. Too busy fingering elaborate doodads on the dashboard.

"A little privacy first," I suggested. "Just a minute or two, if you don't mind."

From the mouth of Gold, the sigh sounded like a foghorn. Then he groused, employing rhetorical singsong cadence: "Why do we wanna camp out in a parked car, when we can relax in a warm booth, like civilized persons, with a waitress serving us *hot chocolate*, on this day as cold as a witch tit?"

"Park the satchel, Manny. C'mon. Join us."

"Give me a break, William. There's tables available."

"For chrissakes, get in the car. It's freezing. Climb in and close the door."

Exasperated, Manny tugged the door wide open and began negotiating himself into the Cadillac. He could have used a few block-and-tackle boys from longshoremen's Local 10. His posterior filled the cab before he'd even gotten his shoulders through the door frame. Daniel was forced closer to me. "Maybe you'd better hop in the backseat," I told the kid, giving him a boost over. Jesus, it was even worse than I'd envisioned. Miserable grunts, groans, and a muffled *shit shit shit* as Gold sank onto the leather to a chorus of protesting springs. Edge of the roof knocked off his fedora, which plopped on the sidewalk. He'd have to get back out to retrieve it.

"Pardon me!" Manny shouted to a passing woman. "Be a doll and hand me that, would you?" She did, with gloved fingers and a smile, because your average San Franciscan is a cut above.

Brim set safely in his lap, Manny squirmed and laboriously hauled in first one tree-trunk leg, then the other, shifting himself to face the windshield. His overcoat bunched and crumpled like a collapsed circus tent. When he tugged the door handle, it didn't budge. Despite superior suspension, the Cadillac had sunk a good six inches. Manny gave up on the door.

"This private enough for you?" he wheezed, face flushed from exertion and embarrassment. The heater, running full blast, wasn't helping him either.

Gold wouldn't get any weaker, so I went to work.

"Manny, listen. I'm asking you to lay off your story of that crack-up at Third and Howard. I need you to do this for me. As a friend—I'm asking."

"I was afraid that's what this was leading to," he said, shaking his head.

Must be why you brought along the kid. Talk about a chickenshit play.

Manny's comb-over had come unglued, stray tendrils dangling limply from his dome. He fished inside his overcoat and produced a flag-sized square of silk, which he used to dab his florid face. "Tough luck some other pal of yours was involved," he said. "But what I saw, I saw. I've already explained that."

"My buddy's screwed six ways from Sunday, Manny. Might never walk again. He needs a break in the worst possible way."

"As if I don't? I'm *not* a buddy? When push comes to shove, you're prepared to cast aside our friendship?" His eyes delivered their own harsh judgment.

Daniel suddenly appeared in the space between us, arms hanging over the seat. "Please, can we go for a ride now?" he begged.

Manny groped for him, to pull him into his arms. My hand came out of a vest pocket with two bits. I flipped it onto the floor in back. "Find that, Danny, and it's yours." When he flopped down to the mats, I bounced another coin off the rear cushions. "There's one more for you."

Gold played sad and disgusted. "What haven't I done for you, William?" he whined. "When haven't I been as good a friend as you've got in this town?"

"Right this moment," I whispered. "'Cause you're lying about having seen that car wreck." I absently rolled up the morning edition while staring off downhill. A flock of pigeons swooped into Union Square, roosting on the monument to Admiral Dewey.

"How can you say that? How can you look me in the face and say that?"

I looked him in the face. "You're lying about the car wreck. I know because Jack Early from the *Call-Bulletin* was Johnny-on-the-spot. Shot dozens of pictures, right when it happened. None of 'em shows you, or your car, anywhere near Howard. Mainly because you weren't there."

What shit *that* was—Jack Early never gave guys from another rag the time of day, let alone his contact sheets. But I was betting my bluff would scare sense into Gold.

"You're turning against me," Manny muttered. "I can't believe this."

"Manny—get with it. Not like I'm asking you to tell a lie. I'm asking you *not* to tell a lie. Get the difference?"

"I found it," Daniel blurted, popping back up and displaying the quarter.

"Find the other one," I told him. "You can keep 'em both."

"You said you wanted to get Ida something special for her thirtieth birthday," Manny kvetched. "Who was it fixed you up with that fox fur? Whenever one of your wife's sisters got married, who found you the best deal on a hall, on invitations, on decorations? That means *eppis* now?" His anger rose, filling the car, spilling onto the sidewalk. "My guy in Detroit got you the first interview anybody out here ever had with Louis—who set that up? Every time you've touched me for a favor, William, each and *every* time—did I once say no? And how often didn't you even have to *ask*? Remind me of an instance when I was less than a loyal and true friend to you. Tell me one *single* instance, and I'll haul my fat ass out of this goddamn car and let you call me a liar in print."

In terms of wholesaling guilt, Catholics had some catching up to do. Daniel was cowering on the backseat, recoiling from his father's roaring voice and ugly words. Passersby gawked at the invective steaming out of Sears' Caddy.

"Manny," I responded blandly, trying to stanch the tide. "We're not talking about our friendship. We're talking about facts."

"So *you* saw that accident? *You* know the facts? Then why in hell aren't *you* giving testimony?"

My skin prickled. I shoved down a heater lever, almost breaking it off. "I'm going to say it again," I snapped. "My buddy is in a brutal spot and I—"

"Fuck you. That clear enough? *Fuck you.* It *is* about friendship. Go ahead, choose this other guy over me. Makes you no better than all the rest. Get whatever you can off the big fat funny Jew. When *his* chips are down, drop him. I can't believe that *you*—of all people—would stab me in the back like this!"

"Shut up or shut the door," I said. Several people now milled in front of the restaurant, rubbernecking.

Gold was quaking, like the mountainside before a volcano. "You were more than just another friend, William. You were my *mishpocha*. You introduced me to Benny Leonard. My God. I shook his hand."

"*Goddamnit!*" I slammed the dash with the rolled-up newspaper, furious. Daniel cringed, then burst into tears, as if *he'd* been hit.

"Why are you pulling this shit, Manny? We're such pals, why do I have to beg you to bag this cock-and-bull story? Dardi's as dirty as they come! Why help *him*?"

"I've got no choice," he bellowed. The Cadillac shuddered when he turned my way. His son's crying became a prolonged wail, an ambulance siren, assaulting my eardrum. Manny seemed oblivious to it.

"She's going to K-I-L-L herself," he said, like it was supposed to explain everything. "Unless I can come up with the money for medical treatments."

"No offense to Peggy—but what the F-U-C-K does your wife have to do with anything we're talking about?"

"At my house, weren't you listening, William?" His voice dropped to a hoarse whisper. "I'm broke. I need cash—now. They've got me over a barrel. There are other things, things they can nail me with. Lies, every one, but what can I do? Peggy is all I care about. I can't lose her, William. She's my whole world, she's who I am. As for Daniel— look what you're doing to him."

"What *I'm* doing to him?"

"Humiliating his father. Before his very eyes. Shameful."

"Using your boy as a shield—*that's* shameful, Manny."

"I should leave him alone with her? Not anymore. I can't."

Daniel's keening had spiraled into a monotonous drone. He was trying to drown us out. Swiping the *Inquirer* across his kisser would have felt pretty good, but would only amplify the hysterics. So I hit his father instead. In the chest.

"Who touched you up for this bullshit story? Dardi himself? You know him?"

"First I'm a liar—now I'm stupid in the bargain? Some *mishpocha* you are." A derisive gust rumbled from his lips, from a shaft deep in the mountain.

"Then who put you up to it?"

"I got nothing more to say."

"How much are they paying you? What's the going rate these days on a *mishpocha's* honor?"

That stung.

"To hell with you. I'm gonna do what I have to do, for Peggy's sake. You wouldn't do the same for Ida?"

Manny Gold was some salesman, trying to convince me that lying through his teeth was an act of valor. No stranger myself to manipulations of truth, I empathized. Too much for my own good.

Across Powell, the Drake's doorman, in full Yeoman of the Guard regalia, escorted a vacationing couple to an idling Luxor. Their faces glowed in anticipation of a fresh, free day. I wanted to jump in the cab with them, headed anywhere, unencumbered. I wanted to go back to work. I wanted to get paid for watching guys punch each other silly and feel absolutely no personal connection to their pain and anxiety and desperation.

Summoning the effort, Gold reached around and hoisted his son over the seat, onto his lap. He didn't seem to care that the kid crushed his hat.

"Sorry for all the shouting," Manny whispered in the boy's ear. "How's a waffle sound? Covered with whipped cream and strawberries."

He may have been on the ropes, but this gigantic bastard wasn't about to fall.

"Okay, Manny," I said. "You do what you think's right. But don't say I didn't warn you if things go bad. But there's something else, too—"

"What? Another favor?" Manny slid me a sidelong glance several degrees colder than the air outside. The kid stared at me, too.

"This Threllkyl family," I said. "They're still in town, right?"

"Far as I know."

"You're acquainted, right? With the wife?"

The kid wouldn't break his gaze. I turned away, focusing on the big, bright facades of Zukor's and the Diamond Palace, all the way down Powell, across Market.

"Astrid," Manny said. "Oh, she definitely knows who I am." From his tone, I assumed they weren't *mishpocha*.

"Give me an intro. Tell her it's about the Mount Davidson Trust. Let her know if she wants—no, no—say if she'd *like* those papers back, she needs to see me this weekend. Sunday at the latest. Tell her that. Tell her today."

Manny solemnly observed the pedestrian ramble returning to status quo after our impromptu sideshow.

"Then we're cleared up on the other thing?"

I flicked my hand dismissively, putting an "in sorrow" more than an "in anger" look on my tired mug.

"Is that the new hat Daddy got for you?" Daniel asked.

25

The night's final bout was decided a minute or two shy of 11 P.M. By half past I'd constructed a trim digest of the evening's amateur action. I handed off copy to a runner rather than phoning it in. I didn't want Ginny Wagner stranded out front, an easy target.

After a show I generally reserve a few moments for the Clingers, regulars who hang on till the bitter end, like grounds at the bottom of the day's last coffee. A troubled conscience was all that waited up for these lonely mutts. Postponing that joyless rendezvous, they'd chew your ear off, recounting every punch in every fight they'd ever seen. Then they'd move on to ones they'd only heard about. Some would keep flapping their gums until street sweepers rousted them, 'long about dawn.

Tonight, shouldering through the Civic's main doors, I ignored the punch-drunk palaver and headed straight for the Roadmaster, right out front. It was parked splendidly, conspicuously, illegally, in the white zone. Marquee lights were kind to its curves. A pair of pie-eyed fans admired the sleek machine.

After brief consideration, their admiration extended to the owner, who lounged against the far fender, insouciantly burning tobacco. Ginny didn't seem remotely fearful for her life.

"How 'bout a ride, dollface?" one goon ventured. A regular Clark Gable, he was.

"Shove in your clutch," Ginny replied. "And get home to Mama."

I slid up while Gable groped for a retort. "McAllister and Larkin," I barked over the gleaming hood. "Five minutes."

My tone knitted her brows. "What's wrong with here?"

"Every mope on this sidewalk knows me," I pointed out. "Get the picture?"

She tossed the remnants of the tar-bar. "Roger," she confirmed, with a mock salute.

Once she'd driven off, I hustled in the opposite direction, down

Polk. Doubling back on Market, I described a circuitous five-block route to the corner of McAllister and Larkin. Panting, I yanked open the passenger door and sank inside.

"Aren't we being a little dramatic?" she said. "Now we *look* suspicious. Before I was only giving you a ride. Now we're up to something."

"Not important." I shoved aside a thick folder and equally fat book stacked on the quilted leather between us. "I can't believe I'd ever say this, but I'd feel safer if you drove. Parked here, we're sitting ducks."

Her eyes assessed me nervously, as she eased into the sparsely trafficked street. "You're more jittery than me. What's going on?"

"My home phone picked up a wiretap," I told her. Removing my hat, I swabbed both the damp inner band and my damper forehead. "I forgot about it when I answered the phone last night. That's why I jumped off so abruptly."

"What's that mean? Somebody's listening in on your calls?"

"The DA's office. They could be scoping us out right now. That's why I had to make with the cloak-and-dagger routine. Besides the obvious."

Several blocks went past in silence, Ginny constantly tossing glances toward the mirrors, scouring streets for any headlights tied to our tail.

"Where are we going?" I asked. She turned onto Market, headed west. We passed the big theaters, the miles of neon tubes, gas and glass burning brightly. Friday's ramble still crackled on both sides of the boulevard.

Something shifted in me. The main stem suddenly seemed anonymous. I struggled for the names of venerable hangouts, but they floated away. All the familiar, glittering gaiety was replaced with a swelling sadness. It clogged my chest, thickened my throat.

"Want me to take you home?" Virginia asked. Innocently, of course, and concerned, but it felt like a shiv between the ribs.

Not her fault: She couldn't possibly have known this was the same route Claire had taken, the day *she* took me home. The day I'd dropped my defenses and made love to another man's wife. Different auto, different woman. But it felt horribly similar. Life repeating itself.

"No. Keep driving. Don't stop."

I picked up the book beside me: *Raintree County*. I'd promised to get her a replacement for the one she'd lost. Couldn't even remember the name.

"Don't bother looking for that Faulkner," she said, reading my mind. "It's sold out. Can't find a copy anywhere in town."

"Maybe I can get you one through the *Inquirer*."

Beneath the book was the cardboard-bound, shoe-laced accordion file containing the complete incorporation papers of the Mount Davidson Trust. Had to assume it's what instigated this clandestine conference. Ginny was probably ready to cash out her stake in this craziness. Couldn't blame her.

Before getting into it, I detoured:

"So—want to hear what I found at Califro's place the other day?"

After a long pause she answered quietly: "I already know."

"Must be why you took off," I said. Then I uttered the line I'd rehearsed for the occasion: "You'd been there?" Plenty of wishful doubt crept into my delivery.

"No. Never," Ginny insisted. She rapped her knuckles on the dashboard's wooden veneer. I hadn't pegged her as superstitious.

She veered off Market onto Van Ness. If you're being shadowed, it makes sense to keep on the wider, busier streets. We held our tongues until we were cruising past the Opera House and City Hall.

Then Ginny let it all out in one gust:

"Claire asked if I knew someplace. I didn't. So I went to Sanders. He gave me an address. Said the doctor was a woman, that it would be safe because everything was squared with the cops. He must have figured it was for me."

"Then when we pulled up outside the other day—"

"I recognized the address." She shuddered. Involuntarily, or so it seemed.

My turn to blab: "I had no idea of the connection first time I went in. Then the other day, like an idiot, I stumbled into the room they use while I was looking for Califro—the esteemed chief counsel of *this* fucking headache."

I backhanded the file.

"Sorry I bailed out on you," she said softly. "Sitting there, I started getting spooked. Something strange is going on, worse than I want to get involved in. I guess I finally put two plus two together."

"How's that?"

She aimed the points of her nose and chin at me. "Sanders *didn't* kill Claire. Neither did that Daws bastard. It was the operation. Wasn't it?"

Mercifully, I found sympathy in her eyes, not indictment.

We paused at the corner of Van Ness and Eddy. A limp array of pennants bordered Sid Conte's Klassic Kar Korral. Center-lot, a shadeless bulb glowed within the peaked-roof Dogpatch hut. Didn't seem likely that Hack Escalante's erstwhile manager would be burning the midnight oil, not when there were joints to frequent, stakes to be wagered, blondes to coax flat. Sid was a shitheel and, like most of his breed, incapable of remorse. Meanwhile, here sat Ginny and Billy, drowning in guilt. We only thought we were doing the right thing.

"I found the doctor," she recounted matter-of-factly. "You paid the tab. Me and you—we helped kill her."

"Claire left me a letter," I said, surprising myself. Nobody was ever going to know about it, I'd vowed. "She had a feeling something bad was going to happen. She said, 'Life just won't leave me alone.' It wasn't just us. It was circumstance. Me, that doctor, Sanders—combined, we were like a net she couldn't get out of."

In the next block, Ginny's tough-cookie act crumbled. "I've had it. I can't take this anymore. Even if I weren't scared out of my mind, there's too many bad memories. I don't want to end up in a net. I need a fresh start. Away from here."

She pressed the bulging trust against my thigh.

"Take it. Sell it to the Threllkyls. Or anybody who's buying. I don't care. Just get something out of it for me. Enough to let me walk away. With a little something for my troubles."

"I told you before. You've got nothing to be afraid of."

This time, the sales pitch was for myself, as well. *Who was I kidding?* Not Ginny. When we reached the next stop, she assessed me through brimming tears:

"I wish I could believe you."

"You should." Something compelled me to say it. I even jerry-rigged a cocky grin.

Insidiously, reassurance had become a staple in my repertoire. Whether I was boosting fighters, editors, promoters, wives, friends—

or desperate strangers—I'd become the man who represented hope. Another of life's practical jokes, concocted for my bitter amusement. Or to drive me over the edge.

The Buick's interior brightened as another car drew up behind. For once, unguarded vulnerability showed in Ginny's expression, despite the harsh beams throwing shadows across her features.

"Don't worry, Virginia," I found myself saying. "You've still got lots of books to read. By writers not even born yet." Canned corn, dispensed without a thought. Coming loose like it does now and then at the Royal. Words, in a certain order. They sound good, at least good enough. Who knows where they come from?

Pinning a toe to the brake, she angled toward me and touched her lips to mine. My fingers tingled, but my hands stayed home. "You're trying your best," she said. "I believe that." Her breath was warm, spiced with a lingering trace of tobacco.

Before I could decide whether this was a benediction or a curse, the eager beaver in our wake leaned on the horn. A brief batting of long lashes, then Ginny returned her attention to the boulevard.

"We're almost to your place," I noted. She drifted into the left lane for the turn onto Pine. "I'll take these," I said, hefting the Davidson documents, "and grab a cab from here."

"Come inside with me," she pleaded. "For a minute, that's all, just to make sure it's safe."

I didn't answer. Suggestion dangled between us as we navigated uphill. She studied the rearview, while I tried to convince myself I could resist whatever temptations might arise. She stopped before her building's awning, rather than pulling into the driveway farther up.

"Give me your key," I said. "I'll open the garage for you."

"That same car's been behind us since back on Van Ness," she whispered, without turning around.

A glance at the side mirror revealed the silhouette of a sedan, idling about twenty yards back, headlamps giving us the third degree.

"Once more around the block," Ginny suggested.

She pressed her pump to the accelerator, propelling the Roadmaster forward. At Octavia, first place to make a right, she did. Too sharply for me to tell if the sedan was in pursuit. When we'd climbed halfway up the block, the mirror caught another car taking the turn.

"Black sedan," I reported. "That what you spotted on Van Ness?"

"I think so," she stammered, with zero confidence.

We topped the rise and spilled recklessly into the intersection. She spurted across California without even checking east-west traffic. Luckily, it was slow-moving and sporadic. Her foot got heavier as the road tilted skyward. The palms of Lafayette Park suddenly loomed above us, deadheading Octavia. Down the slope, the black sedan breached the four-way and gained ground fast.

Hard right onto Sacramento. Wrong choice. The street became one-way at the bottom of the block. Traffic came head-on, practically leaping into the intersection after scaling the ski-run up from Polk Gulch. They had the right-of-way, and employed it aggressively, cars splitting in all directions.

"Daws again?" Ginny asked. Bona fide fear glinted in her eyes. I tried to make light of the situation:

"Maybe he brought a bodyguard this time." It didn't help.

"Think they're really following us?" she asked shakily.

"Best to assume it."

Another look in the mirror and she needed no further proof.

"Here they come."

"Go!" I shouted.

She swung left onto Gough, cutting in front of a two-tone coupe as it blindly crested the hill. Hunkered over the wheel, biting her lip, Ginny grimly noted, "It's Gough."

"What?" My shoes were imbedded in the floorboard.

"It's not pronounced 'go,'" she said. "It's pronounced 'goff,' rhymes with 'cough.'"

Seeing the next intersection clear, she ignored the stop sign. All four tires took leave of the pavement. We were airborne. *Gough* had dropped out beneath us, disappearing at a precipitous pitch. The flight was brief. The Roadmaster returned to earth with jaw-rattling impact. Ginny yelped instinctively, scaring herself now.

"Where's your purse?" I yelled, my voice juiced with adrenaline.

"Backseat," she said, realizing immediately why I'd asked. "You'll see it."

I twisted around to locate the handbag. It was on the floor, and I had to stretch to snag it. On the peak behind us, headlights sailed over the rise, bouncing wild on touchdown. Ginny whipped the wheel savagely to starboard, and I tumbled into her lap. Falling back in place, I got another jolt: cars coming straight at us.

"You're going the wrong way!" I shouted. "Jackson's one way!"

"I know. This oughta clear things up."

She went like a bat out of hell down the right side, nearly sideswiping a long line of parked cars, all facing us. Motorists traveling in the proper direction flashed lights, honked horns, screamed warnings. I peered through the rear window and pawed in the handbag, feeling for a gun butt.

"Son of a bitch!"

The black sedan followed our insane lead into oncoming traffic.

"Oh, my God!" Ginny wailed.

Resplendent red taillights rolled backward from a driveway, directly into our path. She jerked the wheel and the Buick swerved wide, into the middle of the street, tires squealing. Her purse flew out of my hands. A blur of headlamps, smeared across the windshield. The pistol thudded to the floor. I only heard it. Didn't see a thing: My eyes had clamped shut. I ceased breathing and waited to die. The impact was in my ribs: Ginny's elbow.

"Get off me!" she shouted. "How am I supposed to drive!"

Ahead, Jackson was clear. She'd somehow maneuvered a miracle. Approaching Van Ness, she shoved her foot to the floor and rammed a palm against the chrome rail within the steering wheel. The horn shrieked. A southbound streetcar exited the intersection, not a second too soon. We barely had time to be jolted by the tracks, as we clattered full speed across the expanse of Van Ness.

"You should have turned," I yelled, a goddamn backseat driver.

"I've got a different idea." Her teeth were clenched so tightly, I could barely make out her words.

I figured cops would be swarming us by that point—but you know what they say. We strained cylinders up Russian Hill, in plain sight of our pursuers. Ginny hung a left on Polk, with its mix of storefronts and residences, dominated by the blazing neon of the Alhambra Theater. It must have inspired her.

"I'm gonna pull into one of these driveways and kill the lights," she announced, like she'd seen the stunt in a movie once.

"You think they won't spot this showboat?"

"You think?"

"Your luck's running. If we survived that 'Wrong Way Riegels' routine, we can get through anything. Keep driving."

"Where's the gun?"

I fished on the floor but came up empty. "Musta slid under the seat when we came up the hill."

She throttled back until we'd cleared the business district. I couldn't tell if our tail was still attached. Maybe we'd shaken them. I kept hunting for the gun, foraging along the floorboards. Didn't see her make the turn onto Chestnut. Like all gamblers eventually will, she watched the dice crap out.

"Goddamnit!"

Chestnut ran smack into an excavated hill. Ginny'd grown so accustomed to discounting street signs, she'd missed a critical one: "Not a Through Street." The only passage was via a pair of stairways switching back among the trees.

Throwing it into reverse, she wrenched the car around violently, streaking the asphalt with rubber. We'd lost precious time.

Back on Polk, she headed toward the Bay. A dark vehicle neared the intersection, but I couldn't ID it. We sped downhill and fishtailed into a right turn. Ginny's determination was fraying. She pressed too hard on the gas. We shot uphill, where the road suddenly split in two, divided by a bulkhead.

"Which way?" she gasped.

Headlights sprang up over the left grade—answer enough. She gunned it along the right side. The embankment forced us into a tight curve. Shafts of light outlined a huge arrow dictating the direction. The roadway narrowed, bordered by parked cars on my side. Ginny refused to ease off. A once-flawless bumper scraped the stone wall.

"Fuck!" She'd injured her baby.

Night sky appeared at the top of the rise, straight ahead. We sailed into it.

"Don't go right," I cautioned, even before we'd touched down.

Too late.

Her reflexes were remarkable; not her navigational skills. She took the turn—headed directly for an abutment, decorated with a big yellow diamond. She stomped the brakes. We heaved into a screeching, shuddering skid. The Roadmaster's front end dueled the wall. It lost. Metal crumpled.

The missing pistol emerged from under the seat, sliding between my braced feet.

Ginny had driven into the top of the same Chestnut Street hill that had waylaid us below. Now she stared forward, face frozen, eyes wide with shock.

"Back up!" I ordered, shoving her shoulder. "Back up!"

She wrestled an obstinate gear lever. The motor growled ineffectually, like something in the jaws of a bear trap.

Through the rear window, light streamed over the embankment. Our taillights screamed red. Ginny's foot was still jammed on the brake. No matter, they couldn't miss us now. The black sedan reached the summit and leveled out in the intersection. Then it turned slowly, high beams washing over us.

"I'm sorry I got you into this," Ginny moaned.

Cautiously, the sedan crept closer.

"Get out," I said. "Get out and run."

I grabbed the pistol. My fingers pretended the trigger was as familiar as typewriter keys. Over the drum pounding in my chest, I heard car doors open and shut and footsteps quickly scuttle across the pavement. They wouldn't be packing guns, at least not drawn. *We didn't rate guns.* That was our lone advantage, I quickly convinced myself.

Ginny still hadn't moved.

I jerked the handle and flung open the door. Gracelessly, I spun out of the car, barely staying on my feet. A shaking finger nearly squeezed off a round. I jabbed the gun out there into the void.

"Back the fuck up!" I bellowed at the approaching apparitions. "Back the fuck up or I'll shoot you dead!"

Screams. Shrill, piercing, high-pitched. Then they scrambled, turkeys before the ax.

"Oh, Jesus! Oh, Jesus!" pleaded the unmistakable voice of my wife.

"He's out of his mind! God almighty—he's going to kill us!" her loyal sister Paula testified, to witnesses who'd assembled at the windows all around.

26

The waitress angled the coffeepot over Ida's cup. "How 'bout you, hon?"

My wife shoved away her cup and saucer, hard enough to send them tumbling. I hoisted my setup in time. Ida's porcelain spun across the Formica, landing in my lap.

"I don't want coffee!" she said. "I want my husband back!"

Beside me in the booth, Virginia rolled her eyes and fitted an Old Gold into her tight smile. "My, how dramatic," she deadpanned, lighting up.

"I'd watch that mouth if I were you, *slut*." Paula jumped right in, a practiced barroom brawler itching to mix it up with somebody, anybody.

Me, the waitress didn't bother to ask—she just poured. "You're gonna need more than coffee," she suggested sympathetically.

"Don't I know it." I gingerly handed her the rejected cup and saucer.

"Should I confiscate the knives?" she joked. She had a pile of white hair the striped paper cap could barely contain, and the uniform was challenged by the rest of her. The badge on her bosom read GERTRUDE. I wanted Gertrude to take me home, immediately. *Her* home.

"Don't you touch my silverware," Paula cautioned. "I'm having pie. Coffee and a big slice of pie."

"That explains it," Ginny said cattily, giving Paula a thorough once-over as she stepped around Gertrude to fetch an ashtray off the counter. "You don't miss many desserts."

"I'm sure whores have to watch their figures," Paula spat back. "Since that's all they've got going for them."

Gertrude's eyes were about to plop into her coffeepot. "Get the woman her pie, will you?" I pleaded. "So she'll have something else to do with her mouth."

It had required considerable coaxing to herd this group into Paula's car for a powwow at the all-night Florence Café on Lombard. It was my own League of Nations conference, in a front window booth. I regretted there'd been a settlement in the dock strike. I'd have offered my services as a mediator. Steamship owners, port officials, union bosses—they couldn't have been any more hardheaded than this scrappy trio.

On the way over I'd tried to describe Ginny Wagner's predicament, and explain my involvement. Ida sulked mutely. It wasn't the god-damned DA's office listening in on Ginny's call last night. It was my wife. She'd heard me arrange a clandestine meeting with a woman. Paula, of course, immediately suggested a trap. That was right up her alley. I'd told them nothing but the truth, but they weren't buying. Paula kept objecting, like an attorney, reiterating "the obvious": I was with another woman after-hours; we'd fled like fugitives when cornered; so guilty we carried a gun to silence any witnesses. If Paula had half a brain and an ounce of self-control, she could have given Jake Ehrlich a run for his money.

Ida sniffled into a hankie, repeating a muffled refrain about "never wanting to believe the worst."

"Don't be so naïve," Paula said. "You knew it all along—but you couldn't face the truth. Well, here you have it. Like what you see?"

"How long have you been with her?" Ida asked meekly, looking at the reflection of Virgina Wagner in the glass, shunning the woman herself.

"I'm not *with* your husband," Ginny said. She played it calm and collected, having exhausted her hysterics on the Roadmaster's crumpled grillwork. ("How do you think *I* feel?" Ida had bawled back at the crash site. "My *marriage* is wrecked!")

Ginny slid her pack of Old Golds toward Ida, a peace offering. It was ignored. Ginny didn't care. She continued her testimony: "It's like Billy said—he offered to help me out of a sticky situation. That's as far as it goes."

Paula cut in: "And I'm sure you didn't *offer* anything in exchange." The woman had a mind like a Tijuana bible.

My turn to contribute: "Paula—why don't you dummy up?"

"Okay, let's hear your version," she snapped. "Let's hear Mr. Fifty-

Cent Word try to weasel his way out of this one. Go on, we're all ears. This oughta be good."

I took a deep breath, ready to recount the whole damn story again, now that everyone's adrenaline had receded. But Ginny placed a palm against my chest before I could even exhale.

"Save it," she told me. Her sights were trained on Paula. "*You* listen—he's already explained the whole situation. If you don't believe him, that's your problem."

"So you *speak* for him now, too? One of your many services, I assume." Paula had a slight overbite: protruding teeth rendered her smile—especially the mean, sarcastic version—downright feral.

"You do all the talking for *her*," Ginny observed, waving her cigarette at my wife. Ida remained slumped against the window, staring fixedly down Lombard. I nudged her with the toe of my wing tip: like prodding a corpse. "Let's hear from the offended party," Ginny suggested.

"She's in a state," Paula said. "She's had her heart broken. And I can speak for her whenever I feel like it—we're closer than any two people on this earth." Paula liked to regularly note that husbands and wives could never bond like sisters. Paula, in fact, liked to point out any theory that rubbed somebody the wrong way.

"We might as well be twins," she went on. "Isn't that right, Shmoo?" She clutched her sister's limp hand. Shmoo was her pet name for Ida. She'd cribbed it from *Li'l Abner*, I guess because Shmooes followed their chosen human everywhere, silently and obediently.

Ida didn't respond. "My God," Paula said, "she's still in shock."

"If she's in shock," I suggested, "it's from your driving."

Ida's eyes darted my way, the first recognition she'd granted me since I pulled that gun on her. It was an involuntary glance, a split second of instinct: but it reflected years of commiseration concerning Paula's notorious misadventures. And it hinted that there was light at the end of the tunnel. Not that there wasn't a mountain to move first.

"*My* driving?" Paula scoffed. "Look who's talking—we know who was at the wheel of *your* car, don't we?"

Ginny groaned, exasperated, obviously thinking of her glorious machine, broken and abandoned at the top of Chestnut Street.

Patience wearing thinner by the moment, she scanned the street for any sign of the tow truck.

I'd called Willie Egan from the first pay phone we saw. A retired middleweight, he'd invested in a garage over on Fulton, which grew to a five-truck towing service. Had a son fighting in the Gloves this year. Damned if he didn't agree to come out himself. *Wait with the car,* he instructed. I cautioned him that, in this case, it wasn't a viable option. If we'd stayed there, given the caterwauling, Egan might have arrived to find one busted Buick and any number of dead bodies.

Gertrude reappeared, setting an oozing slice of purplish pie in front of Paula. "Hope you like boysenberry," she chirped. "All we got left."

Paula rotated the plate this way and that, assessing it.

Ginny gave the waitress a brittle smile as she tapped ash: "I suspect the issue is size, not flavor."

"I already warned you," Paula said, pointing her fork across the table. I recalled Ginny clipping a piece out of Larry Daws's ear, then crushing his nose with the butt of her gun. I wondered how close my sister-in-law was to receiving similar treatment. Or if I'd intervene.

"Let me get this straight," Paula continued, starting in on the pie. "You expect *us* to believe that *you* believed that stooges from the *DA's* office were chasing *you* to get a pile of *papers?*"

I displayed Exhibit A, the Mount Davidson file. Gertrude refreshed our cups slowly, in no hurry to relinquish her ringside seat. She was visibly disappointed when Ida nudged her sister beneath the table, stifling her sister's oratory. Like her old man, Ida didn't feature strangers getting a gander at the family's dirty laundry. Gertrude stowed her coffeepot behind the counter and took roost on a stool, well within earshot.

"Come *on!*" Paula revved right back up. "You *knew* that was my car! You've been in it enough times! Christ, I've driven you all over this goddamn state! You two were running like thieves because we interrupted your trip to this one's place for a little—"

She pumped the fork graphically in the air, eliciting moans from both Ida and Ginny.

"Admit it!" Paula said.

I knew Paula's game. Keep needling, insufferably, even gleefully, until I lost control and retaliated, blasting Ida for *her* unfaithfulness.

Then it'd all be out in the open, that I wasn't Vincent's father. Ida'd break down. Then Paula'd be—

"Where the hell is Vincent?" I snapped.

"With Phyllis and Jack," Ida quickly assured me. "At their place. It's okay."

"Like he cares," Paula sneered, concentrating on a forkful of pie.

I considered popping her. But then I saw the animalistic expression that had transformed Ginny's face. Oh, Christ—Paula's time had finally come. Ida also noticed the deadly cast take over Ginny's features. She scrambled to rescue her oblivious sister.

"How long have you *known* my husband?" Ida asked, trying to disarm Ginny by rephrasing her previous question in more diplomatic terms. Incredibly, Ginny's icy gaze began to melt.

"Couple of weeks," she said, shrugging. "I don't know."

Ginny shook her head, still visibly rattled by the unconscionable behavior of the specimen across the table. She stared at the imprint of her lipstick on the rim of the coffee cup, just to avoid Paula.

Ida turned to face me. "So you didn't know each other—back then? When we had our little . . . difference?"

That's when it dawned on me—the ace reporter—that Ida'd been seeking clues for *months*. She assumed Ginny was Claire. Not that she knew Claire by name. At first, there'd only been a suspicion. Now it had a shape, a face, a voice. It was sitting right next to me. Ida figured I'd been having an affair ever since she'd gone into seclusion to deliver "our" baby. She was right; just had the wrong woman. While I was running ragged, trying to clean up traces of a mess Ida would never, could never, understand—she was stewing over an imagined liaison, created from her worst fears.

Ginny must have understood my wife's misconception. It was evident in the way she ground down her cigarette and blew the whole twisted scenario away in one last hot exhalation.

"Do you love your husband?" she asked Ida bluntly.

"Of course I do," came the rapid, defiant response.

"Good for you. You're ahead of the game. Some of us don't even know what love is."

"I'll tell you what love is," Paula said. I anticipated what was coming, eagerly, perversely. Paula and her ex had visited our house one evening. After a few nightcaps she began to pontificate on the base realities of love. Now, apparently, we were due for a reprise:

"Love," Paula informed us, "is when a man will eat ten yards of shit for you."

Ginny, not unlike Paula's ex, had heard enough. She stood to leave. I wondered how Paula's flyboy would react when she hung *that* assignment on him.

"Please, sit down," Ida implored Ginny. She stretched a pink-gloved hand across the tabletop, fingers spread. "We've all done things we're not especially proud of—"

"Speak for yourself, sister," Paula said, sucking her teeth. She never quit.

"That's what I am doing," Ida answered.

"Finally." Ginny eased back onto the seat.

"All I really and truly care about is having a good father for our child," Ida said. She kept her eyes fixed on her splayed fingers. "Once I had a man I was proud to call my husband. I want him back. I need to make things right too, I know that. I want to do whatever it takes, so that he's just as proud of his wife." She raised her eyes to mine. "That's really all I want. For us to be in this life together."

Once again, the spotlight swung to Mr. Reassurance. But his words weren't flowing. I took Ida's hand instead and gave it a squeeze. Gesture of commitment? Ploy to cover the silence? Hell if I knew. She squeezed back. It was something.

"Well now, that certainly clears the air." Paula, I could tell, wasn't pleased with this turn of events. "In fact," she went on, "I'd say it leaves at least one question for Billy to answer, once and for all."

We all waited.

"Have you *ever* cheated on my sister?"

Paula's southpaw shenanigans couldn't throw me anymore.

"No, I have not."

I played the wronged defendant with utter conviction. I'd become a brilliant, bald-faced liar—not a rough transition for a writer.

Paula was hoisting some pie remnants toward her slyly smiling lips, but she suddenly stopped.

"*Why the hell not?*" she mocked, her eyes suddenly as wide as two dinner plates. "*It's not like you're gettin' any at home!*"

Paula forked in the pie, belted her sibling on the arm, and shook her head around with a giddy, cackling laugh that threatened to blow boysenberry down her blouse front. She laughed so hard, Ida infectiously began giggling, too. Sisters.

Ginny gaped, slack-jawed.

"Oh, my God, I'm about to pee my pants," Paula said.

"I already did," Ida gasped, clutching her sister's arm. "When we flew over that hill!"

Knuckles rapped the diner window, scaring the beejesus out of us all. Willie Egan stared in, smiling. The cherry atop his truck spun around, washing the street red.

Ginny was out of the gate faster than Citation. She scooped up her book but intentionally left the Mount Davidson file on the bench. I moved it aside and followed her up, trying to figure my next move. Yanking open the restaurant door, Ginny paused to show me a secret wiggle of fingers, down low, signaling she was fine on her own. I wasn't so sure. It seemed wrong to send her into the night, without a car, or a safe place to stay. I started to follow.

"Go with her," Ida warned, instantly the wounded wife again, "and you might not get back in the house."

Ginny was past me before I took another breath. She slammed *Raintree County* on the table, sending Paula's stained pie plate clattering. She hovered over them.

"Your husband put himself in jeopardy to help a total stranger," she said, trying to hold a civil tone. "And he's been a perfect gentleman, even when I've driven him crazy. He's a decent man. Treat him like one. Or a smarter woman will."

As she stormed out, Ginny muttered to me: "You've got your hands full. Do what you have to do."

For a moment I just stood there, watching Ginny explain her forlorn situation to Willie Egan. Talking about the Buick almost brought her to tears. Egan kept glancing at me through the glass, disappointed. He'd expected some chin music, at least, as we dragged the Roadmaster to his garage.

At the counter, our waitress feigned interest in the *Racing Form*. I stepped nearer. "Gertrude, what's the damage?"

"You tell me," she whispered, moving the check from apron to counter. My hand wanted to move along her hip, drawn by some elusive promise of uncomplicated intimacy. That didn't exist, so far as I knew. I reached in my pocket instead, for my roll, peeling off the tariff, plus a generous tip.

"You should be paying us," I cracked. "For the floor show."

I rounded the backside of our booth, as if approaching the para-mutuel window at Golden State. I placed my bet—leaning in between the sisters to give Ida a kiss.

"See you at home," I promised. "I won't be long."

I grabbed the file, bolted, and climbed into the cab of Willie Egan's truck. Ginny was squeezed between us. Quick handicapping had convinced me that Paula was the only runner in tonight's race with no hope of finishing in the money.

27

Sunday morning's paper—printed the day before—predicted a beautiful day in the city. But when Ida and I left mass at St. Brendan's, under the shadow of Mount Davidson's looming stone cross, fog awaited departing parishioners. Ubiquitous fog. If you lived west of Twin Peaks, you got used to the short count on sunny days. You had to go east: chase the sun, outrun the fog. So Ida was tickled, to put it mildly, when I suggested loading Vincent's carriage in the car and driving over to the Marina for a late breakfast and some shopping.

After packing away pancakes, bacon, and eggs at the Horseshoe, we strolled up to Union Street and wove through shops for a while. Ida basked in all the compliments for her beautiful baby. I told her I needed to slip off for a while, to run an errand. Her residual dubiousness was easily erased with a twenty and no restrictions on how it be spent. We agreed to rendezvous in an hour.

I hoofed uphill, reveling in the sparkling turquoise sky, mild temperature, lack of wind. Postcard weather. Refreshed, I sensed things were nearing a conclusion.

The previous night, the Gloves had drawn a huge gate, bigger than Friday, and the kids staged a whale of a show. Fears that Thanksgiving would kill our momentum proved unfounded. Egan's kid even won his match, earning a crack at a novice title in Monday's final. Willie was more relieved than proud.

As for Ginny, she was probably finishing *Raintree County* in a room at the Palomar, next to the new building NBC had spent a million bucks on. She'd been holed up in some fleabag on Ellis, but I had Willie take us to the corner of Taylor and O'Farrell and I gave Ginny the six bucks that'd get her two nights in a decent room with a private bath. I'd also loaned her some extra, to rent a car while hers was being repaired. She intended to load up the rest of the stuff from her Pine Street apartment on Monday, then ditch San Francisco. She'd made up her mind to move, short-term, to Alameda. A friend there had located a one-bedroom in the Neptune Court Apartments, month-to-month.

"Once I'm back on my feet," she said, "it'll be me and the Road-master and no looking back."

I huffed and puffed up Steiner to Vallejo, then another five blocks west toward the Presidio. The briefcase I was lugging felt like fifty pounds of dead weight, and the street ahead loomed like Pike's Peak.

Finally achieving level terrain, I found the house on Vallejo. Entering through a wrought-iron gate, I followed a path lined with pruned rosebushes. The front door was at the rear of a circular porch that resembled a Greek theater. In fact, it looked like a smaller version of the Palace of Fine Arts, which was visible above the trees about half a dozen blocks away. From where I stood, you could see far across the Golden Gate, beyond the Marin headlands. This panorama alone was worth maybe ten grand.

The residence was a three-story mansion. The facade featured elegantly leaded windows and flower boxes that flowered when they had no business flowering. I had a hunch full-time flower-box tenders were on-premises. I leaned on the buzzer and tried to focus on something other than the view, just to surprise whoever answered the door.

"Help you, sir?" It was a colored butler, decked out in a tuxedo. I'd been some places in my day, seen plenty of things. This was the first time I'd been greeted by a butler in full livery—and in my hometown, no less.

"I'm here to see Mrs. Threllkyl. Name's Nichols. Manny Gold told her to expect me." I handed over a card, the one that said nothing more than: Billy Nichols, *Mr. Boxing*.

"Very good, sir. I'll see if she's receiving guests."

He closed the door. Beat that—a colored shutting a door in my face. This was becoming a day of firsts. And it was early yet.

The butler came back a few minutes later and ushered me in. Following him through a foyer bigger than Ginny Wagner's apartment, I absorbed the opulence: the aroma of furniture wax mixed with something freshly baked; walls adorned with perfectly displayed artifacts, each with its own little light; echoes of my footsteps across polished purple hardwood, silenced when I stepped on carpet deep enough to tickle my ankles. Cronies visiting my crib always cracked that I lived like the king of Siam. This place put things in perspective.

The butler escorted me into the living room. More furniture than

W. J. Sloane's. The north forty featured a vast picture window, framing the enormous view I'd only partially seen out front. It looked like a painting the family had added to its private collection. "Mrs. Threllkyl will join you in a moment," he said, his diction more refined than mine. Or the king of England's. "May I take your attaché, sir?"

"No, no, no. I'll hang on to it," I said, redoubling my grip.

"Your hat?"

"No. I'm fine. Thanks."

He drifted. To grab some of whatever was baking in the kitchen, if he was smart. I set the hat on the couch, even though I worried it might set off an alarm. A maid might scramble in to tidy up. Again I ignored the view, focusing instead on a goofy drawing, elaborately framed, that one of their daughters must have done when she was little. I doubted I'd ever go that far for Vincent's youthful doodlings. I'm sure Ida would be bronzing his little slippers and stools before long.

"You appreciated the Miró right off," she said, behind me. "I'm impressed."

Not one of her children, I surmised. I turned, displayed all available teeth, offered a hand.

She was regal. Beyond that—she was imperial. Hair swept up in thick white waves; fine, sharp features, softened by maturity. Tall, slender through the hips, with a decided lift to the triangle of white lace on the bodice of her blue Sunday ensemble.

"Astrid Threllkyl," she announced, placing her hand in mine. "A pleasure."

"Billy Nichols. Likewise."

"You know modern art, Mr. Nichols?"

Like I know gynecology. "I form opinions. And that's a lovely piece." Two minutes near money and I was using words like *lovely*.

"It's only a lithograph, but my dealer has several originals he'd like me to look at. Come, let's sit by the view." She led me there. When we were shoulder to shoulder, I caught a whiff of lilac.

"If only I'd brought my wife along." I made a gesture that encompassed everything. "Ida saw this, she'd probably drop dead."

"And that would be good?" She smiled, knitting her brow. "Your wife dropping dead?"

"Every so often."

That fell about as flat as Buddy Baer against Louis. I'd quickly sunk from art snob to Fuller Brush Man. Small talk wasn't going to get me anywhere.

We sat at a round mahogany table beside the long stretch of window. She must have known this lighting was kind to her. I could say the woman looked like a million bucks and for once not be speaking metaphorically.

"What is amusing you, Mr. Nichols?" She sat back in the chair and appraised me, adopting a slender grin of her own.

"You can see Alcatraz from here," I replied inanely. "Right over your shoulder."

"Yes," she said, slightly craning her neck. She must have been pushing sixty, but the gorgeous line of her throat didn't give it away. Can that be bought, too? "My daughters always enjoyed it when the beam would go round at night. What does one call that?"

"A prison searchlight." I almost laughed.

"Yes. They found it quite magical."

"Did you tell them what it was?"

She gave me a playfully disdainful look. "And ruin their fairy tales? No. We pretended it was 'The Enchanted Isle.'"

I set the briefcase down next to me. She hadn't yet asked what I was doing there, so I assumed Manny had advised her. Before I could get down to particulars, she lifted a small bell from the table and rang it once.

"Would you care for tea or coffee, Mr. Nichols? We also have freshly baked pastries, as we generally do on Sundays."

"You and your husband?" It was a ham-fisted segue, and I instantly regretted it.

She examined the Bay, waiting for her servant to appear. "You are aware my husband is dead." Never heard a flatter voice.

"That's right. I'm sorry," I replied. Something in her manner had shifted, and the sudden coolness was, frankly, a little intimidating. "My sympathies for your loss," I added.

We didn't say another word until the butler arrived. The perfect-hostess routine reappeared with him: "Raymond, we'll have tea—unless Mr. Nichols prefers coffee—and a selection of Winnie's pastries." She eyed me. "Butter and preserves?"

Raymond looked at me, as gracious and accommodating as could be. Wonder how long it took him to hone the act.

"Tea's just fine." I smiled. Don't know why. I hated tea.

"Right away, ma'am. Sir."

Lately, Ida had been dropping hints about a maid, saying since the baby and all, she couldn't keep up with housework. Imagine a *butler*. My father would rise from the grave and cut my throat.

"So . . . I assume you agreed to see me because Manny greased the sk—explained that I needed to discuss a business matter."

"That's correct." Astrid nodded. She felt obliged to add, "The Jewish fellow."

"He told me he'd had dealings with your husband."

"My family socialized with the Winokurs. You've met Peggy? That's how we encountered Emmanuel Gold. I'm informed they're very happy—it's been what, perhaps ten years now?" She widened her eyes, seemingly astonished at the notion of Manny and Peggy together ten minutes, let alone ten years. "I cannot assume this is exactly how Catherine imagined events would transpire."

I was about to ask, *Who's Catherine?* when I realized I didn't give a damn.

"I'm not sure I understand what you mean," I said instead.

"You know." She lowered her lashes.

"The fact she married a Jew."

She showed the disapproving face again. Maybe she'd summon Raymond to wash my mouth out with a cake of expensive soap, for uttering a rude word in her immaculate home.

"Your husband had no qualms about doing business with Manny Gold."

She lifted her eyebrows, turned palms up, and for a split second I thought she was going to concede: *They're good with money*. She held her tongue.

"Mrs. Threllkyl, let me get this out of the way. I haven't much time, and I'd like us to enjoy our snacks and this amazing view. I have in my possession the entire Mount Davidson Trust, the original copy"—I gave her a freighted glance—"all riders attached. I thought the family might be interested in getting it back."

She exhibited a profound lack of interest. She gave the briefcase a dismissive look and said, "Thank you. I'll have our attorney review whatever it is."

"You mean your brother? Is he still handling family business now that he's deputy DA?"

"Are you and Bill acquainted?"

"We've met. Can't claim we're friends, exactly."

Her interest level was rising, along with the color on her cheeks and beneath that lacy bodice.

Just then four feet trundled down the hallway and into the room. They were attached to two pairs of alabaster legs, gleaming beneath revealing hemlines. Identical redheaded twins, in identical pink silk robes. They froze when they realized their mother had a guest.

"Girls, please come over and introduce yourselves." Mrs. Threllkyl seemed delighted by the diversion.

"Ricky invited us over for a swim," one of the twins explained, drawing her silk sheath tighter to hide the bathing suit beneath. Stitched on the robe in scarlet script was her name: *Devin*.

"It could be months before we have another day like this," the other one finished the thought, in a voice indistinguishable from her sister's. Her robe read *Dulcie*.

It took me a few seconds to get to my feet. I was still dealing with the revelation that there were private swimming pools in San Francisco.

"My daughters, Devin and Dulcie. Girls, Mr. Billy Nichols." They double-teamed me with thousand-watt smiles. The family ought to buy insurance now, I thought, to cover all the hearts these two were going to break.

"Mr. Nichols works for the *Inquirer*," their mother told them. "As a sportswriter." She'd gotten advance word, all right.

"Then you must know Mr. Hearst," one of the twins exclaimed.

"Oh yeah," I volleyed, figuring I'd play along a bit. "In fact, I once saved his life."

"You did?" Dulcie was genuinely curious.

"But how?" giggled her sister. "Tell us."

"It was a long time ago," I said, surprised by their interest. "Back when I was about your age."

They traded perplexed glances. Something didn't add up. I was the one unclear on the mathematics—the *real* two-plus-two. Their mother set me straight:

"They presume you're referring to *Randy* Hearst. He's a friend of the family."

Randy, the old man's son. Titular editor-in-chief of the paper. My employer. Astrid's buddy. Tough to impress them now.

From gracefully folded hands, to upturned chin, to merest hint of a smile, to glaze of superiority in her eyes, Astrid Threllkyl wordlessly informed me, over the yawning gap of several social strata, just how out of her league I was.

"My girls are graduating from preparatory school next spring," she volunteered. "And I'm pleased to say they've been accepted at all our top choices of universities. The twins are really quite remarkable, Mr. Nichols—they have virtually identical grades on all their test scores. Without fail."

"Incredible."

"We're torn between Radcliffe and Stanford," Devin or Dulcie said. "Which one would you recommend?"

"I wouldn't know," I muttered, wondering how many people could afford double tuition at top-flight colleges. Ginny Wagner was twice their age and couldn't even make her rent. These girls had risk-free futures completely plotted out, every obstacle paved flat by that inherited greenback steamroller.

The thought brought me back to the briefcase. But Astrid wasn't ready for that.

"Devin is a most accomplished pianist, in addition to many other things," she revealed. "Darling, won't you play Mr. Nichols a bit of that Chopin you've been practicing?"

Dutifully, the redhead gracefully approached a grand piano that dominated the room's southwest corner. She sat, and beautiful music filled the room. Since I couldn't see her hands, I suspected a trick. Maybe she'd flicked on a wire recorder hidden under the bench. It was far-fetched that a teenage kid could play like that. I closed my eyes. Astrid probably figured I was swooning, that I fell for the concerto as much as her Miró. Perversely, I was trying to recall the faces of the two girls outside Mrs. Califro's illegal clinic, wondering what the next few years had in store for them.

When I reopened my eyes I thought I'd slipped into a dream. Dulcie was doing a ballet dance. Guess she'd perform, unprompted, at any moment, and everyone would stop to bear witness to the prodigy. That's when the butler reentered, bearing the tea service.

"Will the misses be joining you?" Raymond softly inquired, carefully arranging accessories so as not to make the slightest intrusive sound. Astrid shook her head, dispatching him with a wave.

I'd detoured into a world as comfortable as a full-body rash. My watch revealed that I'd been gone almost forty minutes. I'd get Ida's silent treatement if I wasn't back on the dot.

Observing the golden duo, I tried to picture the parents of amateur fighters watching their sons spar in the living room. That set me thinking of all the hard-luck scrappers I'd known since I was a boy, my father included, who'd never had a single thing handed to them. Most of the guys in the fight game were still scratching and clawing on the back side of their lives.

Astrid must have spotted me scoping the watch. She clapped her hands, concluding the performance. Dulcie had danced right out of the robe, which was hanging halfway off.

"Girls, get over to Ricky's before it gets too cool. Say good-bye to Mr. Nichols."

"Princeton," I suggested, when they laid out their pampered hands for a parting touch. "That'd be a nice way to honor your father."

They returned blank expressions—identical, of course.

"His alma mater, wasn't it? Wouldn't that be a fitting tribute—since he isn't here to enjoy all your successes?"

"Yes," said Astrid, rising. "Too bad it doesn't take girls." She herded her daughters out before I could inquire any further about their old man. When they'd left, she scowled at me: "They were extremely close to their father. They've had a difficult time adjusting to his absence."

"I noticed their distress."

"Didn't you mention something about a pressing appointment?"

"We haven't finished our tea. Or this delicious . . . cake."

"I don't mean to be rude, Mr. Nichols, but I believe you'd better go. I appreciate your delivering those papers."

"You may have misunderstood, Mrs. Threllkyl—I'm not returning them to you."

"What exactly are you doing then?"

"There are concerns among some of the investors that the assets making up the trust might not be legitimate. In fact, some people have described the trust as 'pure bunco.'"

"That's preposterous."

"Tell it to your brother—I'm quoting him verbatim. Why do you think he'd say something like that?"

"I haven't the vaguest idea. Why did you come here, Mr. Nichols?"

"I'm representing a party who thinks the family would want the papers back. Enough to pay a finder's fee for them."

"You have lost me. Surely my husband had copies. What is so unique about these particular papers?" She was playacting, trying to jerk my chain. Her brother was running Burney Sanders right into jail to cut him out of the picture. She likely knew more about this slick setup than anybody.

"You're probably right," I said, deciding to call her bluff. "I'm sorry to have wasted your time like this."

I prepared to leave, hefting the case, stepping over to pick my hat off the sofa.

"Perhaps if I saw the documents, they might make more sense to me."

I sat back down, cradling the briefcase in my lap.

"I'm afraid I can only part with these papers for a price."

"And why would anyone pay such a price?"

"To avoid an unpleasant situation. Do the twins know that their father is—or *was*—a criminal? Do they realize all this is paid for with money stolen from gullible investors? That their tuition funds will come from the picked pockets of decent, deceived people?"

She only smiled: "You're not making the slightest bit of sense. I'll have Raymond show you out."

"Has anybody been by to ask about the discrepancy between the age on your husband's death certificate and the one in his obituary?"

"Am I supposed to know what you're talking about?"

"I've put a copy of the death certificate, along with the obit, in an envelope addressed to an associate of mine. Francis O'Connor. Captain of Detectives, Homicide Squad. I suggested he try to locate Claude Threllkyl, your father-in-law. I don't imagine he will. There are witnesses who'll testify that Claude lived here, and that he was much closer in age than Dexter to the man described on that death certificate."

"You seemed like a reasonably sane individual when you arrived, Mr. Nichols. But now I'm having serious doubts about your mental health."

"Ring your bell," I said. "If ol' Claude comes down here, I'll apologize on bended knee."

"It's definitely time for you to go."

"Your husband isn't dead, is he?"

She cackled, which seemed to me the last thing a grieving widow would do at that juncture.

"Haven't you left your 'beat,' Mr. Nichols? Shouldn't you be concerning yourself with this week's boxing contests?"

"Listen, Mrs. Threllkyl—here's the gist of it. My friend has gone through a lot of grief over this Mount Davidson stuff. A little recompense would be in order. But my father once warned me that rich people are the tightest wads in the world, so I wasn't sure you'd see things my way. That's why I've got that certificate and obit addressed to O'Connor. Maybe I'm barking up the wrong tree, as you say. But O'Connor can be a real bulldog when he gets ahold of something that stinks. Believe me. I was just hoping we might avoid any messiness like that."

"You're not a reporter," she said. "You're a petty hoodlum. An extortionist. Randy will not be pleased when I advise him of this." Her hand reached for the bell.

"I didn't come here to be insulted, Mrs. Threllkyl. Don't bother with Raymond. I'll find my own way."

I hoisted my goods, donned my hat, and moved deliberately toward the foyer.

"Perhaps we can settle this matter amicably, Mr. Nichols," she said to my departing backside. "Would a thousand dollars satisfy this alleged 'associate'?"

I laughed—it surprised me how easily—and returned to the table. I wished I'd been able to save that guffaw, so I could have pitched it right in her face.

"A grand?" I scoffed. "What's that? A peanut you're throwing to a peasant? This trust contains more than two million dollars in assets—as you're well aware. And I know it's real, at least in part—despite the dummy corporations your husband used to bilk his suckers. Despite your brother's best efforts to bury the truth. But Burney Sanders—grubby little hustler that he is—he outsmarted your dear departed and finagled himself a chunk of that money. You'd hate to lose it, wouldn't you? Mirós must be expensive. So don't insult me with an offer of chump change."

I'd never seen a she-devil before. At least one this rich and beautiful. "Ten thousand," she said.

Ten grand would let Ginny pay for most of a nice spread far away from these troubles. I looked at Astrid Threllkyl's compressed lips and Arctic eyes and saw the arrogance of people who took entitlement as a birthright. She expected me to take the payoff and shut my mouth. She assumed she'd get away with everything, she and her brother—maybe even her "late" husband.

But all that made sense, sick as it was. None of it rankled me half as much as the impromptu recital. That's what turned it. If she hadn't rubbed my nose in her daughters' perfection, I might have let her skate. What can you do? It was the Irish in me.

"I've changed my mind." I gave her a chilly grin of my own. "I'm going to keep the papers. See who else might be interested in them."

I turned to see Raymond entering the room.

"Raymond, Mr. Nichols is attempting to leave with property that belongs to me."

This black-tie boo was actually going to brace me. My first shake-down ever, from a dinge in a tux. I didn't know whether to be honored or insulted.

"The briefcase," she instructed him.

Raymond got ready for me to take a poke at him. Instead, I calmly handed over the attaché, minus any fuss. He eyeballed me menacingly while his big, white-gloved hands went through the contents. He withdrew several thick tomes.

"They're books, ma'am. Are these what you wanted?"

"Let me see them," she said.

"*Intruder in the Dust* was for a friend," I explained. "But you can keep it if you want. The rest are *Ring Record Books*, years forty-one through forty-three. I don't need 'em anymore. Give 'em to Devin and Dulcie. Broaden their horizons."

"You don't have the papers," she said, sighing. She swung a hand at Raymond, almost knocking the books from his grasp.

"Sure I do. Under lock and key," I said. "Am I gonna walk in here and just hand 'em over? You think I'm stupid?"

Her voice, serene and modulated moments earlier, now slammed words like a rigging ax driving down a nail:

"Yes. I. Do."

28

The deputy District Attorney's office had a totally different feel when I shaped up, front and center, the following day. Same cramped confines and government-issue fittings as on my prior visit, but this time the walls and woodwork glowed, warmed by sunbeams streaming through the open blinds. I could have counted the dust motes drifting around Corey's empty chair.

It had been fifteen minutes since the receptionist decamped, without offering any encouragement or refreshment. Compared with his sister, Corey was a lousy host. Astrid had surely provided all the details on our lovely high tea the previous afternoon—why else would he have cleared a space on his schedule, given such short notice?

Minutes crawled by. Pigeons cooed on the ledges. The asthmatic ventilation system wheezed. Particulate matter settled. Corey's ostentatious marble-based fountain pen set cast a creeping shadow, recording my wasted time. The waiting game was nothing new to me. Boxers practically invented it. The champ routinely makes his opponent enter the ring first, then lets him dangle. He'll think too much, tighten up, get exasperated. Fanfare: The king blows in on a wave of cheers. It's supposed to scare the challenger into submission before the opening bell.

I unfurled the morning *Inquirer* and reread the item about Jake Ehrlich taking on Burney Sanders's defense a mere three days before the trial jumped off. A worrisome prospect, more so for Corey than me, or so I kept telling myself. Adapting one of my sport's cruelest axioms, I'd concluded Corey had to be flattened fast, when he was on the ropes and vulnerable.

Half past the hour we'd agreed to meet, Corey sprang into his office, coattails flapping, trailed by a pair of underlings. One spewed an incomprehensible commentary about this case and that, then blew. The other lurked behind me, like the guy in an escalating bar beef, prepared to land a sucker punch.

"My schedule's out of control," Corey said, not bothering with pleasantries as he dropped into his seat and inventoried the papers lined up on his desk. "I hope whatever's on your mind won't take long."

I swiveled for a glimpse of the lug against the wall: Muscle gone to seed. Belly over the belt. The practical, thick-soled footwear of a professional legman. "We haven't been introduced," I noted, getting no reply. His hands went in his pockets and he repositioned his considerable weight on the balls of his considerable feet.

"That's Frank Moran," Corey said. "He's not leaving. So you might as well get on with it."

Moran had proud, obedient, but slightly moronic features. I thought I'd seen his face before. Maybe in a newsreel, above a brown shirt and black armband.

"You sure about him?" I pressed Corey.

"Mr. Moran's my assistant," the deputy DA declared, pencil tapping four-four time on a file folder. "He's aware of everything that goes on in this office."

"If you say so. Guess that means he knows you're railroading Burney Sanders into the pen, so the truth never comes out about your brother-in-law's bogus financial racket."

Corey pursed his lips and eased off on the pencil solo.

"What exactly did you hope to get out of this misguided ploy?"

"*She* said that, didn't she? Astrid. About my visit yesterday. That line suits her more than it does you."

"Trying to show how smart you are, Nichols? Is that it? You're proving exactly the opposite. And by the way, bother my sister again and I'll make sure you're arrested."

"Don't worry. I think we exhausted our conversational possibilities. But let's go back to your first question: I don't stand to gain a thing. I'd like to see the people who sank their savings in those so-called corporations get their money back. Shouldn't be that tough. Advise your sister to dissolve the trust and reimburse the original investors."

"A moment ago you made a very serious allegation about the integrity of this office. In the first place, it is unfounded, in the second, it's slanderous. I don't know where you get off, Nichols—and frankly I'm not all that interested. I'm not going to dignify this charade by suggesting I have a clue as to what you're talking about—"

"Right—you agreed to this visit so you could tell me—in person—how much you enjoy my coverage of the Golden Gloves."

"—but I am willing to give you one last chance to walk out of here. Go back to scribbling about broken-down pugs and their cauliflower ears. I suggest you take me up on this. Walk away. Keep on playing the big shot in your sporting circles. Stick to your own tawdry piece of turf. Am I clear enough?"

You just stay there like a good little boy—what the goon who murdered my father said to me, leaving the beaten body.

"Okay, I'll go," I told Corey. "I'll hand over those trust papers to a city editor. He'll start an investigation that will blow the Sanders trial to hell. Not to mention what'll happen when Jake Ehrlich gets hold of this stuff. Might cause a ripple or two in the DA's office. When Brown sees the conflicts of interest everywhere, he won't be able to dump his deputy DA fast enough."

"Your current employers aren't going to be all that interested," Corey said. "Call it a hunch. But bet on it."

"Who said anything about the *Inquirer*? Does Astrid have friends in high places at the *Chronicle*, too? And the *News*? And the *Call-Bulletin*?"

Corey rose, glanced at the bulldog behind me, then took a leisurely survey of the street below. Pigeons took wing when he tapped on the window. He returned to the desk and tented his fingertips above the blotter.

"You're actually too stupid to turn loose of this, aren't you?"

"Tell her to give the money back. Liquidate it all—before Ehrlich runs your ass ragged and Sanders ends up *keeping* his share."

"You think I'm scared of Jake Ehrlich?"

"You ought to be. If you've got any sense."

He stabbed a lever on the intercom.

"Send him in. The stenographer, too."

Moran moved a chair from the back wall and crammed it into the space beside me. Corey removed his jacket, hung it on a coat tree near the file cabinet, and shot his cuffs. He then settled himself on his creaking, cracked-leather throne.

A middle-aged woman in a dowdy dress and shapeless sweater came through the door, pushing one of those new key-punch machines that are faster than shorthand. I'd seen one in court, when I was watching Ehrlich work, and wondered how any operator could keep up with him.

Then Manny Gold crept in, nervously spinning his doffed fedora with his fleshy fingers. Moran pointed to the seat next to mine and Manny filled it.

"What the hell are you doing here?" I asked.

Gold stared straight ahead and played deaf.

"All right then," Corey said, as if he were bringing a courtroom to order. He nodded at the secretary. "This is the deposition of Emmanuel Gold. The date is Monday, November 29, 1948. The location is the office of San Francisco Deputy District Attorney William Corey—"

"What the hell is going on?" I snapped. "Manny, what's this all about?"

"In attendance are Frank Moran and—should it appear as 'Billy' in the transcript? Or do you legally go by William? And is Nichols your legal name, or should we use the original—Nicholovich?" He glanced up from his notes. They hadn't told him where to put the accent.

"What are you staging?" I protested. Rapping Manny on the arm, I leaned toward him, whispering: "What's this clown up to?" Gold didn't flinch. Corey went on running his legal spiel:

"Strike the last two questions. In attendance are Frank Moran and William Nicholovich, also known as Billy Nichols, as well as William Corey and a certified court reporter." He then looked at Gold the way a manager checks his fighter before the bell: encouraging, imploring. Manny needed it. He was as haggard as a three-hundred-pounder can be.

"Mr. Gold, do you swear that the testimony you are about to give is the truth, the whole truth, and nothing but the truth, so help you God?"

"I do."

"And you are appearing here today voluntarily and not under duress?"

"I am."

"Please state your name and address for the record."

"Emmanuel Benjamin Gold—2212 San Jacinto Way, San Francisco, California."

"Please tell us where you were on the night of November 3, 1948. It was a Wednesday if that helps you to recall."

"I was downtown. Downtown in San Francisco."

"Were you anywhere in the vicinity of Third and Howard Streets on that evening?"

"Yeah. I drove past there about a quarter after eleven."

"You're referring specifically to the intersection of Third and Howard?"

"Right. I'd parked over on Sutter, and crossed onto New Montgomery. I missed the turn at Mission, so I took Howard. I was headed home."

"You were traveling west on Howard, is that right?"

"Well, yeah. It's a one-way. That's the only way you can go."

"Please just answer the questions."

Gold's face was blotchy, his lips trembling, sweat running. I couldn't fathom why Corey wanted me to observe this inquisition.

"When you passed the intersection of Third and Howard at approximately eleven-fifteen that night, were you witness to an automobile accident?"

A tear seemed to be gathering in the corner of Manny's eye. His meaty hands gripped the arms of the chair, knuckles white. It was one thing for me to give Manny a going-over like I had the other day: We were friends, we shared history. This was ugly. I watched the stenographer's flashing fingers, for distraction.

"Answer the question, Mr. Gold, if you would."

"No."

"No what?"

"No, I didn't see any car accident."

Incredulous, I turned back to Manny. The tear rolling down his cheek was the only part of him that moved. That, and his still quivering lips.

"Yet in a statement you previously gave to attorneys representing the Major Liquor Company"—Corey shuffled a few papers for professional effect, then continued—"dated Friday, November 12, you alleged that you saw a truck belonging to that company, headed north on Third, run a stop sign and collide with a passenger vehicle that had already turned onto Third Street from Howard. Isn't that consistent with what you stated on that occasion?"

"Yes, that's what I said before."

What the hell was this? That was the exact *opposite* of what Manny claimed he'd told the lawyers.

"But now you are informing us that your previous statement was not true?"

"No. Or yes. That's right. It was not true."

"Then what is the truth, Mr. Gold?"

"I was told to say that. What I said the first time."

"Told to by whom?"

"By Billy Nichols."

"The sportswriter? Also known as William Nicholovich? Present here today?"

I shoved my chair back and leapt to my feet.

"This is horseshit!" I yelped. I stood over Gold and glared down at his shuddering face, fleshy cheeks shiny with tears. "What do you think you're doing, Manny? Huh?"

I hit him. So help me God, I buried a left into his chest with all my might. He sucked wind and grimaced. Not the choking, spasming death I'd envisioned. Moran pinned me in a second, but from the corner of my eye I saw Corey wave him off.

"Let the record show that Mr. Nichols assaulted and battered Mr. Gold, physically striking him, following a verbal outburst. Mr. Nichols, you might want to think twice about speaking again during these proceedings without a lawyer present."

"*Fuck you,*" I stated for the record.

"Return to your seat, Mr. Nichols, or Mr. Moran will escort you downstairs, where you will be charged with assaulting this witness. Now, Mr. Gold—did Mr. Nichols inform you why he requested that you perjure yourself about this incident?"

Manny started sniveling, unable to hold his shit any longer. Even if he was a no-good conniving bastard, it was painful to watch a man that big bawl his eyes out. "Billy—Mr. Nichols—said that he wanted to help a buddy get a big settlement from the Major Liquor Company. He was due for a share if he could come up with an eyewitness to back his guy's story."

The stenographer looked terrified when I spun toward her: "Put down that Gold's crying like a baby while he lies his ass off. Make sure that's in there!"

She looked toward Corey, who waved off any such notions. "People often lose their composure during depositions," he advised, with an undisguised smirk. "It's a form of release."

"Did they come to your house last night, Manny? What was the pitch? They freeze your bank accounts? Offer Peggy room and board on the state's tab? What'd these sons of bitches promise you?"

"I've warned you against incriminating yourself further, Mr. Nichols. Disregard him, Mr. Gold. What else did Mr. Nichols tell you when he proposed that you lie about the accident?"

"He said he'd cut me in for a piece of the pie. That was part of the arrangement he had with this guy who got busted up."

"Pretty work, *mishpocha*," I sneered at my former friend. "You'd have been first in line to lick the gestapo's boots."

Manny struggled upright. *"You have no right to say that to me!"* he cried.

Moran wedged himself between us.

"Frank, take Mr. Gold outside. Let him calm down. See if he wants to press battery charges."

I clutched the arms of the chair Manny had vacated and considered crushing it against his hippolike back as he shuffled away. "You got nothing, Manny," I called after him. "You sold out the last shred of your soul. Daniel's gonna grow up real proud of his old man."

"Sit down and shut up," Corey ordered. The steno operator had finished and was wheeling her equipment out. We were now off-the-record. I didn't sit. I didn't do anything. I stood there, shaking.

"You will immediately surrender all documents in your possession relating to the Mount Davidson Trust," ordered Commandant Corey. "If you fail to do so, this deposition will be filed in the case of *Anthony Bernal* versus *Virgil Dardi* and the Major Liquor Company—then we'll see who stands to lose his job. Mr. Moran will drive you to wherever it is you have those documents 'under lock and key.' We're going to settle this matter as rapidly as possible—so I can return to the job of prosecuting criminals. Not reprimanding puffed-up sportswriters. Now get out of my office."

29

Booze was the lubricant that greased many important wheels in my career. Knocking back Ward Eights with the mayor in Parente's after the Corbett-Fields fight, on his tab. I'd saved hizzoner a bundle warning him to lay off Fields. That got my calls through for as long as Angelo Rossi held sway at City Hall. Learning which scotch to drop on a visiting manager, to score exclusives with fighters passing through on the sly. Matching boilermakers with wild-eyed Conn-men in Toots Shor's before Billy's second fight with Louis, filing my account from ringside, then surviving the subsequent all-nighter with local heavyweight scribes like Dan Parker and Frank Graham. The story ended up a prizewinner. I deserved a Purple Heart for making the train with *that* hangover.

I'd learned early that holding your liquor was as essential in this racket as the ability to crank out an instantaneous, arresting lead. Just as fighters conditioned their bodies to withstand the rigors of the ring—soaking hands in brine to toughen the skin, snuffing salt water up nostrils to tan the tender membranes—I trained with snorts of single-malt, blasts of bourbon, jiggers of gin, miscellaneous libations in between. Along the way, I wised up to alcohol's wiles and managed to slip its more severe surprises.

This paid off. It meant that after too many Manhattans with Jimmy Cannon at Dempsey's, I could still follow his lead to Table 50 at the Stork Club—and know *not* to buy a round for Runyon's table. I recalled through my sour mash haze that Damon only allowed coffee when holding court after-hours at the "blasting block." It was to be my one and only meeting with the top dog. If I were a name-dropper, I'd run down everybody at that table, and what they said that night. Winchell himself was there, for half an hour.

I'd evolved into a *professional* drinker. It was a matter of management. Don't abuse the sauce, it won't abuse you. I had contempt for teetotalers who proselytized against demon rum. A dim gin mill stocked with ranks of gleaming glass soldiers, awaiting their screw-loosening assignments—for me it was the sanest sanctuary in the world.

Until I entered the Daily Double at four o'clock that Monday afternoon.

California Joe Lynch was behind the plank, picture-perfect: brilliantined black hair, lantern jaw, muscled torso in a starched white shirt, checkered bow tie, razor-sharp pleats. I'm sure there wasn't a wrinkle in his skivvies. The man mixed perfect cocktails; remembered faces, names, and usuals; was disinclined toward larceny; and wouldn't hesitate to flatten anybody who got out of line. He'd been a top-tier bantamweight in the thirties. He was also an artist out of the ring: brushes and oils. He painted the portrait of me that hung over the mantel at home.

When I slumped against the bar, worn and wilted, Joe took it upon himself to console me. Not just with a generous pour. I got a benediction, in the same full-throated voice that boomed out of the St. Bonifice choir every Sunday.

"I'd be privileged and honored to buy a drink for the man who's done more than any other to promote the art and science of pugilism in this city," Joe announced to everyone riding the long bar's rail. "Your commitment to amateur boxers is particularly commendable, as the physical and moral fiber of our youth is a great concern in society today."

Last thing I needed, desired, or deserved were testimonials. I turned away from my reflection in the silvered mirror and gave the bourbon little time to fraternize with ice cubes. The burn in the throat and kick to the head were a welcome but brief distraction from my misery.

Joe's brows rose, nearing his slicked-back hairline. "You're in that much of a hurry?" he said with mild alarm. "I'd have poured the cheap stuff."

I motioned for another.

After I'd killed that one in morose silence, I surprised him by planting my ass on the stool, taking up residency. He diluted the third with extra ice, and delivered a sneaky short pour.

"Save the tributes," I said, as the pain started to pulse behind my eyes. "It's all a pile of shit. A sham. Today was the proof."

Joe looked perturbed and didn't ask for details. He slid away to serve other customers. On his return, I exhibited my empty glass. He didn't attend to it right away. No matter. I wasn't going anyplace.

"All the clippings, the awards, they don't add up to a damn thing when you get right down to it," I said, lips and tongue starting to act independently. Couldn't wait for the brain to head out on its own. "Am I wrong about this? When you fought the other Joe Lynch—did it matter what people said about you, or what reporters wrote? Did you bring any of that in the ring with you? What's a reputation matter, when you have to put it all on the line?"

"You are right, as usual. Comes time to do the job, a fighter can't dwell on past achievements. He's a fool to look to future rewards. He needs to confront his challenge squarely, in the here and now, and rise to the occasion."

"Perfectly put." I pointed to my glass, and clumsily jabbed a finger into the melting ice. "Freshen this, wouldya? What you're talking about is guts, my friend. You're putting it out there for the world to see—exactly what you're made of. . . . And I let her down. Again. I couldn't come through."

Joe spent a good while wiping his hands on a rag, postponing a reach for the bourbon.

"That fat-ass gorilla walked me in there and right in fron'a the whole crew—including one teller who thinks I'm the second coming of FDR—I handed it all over. Jus' like that." My fingers made a moist, sloppy sound, much less crisp than the snap I intended. "A forfeit. A fuckin' embarrassment. Right? To not even fight? To quit like that? You know why? Know why I did it?"

"Sad to say, I wouldn't know." Lynch coolly looked away, toward the end of the bar. He disapproved of bad language. A guy who could have been Jimmy Ryan had entered from the back and was mingling with some barflies. Couldn't tell if it was him; he wouldn't stand still.

"'Cause I want it too much. When there's somethin' you want too badly—makes you weak. You worry 'bout holding on to somethin', you hold too tight. Then they got you right where they want you."

"Not sure I follow, Billy." Joe looked me in the eye. He slickly whisked away the glass.

"When you were champ," I blathered on, "I bet you never thought 'bout losing the crown. You prolly just took each bout one by one. See, see—that's *it!* You didn't act like you even *had* a title belt, that way you weren't afraid of losing it. Right? That's the way to go 'bout it. 'Cause in the end, what's it really boil down to? Who you *are*—*that's* what counts. Not a title somebody gives you. Pppfftt—*Mr. Boxing!*" I sneered.

"I was never the champ, Billy. You know that."

"Do I? What'da I know, Joe? You tell me."

"Excuse me a moment."

It was doubly humiliating getting shit-faced in front of a guy like Joe Lynch. I'd visit him on occasion in his residence hotel, and he'd show me his immaculate scrapbooks. His easel, paints, and canvases. I'd never seen a room so orderly, so dignified. Maybe he lived out of a single steamer trunk, but he had more class than Astrid Threllkyl could ever buy. I suppose I'd failed him too, in a way.

Joe was down the far end of the bar, conferring with the personage who might be Jimmy Ryan. They glanced over. All the mugs in attendance had swiveled to observe me. One guy held up his drink in a comradely toast. I reached for mine. Nothing there.

Hey, Billy, gonna see you tonight at the Gloves? somebody asked. A hand slapped me on the back. Somebody passing by, a blurry shape. I stood up to peer over the hardwood, looking for another nervous glass. The quality product was on the back bar, out of reach. The well hooch would have to suffice. I groped around for it, so I could return that guy's toast and not be rude. *Hey, Billy, you think Gonsalves is gonna take another title this year?* I lost purchase and accidentally kicked my stool backward onto the floor. *Hey, Billy, whatd'ya think about Jake taking Burney's case?* My fingers couldn't quite reach the goddamn bottle. *Hey, Billy, how'd you manage to louse everything up by trying to do somebody a favor? Hey, Billy, why don't you tell Fuzzy you're quitting, before goddamn Randy Hearst fires your stupid ass? Hey, Billy, what the hell happened to you?*

"Hey, Billy—"

"Piss up a rope."

Jimmy Ryan gazed at me, crooked smile frozen on his placid face.

He was dressed all in black, except for the red carnation that seemed to be revolving in his lapel.

"My friend—you'll always be welcome here." He laid a hand on my shoulder. "But at the moment I'm going to suggest you head down to the Civic. And find yourself some coffee on the way."

"How 'bout a bottle, sport? Short one. For the road."

"No chance. I'm not joking. You got a job to do. Currently you're in no shape for it. These are the finals tonight. Pull yourself together." He shot his cuff and checked his watch. "Show jumps off in a couple of hours, for chrissakes. Either walk yourself sober, or I'll give you a ride. But you're cut off at this establishment."

"No, no, no, no, no . . . I don't need a ride." I tried reading my watch, certain his was wrong. The hands wouldn't stop floating around. "I'm gonna walk, like you say. I got someplace I gotta go first. Something I gotta do."

On my way to 1770 Pine I stopped in a corner market and bought an unnecessary short dog. I detoured shakily past the tall white building once or twice, wrestling with elusive excuses that snaked around my mind, alibis that helped explain my total, dismal failure. Dusk turned to darkness as I staggered back and forth along Pine Street, avoiding the eyes of more sober pedestrians.

It took about half an hour and half a pint of fortitude to muster sufficient courage to climb the tile steps and face what had to be done. *Who am I fooling?* It was shame, not guts, that made me push that buzzer.

Ginny was wearing dungarees and canvas shoes and a man's white sleeveless T-shirt. Her hair was piled up inside a baseball cap with an S.F. Seals insignia. She was a smudged and sweaty mess. She never looked better.

"I'm cleaning up the apartment so I can get my deposit back," she said, pulling me inside by my overcoat sleeve. She pranced down the hall before me, giddy as hell about something. "You'll never believe what happened this morning," she began. Her voice punished the damaged lobes of my liquored brain. She flashed a wide smile, happier than I'd ever seen her.

"Where'd all your books go?" I asked, trying not to slur the words. The skyline of stacked tomes that ran around the baseboards had vanished. The walls, too, were stripped bare.

"Sold 'em. To a dealer on Irving Street. That's what I was doing out by Stow Lake the other day. He came and hauled everything away earlier today."

"Tha's your big news?"

"No, no, no. Get this—Jake Ehrlich was here. *In the flesh*. He is one slick article, let me tell you. Very suave. Really quite charming. Much more likable than I expected."

I wobbled to the chesterfield in the living room. My legs weren't performing too well.

"Ehrlich came here?" I moaned, falling onto the cushions, flipping aside my hat. It was squeezing my head like a fully laced corset. She looked at me dubiously. Must have assumed I was clowning around. She hadn't gotten close enough yet to inhale the fumes. She sat on the little ottoman and leaned over, elbows on her knees. I squinted, trying to turn multiple images into a single woman.

"You were so right, Billy—he asked all about the Mount Davidson Trust. Sat right where you are and tried to smooth-talk everything out of me. And I wouldn't bite! I didn't panic or get intimidated or anything. Told him I didn't know what he was talking about. Said he could look all around the apartment if he didn't believe me. He was suspicious at first, because I was packing up to go. 'Seem to be leaving in an awful hurry,' he mentioned. And I said, 'Mr. Ehrlich, the last thing I expected was for you to sound like a cop.' He got a chuckle out of that. I'll tell you what helped me be so calm—giving *you* that file. It made it so much easier to bluff my way through. I really *didn't* have anything to hide! Can you imagine? The famous Jake Ehrlich! Left here with nothing, Billy. I fought him to a draw. How do you like that?"

"Let's celebrate your stunning victory," I proposed, pulling the short dog from my overcoat pocket. "Have one on me."

Ginny laid a look on me fiercer than what Paula got at the diner. She rose up, fuming.

"I'm an alcoholic, Billy. I thought you were supposed to be good at recalling little details like that."

"Have one. Go ahead."

She stalked from the room. Dimly, I heard what sounded like water sloshing in a bucket, back in the kitchen. The squeak of rubber soles on a wet floor. I tipped in another belt. Some of it trickled onto my shirt. A cupboard door banged. Noises like stuff being shoved and slammed.

Then she was back, standing over me. Water was splashed over parts of her.

"Okay, there's two excuses I'm willing to buy," she rasped. "One, that wife of yours and her sister, maybe they've been cutting into your ass. That I'll *almost* accept. Or, number two—and I hope to hell this is it—you got a fat check out of those Threllkyls and you started celebrating without me."

She waited. "So . . . which is it?"

I got to my feet unsteadily, but couldn't quite detour around the edge of the coffee table. I stumbled, falling to a knee. She stood there, hands on her hips, glaring at me. Kneeling seemed like my only chance at stability.

"This is truly pathetic, you know."

My head was barely four feet off the floor, but I was wavering like I was on a high ledge. I pitched forward. If her thighs hadn't been in the way, I'd have done a face-first header into the carpet. "Ginny," I mouthed into the rough denim. "I . . . I got a confession to make." I drew my head back. My eyes were cinched by taut rubber bands and a trip-hammer was tattooing my temple. "Something I've known for a long time, but I can't hide anymore. I've tried, you know I've tried. But I'm not the stand-up guy you think I am. I want you to for—"

She slapped me across the face.

"After all that's happened, *this* is your play? You gotta get pie-eyed to put the make on me? To hell with you. You think I have any interest in screwing somebody in this condition?"

She hauled me to my feet and muscled me through the doorway of her bedroom. I was a bundle of soiled laundry she heaved onto the naked mattress.

"When I'm done cleaning, I'm leaving. Sleep it off till then. After that, beat it."

30

The ring was a mile away. Characters I didn't recognize, Joes with no juice at all, kept filing past, laughing too loudly and sloshing beer on the steep concrete steps. I felt a hand on my knee. Long, tapered fingers with manicured red nails. Warm breath conveyed a familiar voice to my ear.

"Surprised you couldn't do better than this," Claire teased. "Lucky I brought binoculars."

Her voice, no mistake about it. Couldn't really see her, however, even though she sat beside me. My head was stuck in some kind of invisible vise. Wouldn't budge, not an inch. I started panicking when I couldn't form words, either. Plenty to ask her, but somebody'd stuffed a bourbon-soaked rag deep down my mouth. That's how it felt, at least.

Fellow in the row ahead turned around: Mickey Walker, greatest middleweight I'd ever seen. Out of the dodge almost thirteen years; successfully blowing the last of the millions he'd made. He cradled an ugly, flat-faced dog in his arms. Mick's handle was "The Toy Bulldog." Didn't want anybody to forget, I guess.

"Who you like in this one?" he asked, showing his trademark Irish smile.

I remained mute, another anonymous chump.

"Bet on my husband," Claire said. "Or else I'll belt ya one."

She leaned forward and scratched the short fur between the dog's ears. I saw only an indistinct edge of her profile. It was Claire, I could tell, but she wouldn't turn to face me, which is what I wanted more than anything. All I got was a red wool coat and a hat with fake plumage. The bulldog sloppily tongued her fingers, which widened Mickey Walker's grin. "He likes you." Mickey laughed. Then he eye-balled me: "Who's this mug?"

I tried to protest, to advise Walker of the time we'd spent bantering about his glorious career. *Need I remind you of the week-long series I did on you a few years back?*

No sound came out of my mouth. Claire answered instead, as she let the dog lick her face: "I gave him a ride a couple of times," she said slyly. In hushed, conspiratorial tones, she added: "But he got me pregnant."

Walker glowered. The flammable, pugnacious part of him suddenly crowded out his good-natured side: "You're screwing her while her husband's in there risking his neck?" It wasn't a question. It was a declaration of disgust.

Unable to devise any verbal defense, I pulled the binoculars from Claire's hand and trained them on the square of light. Big cheers. Spotlights. Walker and his drooling mutt redirected their attention. The fighters were entering the arena. Something wet tapped my face: raindrops. Made no sense, since we were in the Cow Palace. Moments earlier I thought we were at the Civic, but now I recognized the place was cavernous and packed to the gills.

Had to be a major fight. And I was in the cheap seats.

I ran the binoculars around ringside. Found my empty seat. Right beside Alan Ward of the *Trib*, like always. The Royal was there; I'd forgotten to load paper in it. Tried to stand up. It was as if my keister were grafted to the hard seat. The rain was coming harder now. Had to make it down there. Somebody needed to stall the introductions till I got properly situated. But there wasn't a single connection up here in the nosebleed section. Surrounding us were nothing but hollering, oblivious ticket buyers.

Suddenly it started pouring. Sheets of it, drenching the spectators, ricocheting off the bright canvas square. A torrential Old Testament rain, right inside the arena, trying to wash everything away. People scrambled madly for cover. Still unable to rise, I peeled off my jacket, handing it to Claire, so she could use it for protection.

Her seat was empty.

The Cow Palace was draining fast, people literally streaming to the exits. I turned my face upward, letting the stinging needles pelt me full-on.

Then pounding, repeatedly, through the mud in my skull.

"Hold on, hold on!"

Ginny's voice.

I cracked an eyelid. Across the hallway, the bathroom door was ajar. The shower was running full blast. The pounding began again, a series of three hard knocks. Ginny rushed into the bedroom, a blue bath towel barely covering her glistening body.

"Hell's bells," she huffed. "I said, '*Just a minute.*' You ugly, impatient bastard."

I raised myself on an elbow, which pried the throbbing gap in my cranium apart a couple more inches. My other eye opened to see Ginny wrapping herself in a long white robe.

"Great timing," she muttered. "All I need is for the super to find some guy drunk in my bed. Makes me look *so* classy." The towel dropped away beneath the robe. She kicked it onto a pile of other linens, while cinching the sash at her waist.

More hammering.

"*All right already!*" She scowled over me on her way to the door. "If you can't be useful," she said, "at least lie there and be quiet." She moved back to the hallway. "Maybe he won't look in here." She shut the bedroom door behind her.

At the moment, that throwback of a building super was the least of my worries. I strained to read my watch in the gloom. I could only see one hand, straight down. Half past six? I tried to assemble anarchic thoughts. Four hours earlier I'd turned over the Mount Davidson Trust, specifically so I could keep my precious job. The Golden Gloves finals began in thirty minutes. I'd never blown an assignment in my career.

I rolled onto my back and used both elbows for support. A blanket was draped over me. Ginny'd put me to bed. When my eyes finally focused, I saw my overcoat, suit, and hat folded on a chair in the corner. Beneath the quilt I was wearing only shorts and socks and a thin T-shirt. Even enduring a murderous headache I realized Ginny Wagner was no purebred Nightingale: she'd riffled my clothes, looking for that payout from the Threllkyls.

I heard a couple more muffled knocks, cut short by Ginny's protesting voice. A bolt unlatched. The bedroom door abruptly hugged tighter to the frame. A louder thud down the hall, as something banged against a wall. I tried to get up, but couldn't manage it in one go. The room pitched wildly.

Ginny was yelling. A dull smack. Grunts and moans.

I forced myself upright, stumbling across the room, trying not to make too much noise. My brain was in the grip of a giant fist. I pressed an ear to the door.

Sounds of struggle, only inches away.

"Okay, bitch," threatened a guttural voice. "Now we settle up."

Larry Daws.

Ginny fell to the floor. Or was thrown. Weight, dragging. "Let's see how tough you are now, okay?" She was thrashing, legs banging against furniture, floorboards.

"No!" she wailed. "Get the fuck off me!"

A sharp, sickening slap. Then an unmistakable sound: a head hitting the mat. I'd heard that enough times. Ginny was conscious, but sobbing.

I was in no shape to fight this thug again. He'd probably wised up and packed a gun this time. It might be pressed to her head right now. Although the room was tilting, I could see it was devoid of useful implements. Nothing but boxes, a couple of garment bags. A pile of clothes. Not a damn thing to use as a weapon. I had to do something— something that wouldn't result in getting both of us killed.

Think. He wasn't here now to find that file for Corey. This was payback. Avenging his humiliation. I couldn't let him get away with it. He couldn't abuse her and leave her lying on the floor. To die.

The way Claire died.

Daws did it. In Claire's own home. Punched her till her wounded insides hemorrhaged. Left her on the floor, as the life drained out of her.

I examined the room, struggling to control the spinning, get the world back in balance, like a fighter trying to regroup from a knockdown. I needed to go out there, no matter what. If he was going to kill Ginny, he'd have to kill me first.

That's when I spotted it, by the side of the bed, knocked onto the floor—her handbag.

Daws was straddling Ginny's chest. Her robe was pulled loose, legs and everything else completely exposed. There was a decorative lamp nearby, throwing faint light through a beaded shade. Choking gurgles told me he had her by the throat. "Pretty face," he kept repeating, over and over. He rose up slightly on his haunches. Sound of a zipper dragged down.

"Get off her," I shouted, trying to sound sober and deadly. "Don't make me shoot you in the back."

His broad shoulders tensed. Daws didn't turn, or ease off. His head bobbed once, then he chanced a glance over his shoulder. There was a pulpy, overcooked vegetable in the middle of his face: broken nose. Purple smears ringed his eyes. Stitches protruded from his busted-up ear. He managed a stupid grin as he sat back on her naked stomach.

"Kill this dumb fuck," Ginny commanded through a constricted larynx.

He didn't recognize me right off, having never seen *Mr. Boxing* in his underwear before. I leveled the gun, close to my body, trying to hold it steady. I was on the deck of a ferry in extremely choppy water.

The dimmest of bulbs finally illuminated. "You shitheel," Daws said. "You're married." Amazing what people will focus on, any given moment.

"Get the fuck off her."

He inhaled deeply, like he was in his corner, getting set to answer the bell. "Shit," he said, heaving air back out. "I only wanted to even things up. Now I'm in a different spot. Gonna hafta deal with the both of ya."

Ginny tried to hammer fists into Daws's chest. Her wrists were bound with the sash from her robe. He squeezed tighter on her throat. She let out a strangled squeal, which was quickly suffocated.

"Let her up now," I bellowed. "Or I swear to Christ, I'll blow your head off."

Still gripping her throat, Daws jerked Ginny's head up. Then he banged it against the floor. The fight went out of her, but she whimpered, still alive. My finger tightened on the trigger. One more pulse would make me a murderer. I had no choice but to kill him, I told myself.

"You don't scare me," Daws said. "And guns don't scare me." He started to rise, convinced Ginny was no longer a threat. "Nothing scares me." A demented expression spread across his battered face. I'd seen it before, in that early fight.

The notion flew in at that moment, like a wren sailing through the alcohol haze to roost in my brutally throbbing brain. It spread its wings and suddenly became a hawk. I eased my pressure on the trigger. Something remained of my brain.

"Kill him," Ginny wheezed, as Daws got to his feet.

I came right at him, before he had a chance to get his balance. He went into an instinctive fighting crouch, hands hoisted up. I threw out a sorry excuse for a jab, but it surprised him just enough. Up came his right, pure muscle memory. I swung the gun in my other hand. He blocked most of it, but the barrel nicked his temple, angling him sideways. Ginny rolled over, taking Daws's leg out from under him. He banged a knee into the coffee table and had to use both hands to stop himself from tumbling over.

It was my opening, and I took it. Flipping the Baretta so the barrel was in my fist, I cracked the butt against his head. Hard enough to kill an ordinary man.

Then I did it again. And again. And once more.

There was a small serrated steel tongue at the bottom of the gun butt. It tore divots in Daws's head. With each recoil of my tomahawking arm, blood spattered my face and clothes. Ginny shuddered at each sodden, sickening crack.

I expected her to put the brakes on me, like I'd restrained her in the park. She didn't make a move, didn't even look away.

"Keep killing him."

That snapped me out of it.

I stared at the syrupy red mess irrigating the carpet. A long strand of saliva swung from my panting mouth. My stomach surged up. No chance of Ginny getting back her cleaning deposit now. Amazing what people will focus on, at a given moment.

Finally, thankfully, I saw a bubble of breath appear between Daws's bloody lips.

"He's no good dead," I told Ginny. "Believe it or not."

31

"Where's the telephone?" I croaked, reeling backward.

Didn't occur to me to untie Ginny, but she didn't need my help. She'd used her teeth to undo the sash binding her wrists. Back on her feet, she drew the robe closed, tightly, then tighter still. She was trembling and looked ready to be sick herself. She pointed toward the beaded lamp. The phone was next to it, on a small end table.

"Oh, dear God," she sobbed, surveying the devastated apartment.

I gave her the gun and picked up the phone. My hand was shaking so violently I could barely dial.

"Hold it on him," I instructed. "If he comes around and starts going crazy, *you* get to kill him."

"No bullets," she said.

Good thing there wasn't time to think about that.

"Hello?" said the woman's voice.

"Mrs. Bernal, this is Billy Nichols. Is Nate there?"

"What?"

"Nate, *Nate*. Your son. If he's there, put him on."

"He's on his way out. Why do you want to talk to *him*? I'll get you Tony."

"*No!* Please, put Nate on the line."

She probably thought I was auditioning new drivers. If only. Seconds later, the kid grabbed the phone.

"You're headed for the Gloves, right?" I wasted no time. Adrenaline really pumps when you've pistol-whipped somebody. "Got a ride? Okay, listen. I'm not gonna make it. You're covering me, got that? I'm not joking, not a bit. You wanna be a writer, you get to start tonight. Shove the good shit up front, spell everybody's name right—check, don't guess—and don't decorate. Make sure you include the attendance. Get a towel or something—put it under his head. No, not you. You got a typewriter, I hope? Take it with you. No, you don't sit at ringside, you sit where you've got a ticket. Take notes, type it all up in the car after. Remember how to head it and all that? From that story I gave you? Make sure you put *my* name at the top of each add. When you're done, drive it over to the *Inquirer* and take it to Sports, like you did after the Carter fight. Got it? And Nate, listen to me: This ain't Dempsey versus Firpo—just make sure you get the winners right."

I hung up and groped my way toward the bedroom. There was a dark hat lying in the corridor, which must have fallen off Daws in the struggle. As I passed the bathroom, my stockinged feet squished into the sopping carpet. That's when I realized the shower was still running.

"I thought you were calling the cops," Ginny said, following right behind. "What the hell's going on?"

She peered in the bathroom. "Oh, shit!"

The tub was overflowing, its drain stopped up. There was water covering the gray-and-white tile floor. She'd worked all day cleaning the place and in minutes it had become a disaster area *and* a crime scene.

No time to ponder our collective misfortunes.

"Did you get your car back?" I yelled from the bedroom. Nearly toppled over pulling my trousers on. Adrenaline hadn't burned off all the booze. Her bare feet slapped around in the flooded bathroom. The shower cut off. More sloshing, then a sucking sound as the drain was freed.

"Still got the rental. In the garage downstairs," she called back, voice echoing off the tiles. "It's got a bunch of my shit in it already. Why?"

"It's gonna have some more shit in it," I said. "We're taking your man for a drive. Get some clothes on."

"Are you serious?" She entered the bedroom and stood with arms akimbo. One hand still clutched the bulletless Baretta. The robe adhered to her, saturated. She may as well have been naked.

"Have any bullets for that thing? Just in case?"

"No."

"Was it ever loaded?"

She shook her head. "I'm getting the police over here to take that bastard away," she said. "You won't have to worry, I'll testify you did it in self-defense."

"Doesn't do me any good. I'll explain on the way. But we gotta get him in your car before he comes around. Look it, I'm at the end of my rope here. I got one more shot. Can't do it without you. C'mon, Ginny."

We cleaned Daws up as best we could without reviving him. I didn't give a damn if he woke up in the trunk. I didn't want any resistance between Ginny's apartment and the basement. She swabbed the blood off his head with a bath towel. It didn't do much to improve his busted-up features. She winced when she saw the dents I'd put in his skull.

Daws's hat was soaked with bathwater, shapeless. I shoved mine on his dome instead, pulled low to hide the damage. I wouldn't need it anymore. It'd only remind me of that lard-ass turncoat Manny Gold. I hurriedly washed my face and stashed my blood-speckled T-shirt in with Ginny's laundry. I redressed sloppily. Ginny wasted precious time searching for a specific pair of shoes.

"We don't have all fucking night," I snapped.

"Then drive him yourself," Ginny said, tugging on a pair of flats. Only thing else she'd managed to don was a slip. "Give me your overcoat," she demanded.

"I can't carry him by myself," I complained. "You get under this other arm and we'll move him that way. Anybody sees us, we'll act like he's passed out drunk and we're hauling him to your car."

We managed to angle ourselves through the doorway and into the dim corridor. She kicked the door shut behind us. It slammed. Daws moaned. Ginny grimaced.

"Let's go," I said.

It was like dragging an unconscious fighter to his corner, but in this case we had considerably farther to go. Past doorways I expected to spring open, around the bend of the hallway, down the long stretch of green carpet, beyond the stairway, to the elevator. It seemed preposterous to imagine we wouldn't run into anyone. It wasn't even seven o'clock. People would be arriving home from work, getting off on every floor.

"Maybe we should take the stairs," I grunted.

"Maybe I should just drop the son of a bitch right here. 'Cause I'm not carrying him down five flights. I'll push him down, but I won't carry him."

He *was* heavy, and listing toward Ginny. "You should have worn heels," I said. "Would have made us more balanced."

"Just hold up your end. Spare me the commentary."

The elevator arrived. Miraculously empty.

We struggled aboard, Ginny again deftly using a foot, this time to slide the gate closed. "Push One," she instructed.

"We want the garage, don't we?"

"You see a button for it? We can only get there from the lobby."

"Shit, we might as well be walking him through the SP depot."

"This was your brilliant idea, remember."

We slumped against the back wall as the cage began its rumbling descent. I sneaked a sidelong glance at Daws. The gray felt above the hatband was seeping red. His head lolled toward Ginny, a groan escaping his gaping mouth. Blood was leaking from beneath the fedora, trickling through his stubbly sideburn, down his jaw.

"He's still bleeding, goddamnit."

The elevator lurched to a stop. Third floor.

The door swung outward. The gate clattered back and a balding guy in a three-piece suit stepped in. He barely acknowledged us, slamming the gate shut and jabbing One.

"Gorgeous weather," he noted.

Daws twitched and let out a moan. The guy had to look.

"Beautiful," Ginny said. "I'm hoping it stays nice tonight."

The tenant's eyebrows lifted curiously before he even looked at Daws. He flushed, then went back to studying the passing floors. His ears were red. Leaning forward, I noted that Ginny had allowed the overcoat to fall open, giving her neighbor an eyeful.

We reached the first floor. Mr. Three-Piece stepped out, graciously acting as doorman. I managed to prop the gate and wrestle with Daws simultaneously.

"Is he all right?" the guy inquired, finally taking his eyes off Ginny.

"Has a case of narcolepsy, the poor sap," Ginny explained.

Not wanting to appear ignorant, the guy asked nothing else. Once we were clear, he let go of the door and headed for the lobby exit.

"Up those stairs to the mezzanine," Ginny said. She was struggling to help keep Daws upright. "Then around the corner and down the steps, to the garage. My car's not far."

"What the hell is narcolepsy?"

We didn't get one step farther. The super appeared from around the corner at the head of the stairs, then motored straight for us. No way he could squeeze past. He saw Ginny, but wasn't the least bit interested in her slip or anything beneath it.

"What the hell are you doing up there in five-oh-six?" he barked. "Lady below you is calling, says she's got water pouring down the ceiling of her bathroom. Five-oh-eight is griping about shouting and some big ruckus. And what the hell is wrong with *this* guy? What kind of trouble are you causing up there on your last day?"

"Everything's fine," Ginny said, in her calmest, coolest voice. "My friend here had a few too many; now we're taking him home."

Daws spasmed, and his head snapped back. He gurgled like a guy awakening from a fitful sleep.

The super stepped closer. Damn good thing he was blind as a bat. "Whew, this guy stinks like a distillery," he reported, qualifying himself for a job at the *Chronicle*.

"We're just gonna get him in the car real quick," I said. "He can be unruly when he snaps out of it."

The lobby door opened behind us. Several tenants entered, chattering away. We were still planted in front of the elevator. They'd be swarming around us in several heartbeats.

The super's imbecilic eyes, magnified by the thick lenses, settled on me. "I remember you," he said. Then his gaze shifted to Ginny. He was gamely trying to form simple equations in his under-equipped mind.

Daws's hands, draped over our shoulders, began twitching. Voluntarily or not, I couldn't tell. A doctor might have known whether he was waking up or dying, but not me. The scarlet spot on the fedora was widening. I shifted my weight so Daws's head rolled toward me, hiding the thickening trail of blood down his face.

Ginny started toward the stairs. The super put out his arm to stop her.

"Let your boyfriends fend for themselves," he said. "You're coming upstairs with me. You're not skipping out, not if there's damage to that apartment."

"Get your hands off me!" she said. "Look at me—you think I'm running off dressed like this?"

Behind us, mailboxes swung open and closed. Footsteps approached.

"Look," I said, "she's just helping me get my brother in the car. Then I'll drive him home and she'll come back up to finish cleaning. Okay? Better let these people get on here."

While he held the elevator door for the arriving residents, we forged past him.

"I'm going up there now," he cautioned. "If anything's damaged, you won't get back a penny of that deposit."

We hauled Deadweight Daws up the mezzanine steps. If we weren't in the process of committing a felony, I might have grinned when Ginny grunted, "Go fuck your own miserable self, you stupid four-eyed freak," as the elevator door wheezed shut.

32

Daws didn't come off Queer Street for nearly two hours. When he rejoined the living, his first thought must have been that he'd died and gone to hell.

"They tol' me you some kinda tough fighter," mocked Nightbird Jones, inches from Daws's mutilated mug. "Not scared o' nothin' or nobody. Won't step in a ring with a colored man, though. Don't even like being in the same room with a Negro, do you? So how you feelin' now?"

The Bird raised himself unhurriedly from the edge of the desk. He'd been perched there for around thirty minutes, monitoring Daws's shallow breaths and fluttering eyelids, checking for signs of consciousness. Moving backward, he let Larry's puffy, slitted eyes squint at the oddly shadowed confines of the manager's office. Ordinarily it held little: a desk, two chairs, watchful head of a trophy deer, antlers crisscrossed with cobwebs.

Currently, however, the place felt more like a rush hour streetcar: more than twenty strapping black men, craning their necks to peer at their unpopular, pale-faced guest. Several wore scowls that suggested Daws could readily stand in for every white man who'd ever shit on them, their fathers, their granddaddies—all the way back to that first mercenary slave-ship captain.

You might say I had something to do with the frosty reception. Daws had been singlehandedly dragged by Nightbird across the lobby of Cold Springs Resort, his wrists bound with the belt from my overcoat (a service performed with relish by Ginny in her Pine Street garage). A few resort residents showed genuine alarm and concern: "What happened to *him*?"

No cause to recount the whole saga. I announced, distinctly enough for all to hear: "He called Joe Louis a no-good . . . well, I'd rather not repeat the slurs he applied to Mr. Louis."

Any remnants of compassion for Daws's sorry condition instantly evaporated.

Nightbird Jones didn't need my cheat sheet on the racist fighter. "This peckerwood fool ducked me twice that I know of," Bird said, as we crammed Daws's carcass into the chair. "Used to get on his soapbox in the Royal locker room, going on 'bout how them Rebels and Nazis had the right idea, y' know what I mean?"

It didn't take an elaborate pitch for Jones to back my plan.

"Not a single soul knows you're here, Larry," I began, stepping away from the wall when I saw—finally, gratefully—that Daws would survive. "Then too, I can't imagine who might miss you if you didn't leave this room alive."

I hunkered in front of him, blinding myself to how badly injured he was, or whether he could even fathom what I was saying. He was a battered, trapped, confused animal—that was clearly evident in his eyes.

I had no time to waste.

"So here it is—the only way you're getting out of here is if you put down, in writing, exactly what Corey told you to do."

I uncinched the belt around his wrists. Daws moved a hand to his head, probing the grisly damage. *My* spine twitched when he fingered the depth of the dents.

"My fingers are broke," he realized, staring at two oddly angled digits on his left hand. Ginny had accidentally smashed them while closing the trunk.

"Good thing you're not a southpaw," I noted. "You can still write this up."

"I'm messed up," Daws said. "I don't know what you want. I can't write nothing like you want."

"Don't worry, Larry. I'm a professional. It'll be like an interview. You give answers, I'll make sure it reads right. We'll just go through it first, that way you won't have to cross anything out later. One more time—what deal was Corey offering?"

"Who's Corey?" Larry ventured weakly. He winced, an involuntary revelation of pain.

"Why play dumb, Larry? You need a doctor. Can't afford to wait long, either. You're going to say, short and sweet, what Corey cut for your grand jury testimony. Do that—you spend the next few nights in a comfy hospital bed. Or, you could go the other way, in which case . . ."

"You're talking bullshit," he groaned. "I went in front of the grand jury already."

"Larry, take a look around. This is the only jury you need to worry about now. You talk, you walk. That's it. Understand? Now, after Corey had you finger Burney, he gave other orders, didn't he?"

"Wasn't Corey," Daws finally croaked, his features contorted in agony. "Some other guy put the screws to me."

"So's you'd do what?"

"You know."

He tried to nod over my shoulder. Ginny slouched in the corner, overcoat wrapped tightly around her, though it felt about six hundred degrees in that room.

"To juke up Miss Wagner for some paperwork, right? How 'bout the hired hand's name? Frank Moran, right? Corey's pot-bellied stormtrooper."

He gave a brief flicker of surprise. I'd nailed it.

"What were the terms? Cash money for bringing back the file?"

"No money. Said I had to do it, or Corey could nix my deal with the DA."

Toss the dog a bone, then threaten to take it away. Corey was a miserable, masterful manipulator.

"When you write it down, you'll have to say Corey himself gave the marching orders. Got it? What about Montague? They tell you what to do with him, too? Run him off the road? Try to kill him?"

A hot glare was his response.

"I ain't writing nothing down," Daws whispered.

"Why not? You *can* write, can't you, boy?"

Several dusky youths stationed near us chuckled knowingly, familiar with such cruelty and the terminology. Must be satisfying when a white guy swallows it for a change. Larry didn't cotton to being laughed at—especially if it came from black faces.

He glowered like he wanted to shove the ridicule back down their throats, make them choke on it. But he wouldn't. Even at 100 percent, with hands free to attack, he wouldn't. He couldn't. That's how terrified he was.

Daws slumped and mumbled something I couldn't decipher.

"Didn't hear you," I said. "What was that?"

He gestured with his head, summoning me closer. I leaned in, ready for a desperate confession.

"Nigger lover," he hissed through clenched, bloody teeth.

Then he spat in my face.

An ominous rumble coursed through the room. About half of Nightbird's boys surged forward. I straightened up, arms out-stretched, protecting Daws. I had to stifle a smile as I pulled out my crumpled display handkerchief and histrionically swabbed spittle from my cheek.

This is actually going to work. I silently offered thanks and praise for the ignorance, cowardice, and, most of all, for the pitiful predictability that lives in the worst of us.

"Keep your eyes on him," Nightbird directed the group as he exited. Daws sensed many pairs of eyes on him, none sympathetic. If there's justice, he was quaking like some poor colored farmhand, surrounded by the Klan, the noose being knotted. A few moments alone in there might prove persuasive. I followed Bird out.

From the desk in the lobby, Jones slid sheets of blank foolscap. No letterhead, no watermark.

"Envelope, too," I requested. "And a stamp." Bird delivered, stony and implacable. I produced a pencil from the *Monarch of the Dailies* pocket protector I'd be discarding once I changed my shirt.

Ginny tottered up behind us. She hugged the desk, distressed. "That play won't work," she sighed, clearly repulsed by the sickening spectacle. "Those are *boys* in there, not a cell full of hardened crimi-nals. They'd never hurt him like you say they would. He'll realize that."

"Mor'n that, they're *good* boys," Nightbird said. "But with all due respect, miss, you didn't feel any too safe round 'em when you was up here one time before."

"That was different."

"Sorry to say, Miss Wagner—it ain't. You an' me both know those boys doing nothin' but standing 'round, and tha's all they gonna do. 'Massuh' there, he feel like he's locked in a cage at the zoo. When he look at a man like me, he don't see a person—he see his worst nightmare. I don't like it, but I'm wit' *Mr. Boxing* on this one. That jackass gonna cut loose with whatever Mr. Nichols wants."

Ginny flushed and stared at the floor.

Once I had the stained, scrawled statement folded inside the envelope Daws had shakily addressed to Jake Ehrlich, Bird helped load him back in the car. Daws was so far gone by then, Ginny could have laid him out with a love tap.

"Wait a minute!" Nightbird called as we swerved the car around, headed back downhill. "You don't need no loose ends when you drop him," he explained, hustling to the rear of the car. In the glow of the taillights, he rubbed mud over the license plate. Some of the boys pointed, smirked, or laughed out loud. They recognized that their Good Samaritan's past was checkered, if he was savvy to such precautions.

I wanted to tip him every last dollar in my pocket, but I knew it'd be an insult. I shook Jones's hand through the window and said, "I owe you."

"Yeah, you do," he responded flatly, before waving us away.

Ginny and I drove to the Emergency entrance of the Napa County General Hospital. While orderlies muscled Daws from the car and hoisted him on a gurney, I fed the admissions clerk a dose of bullshit that left Ginny in awe. Soon as Daws got rolled down the hall, I pulled on her arm and we bolted.

"You must still be drunk," she decided as we ducked back into the rented Nash. "He'll eventually tell them what really happened."

"No, he won't. He's going to say he can't remember a thing. Then, first chance he gets, he'll rabbit."

"What makes you so sure?" She switched on the ignition and pumped on the gas pedal. It was no Roadmaster.

"'Cause I know guys exactly like him," I explained. "He'd rather be dead than have his fatal weakness come out. Think he'd ever admit writing up that statement on account of he was in a room full of colored kids *looking at him*? Daws'd open his wrists instead."

"*See, we're not from around here*," Ginny suddenly parroted, dropping her voice a couple of octaves to better imitate me. "*The wife and I missed a turnoff. We were sightseeing, when we come across this poor fella by the side of the road. No, can't say where exactly—we're not locals. This must be his wallet. He was lying on it. No money. Think he might have gotten robbed? Hope he'll be all right.* My God! How do you come up with this stuff?"

"Tell stories for a living." I was using dim light off the dash to count out the nine lifted singles from Daws's billfold. "Not much different from the big shots who write those books you read. 'Cept I'd like their deadlines. And their paychecks."

Recognizing the road we were on, I had Ginny pull into the lot of the Dew Drop Inn.

There was a telephone booth in front of the roadhouse, at the top of the stairs.

"You're not having another drink," Ginny said. "Believe me."

"No argument there. Gotta make a phone call."

The night's last story, I hoped.

"Hey, hon. Look, I'm really sorry, but I'm gonna get back later than I thought. Probably won't be home for . . . least a couple more hours. Hey, *hey*! Cut it out—don't start with that. No, I am *not* with her. We've been over all this."

Through the booth's grimy glass doors, and the inn glass, I observed Ginny. She decorated a bar stool, dragging on a smoke, oblivious to customers gaping at her provocative undergarment-and-overcoat ensemble. She was drinking what looked like a ginger ale, which my stomach found very appealing.

"Listen to me," I lectured Ida. "We had an injury tonight. No, not me. A fighter. He got hit pretty bad, concussion. They had to carry him from the ring. I'm heading over to the hospital, see how he's doing. First I need to notify his family, tell them what happened. Called because I didn't want you to worry where I was. Okay? I'll be home soon as I can. It'll be all right. Don't do that. C'mon, it'll be okay. Ida. I said stop now. It happens. He'll be all right."

She was sobbing, demanding to know how any mother could allow her son to become a fighter.

"Hey, guess what?" I tried to soothe her. "I don't have to work tomorrow. It's my day off. Know what I'd like to do? More than anything else? Sleep late. We'll haul Vincent in the kip with us and sack out till ten or eleven for a change. How's that sound? Then I'll whip up your favorite: pigs in a blanket. Doesn't that sound great? No, no, that's okay. Don't wait up. I'll see you in the morning. Love you, too."

33

San Francisco Inquirer December 1, 1948

MURDER CASE MISTRIAL!

DEPUTY DA SUSPENDED

Surprise Evidence Submitted

By William Sonlich, Inquirer *staff reporter*

The Burnell Sanders murder case ended shockingly in a mistrial on its opening day, when defense attorney Jake Ehrlich presented Judge Harlan White with evidence that a key prosecution witness provided tainted testimony to the grand jury.

Within hours of Ehrlich's stunning disclosure, District Attorney Edmund G. "Pat" Brown conditionally suspended deputy DA William Corey, the lead attorney in the city's prosecution of Sanders, a San Francisco businessman and boxing promoter. Sanders had been charged with murdering the wife of local heavyweight boxer Hack Escalante.

Judge White received the signed statement of Lawrence Daws, also a boxer, in which Daws maintained that he had been coerced by the prosecution into delivering grand jury testimony that directly led to Sanders's indictment. Sources close to the case provided the *Inquirer* with a copy of the handwritten document. In it, Daws also claimed he later was instructed by the deputy DA to physically intimidate potential witnesses. "I was Corey's goon," Daws's statement bluntly alleged.

"These are extremely serious allegations," DA Brown confirmed during a hastily called press conference at the Hall of Justice. "We are launching an internal investigation to determine the validity and admissibility of Mr. Daws's statement.

We believe Judge White is acting in the best interests of all concerned at this time, prudently declaring a mistrial, so the facts of this matter can be determined."

The *Inquirer* also learned that police, responding to an anonymous tip, took Daws into custody yesterday in Napa County, the location from which he had mailed Ehrlich his "confession." In addition to perjury, legal analysts say Daws could be charged with obstruction of justice, assault, extortion, and possibly attempted murder.

Little is known about Daws, described by *Inquirer* boxing editor Billy Nichols as "a journeyman fighter, with a jab like a men's room attendant brushing off a customer. Seems like he lived up to his potential."

Ehrlich hinted that he intends to prove Daws was equally culpable in the death of Mrs. Escalante, and that the prosecution illicitly offered him immunity in exchange for testimony against Sanders.

"I hope that this will lead to a clear understanding of the circumstances surrounding the death of Mrs. Escalante—and the acquittal of my husband," said Mrs. Florence Sanders, wife of the defendant.

Several Hall of Justice veterans think Corey's career may be irreparably damaged. "They're going to cut [Corey] off like a gangrenous foot," said attorney Steven Vender. "They'll do whatever it takes to make this appear to be an isolated case of corruption within our city's judicial system."

"Incredible," marveled Susan Montague. She'd been reading the article aloud. We were on a glass-walled sundeck of S.F. General Hospital. "Ehrlich is on the case less than three days and he manufactures a mistrial. It seems like he has the whole deck up his sleeve before they even start dealing."

"Could be why they call him the Master," I said. I repositioned Woody's wheelchair, so the sun wouldn't hit him across the eyes. One of his arms was in a curved cast, one leg immobilized on a rail. Worst of all, though, was his face: Surgeons had reconstructed the jaw, but he wasn't handsome anymore. His mouth was wired shut to give the remodeling a chance to heal. Meals came through a straw.

"You suppose Ehrlich might want to step in and help me out on this Dardi case?" Susan was only partly joking.

She wanted to go ahead with Tony Bernal's claim against the Major Liquor Company. Tony was dubious about a female lawyer. "You could do a damn sight worse," I'd counseled him. Truthfully, I wished they'd drop the whole beef—I had no idea how that rigged deposition Gold recorded could replay and haunt me. Not that anything with Corey's stink on it would have much credibility anymore.

Susan quartered the newspaper and laid it on her husband's lap. "Pretty snappy quote in there from *Mr. Boxing*," she said. "Guess you've seen this Daws character fight plenty of times."

"Once or twice. But I had a ringside seat."

Woody gave me the fish-eye, thick horn-rims slightly lopsided on his long, bony face. His mouth might have been out of order but the brain was working overtime.

With his good, long arm he reached up and pulled a pencil from my shirt pocket. He scrawled along the newspaper's margin, then held a message up for me to read.

Nice work. Buy this Sonlich a drink on me.

Wasn't easy, but he managed a wink.

That Sonlich character sold some extra runs of the *Inquirer* with his week-long investigative series on the Mount Davidson Trust, and how it spawned a blackmail ring and ultimately led to the death of Claire Escalante, an innocent pawn in the scheme. Several intrepid staffers from cityside were sent digging into the dealings of the deceased Dexter Threllkyl. They uncovered a voluminous paper trail of bogus corporations dating back to the early 1930s. Featured in the stories were multi-column halftones of the opulent Threllkyl mansion, one above the crafty caption: BUILT ON A FOUNDATION OF LIES. A few shots of Astrid were extracted from the society files in the *Inquirer* morgue, to lend a bit of much-needed glamour to the dry accounts of financial malfeasance.

Yet you never saw a single picture of Dexter Threllkyl. The renowned attorney must have been the most unphotographed man in San Francisco. With good reason, if you bought our reporter's unsubstantiated speculation about Threllkyl faking his own death—not once, but twice.

Dex was the piece missing from the jigsaw, from managing editor Marty English's perspective. English wanted to track down the villainous mastermind, thereby keeping the story fresh and juicy.

Even SFPD Captain of Detectives Francis O'Connor got into the spirit of things. He was quoted as recommending, "Let's dig up the corpse and see just who this old Okie really was." The revelation (conveniently withheld until a later commuter edition) that "Dexter Threllkyl" had been cremated only added fuel to the fire, so to speak.

Despite the paper's best efforts to resuscitate him, Dexter Threllkyl remained resolutely dead.

His widow absconded from her Vallejo Street mansion after draining every last drop of liquidity from all bank accounts the *Inquirer* was able to trace—including, of course, the sizable sum she'd inherited upon her spouse's demise.

Conspicuously absent at the same time was disgraced, suspended Deputy District Attorney William Corey. This caused wild conjecture in the newsroom that Corey and the widow Threllkyl weren't brother and sister at all, but lovers who'd bumped off ol' Dex in order to share his fortune. There wasn't enough evidence to run with that one. So although it would have sent the paper's sales into the stratosphere—such suppositions never reached the composing room.

If he wasn't careful, "William Sonlich" was going to end up with a steady job on the news desk. No small feat for a guy who'd never spent a day cityside. The section editor wanted to put Sonlich's real name on the series, give credit where it was due. Fortunately, English nipped that in the bud, before it got anywhere near editor-in-chief William Randolph Hearst, Jr.

Before "Randy" could do anything to squelch it, the genie was out of the bottle regarding Dexter Threllkyl, his wife, her brother, and the entire ugly conspiracy of fiscal fraud that had kept the family floating atop San Francisco's social elite.

When the chips were down, Hearst proved to be a newspaperman worthy of his illustrious name. When street sales spiked on the second day of the series, Junior swallowed any allegiances and ran with it. Forced to choose between hot copy and loyal cronies, his appropriate response was "Dexter and Astrid *who?*"

Burney Sanders and Larry Daws wound up being tried separately for the killing of Claire Escalante. Change of venue for each, to Los Angeles and Sacramento. With all the publicity generated by the *Inquirer* series, the defendants needed to be taken out of town to get a fair shake.

Burney was one of the few people outside the *Inquirer* who knew the true identity of William Sonlich—and he evidently understood what he owed the reporter. References to a certain *Mr. Boxing* never arose during his trial.

Verdicts and sentences came back identical: Guilty, voluntary manslaughter. Sanders and Daws each got ten-year jolts. One day I'd be seeing them again, I figured. I also assumed Burney would be grateful as hell, at least enough to send a thank-you card. I'm still waiting.

If Sanders was lucky, his wife would wait, too, while he served his time. Not likely. Florence began receiving suitors as soon as she moved into classy new digs in Pacific Heights, underwritten by the payout from the Mount Davidson Trust. Once the trial went to L.A., Ehrlich dropped Mr. Sanders cold. He decided to represent Mrs. Sanders instead.

She got Jake to dig through a certain accordion file of documents, part of the heaps of paper impounded in Corey's office. Amid all the card-trick corporations and fraudulent foundations, the Mount Davidson Trust was deemed oversold, but essentially legit.

And wouldn't you know, it was the only one of Threllkyl's fronts and flimflams to which Burney Sanders was legally connected. So, even though the signatory was doing a dime in the joint, his wife received a spousal share when the trust was liquidated by court decree.

Last I heard, Jake was handling the finer points of her divorce petition.

When the trust was liquidated, Cold Springs Resort was put up for sale. Nightbird Jones's "Young Men's Vocational Camp" got the bum's rush. When I approached the Hearst Foundation about a charitable donation to such a worthy endeavor, the rubber stamps pounded proudly. When they found out the camp was exclusively for Negro boys, the paperwork got lost. When I argued that sponsorship of the camp would be a good marketing ploy to help the *Inquirer* compete with the *Oakland Tribune* in the increasingly colored East Bay market, Nightbird finally got his money.

Tony Bernal's lawsuit against Virgil Dardi stalled when he passed on Susan Montague's offer of pro bono counsel. He decided to wait for Woodrow's recovery. While both men struggled with medical bills that nudged them nearer the poorhouse, Dardi strengthened his liquor monopoly in the city.

Peggy Gold was committed to a private sanitarium, one of the Golden State's best, I hear. How Manny comes up with the monthly nut, I don't ask—on those occasions he shows up at the fights, still pitching. And I'll say this for him: He never shows up without the kid in tow. Breaks my heart when Daniel's big eyes recognize me, a familiar face among the gruff, yapping pugs towering all around him.

Not that I carry a grudge. Gold did what he had to do. One day I might allow myself to forgive him. Doesn't mean we need to talk in the meantime.

Virginia Wagner? She didn't get much out of the whole mess. Except for freedom and car repairs. With Sanders and Daws locked up, and her name edited out of all *Inquirer* accounts of the Threllkyl affair, Ginny finally relaxed enough to return from Alameda exile and walk the city's streets without a pistol in her purse.

She felt sufficiently emboldened, in fact, that she applied for a job in the *Inquirer* library. I'd called to advise her of the opening.

We see each other every once in a while, coming or going around Third and Market. We shoot the bull. Sometimes we'll grab a bite nearby and have a good laugh about it all. "I can't believe it was only three weeks," she invariably says. "It felt like we did it *all*. Except, of course, for . . . well . . ."

That's why I like her. And it's why I keep my distance, too. We carried some markers, but those debts were squared.

I'm hoping she meets a decent guy who can handle her, or even make heads or tails of her. That's a wedding I won't miss. Might even break out the dancing shoes. In the meantime, it's good to know she's toiling in the same shop, just another drone turning in an honest day's labor. She ought to save her money and keep that cute nose clean.

'Cause nothing beats working at the paper.

Take my word for it.

Epilogue

Next spring, I received a local Press Club award. Best Sports Story of 1948, for coverage of the Carter-Escalante title fight. This was my third such honor, but it meant the most, by far. After an unusually rocky acceptance speech during the banquet, I took a brutal ribbing from colleagues at our table about how many times I'd choked up or took off my glasses to wipe my eyes.

"You wanna see tears?" Fuzzy Reasnor heckled. "How's about I tell him how close he came to getting bumped down to Prep a few months ago? The big man was just going through the motions then. Shoulda seen a piece he filed, for the Golden Gloves finals no less, before I cleaned it up. Amateur Night! Now look at him!"

"Yeah, that one was pretty sad," I admitted. "You'd have thought a fifteen-year-old wrote it."

Everybody broke up. Ida gave me a big hug. The roasting continued unabated.

"That's enough, now!" My wife tried to call a halt, not realizing this was how veterans of the dodge showed their love and admiration.

A bit later we repaired to the bar for brandy and cigars, where I dutifully greeted well-wishers. Some were pals from the job, or friendly rivals writing for the competition. Others were strangers, simply eager to glad-hand over a nightcap.

"Congratulations on a job well done," pronounced one distinguished, gray-haired gent, pumping my hand. I didn't place the accent right off.

"Thanks," I said. "It's not hard when a fight's that good."

"No doubt. But I'm not referring to the boxing story. I meant that series of yours on the investment swindlers. What a read! Heading in I was so confused, I didn't know whether I'd lost my mule or somebody'd handed me a rope. But by the end, I'll be damned if you hadn't pieced it all together. Almost all of it."

"Afraid you're misinformed," I said, transfixed by the icy glint in the guy's blue eyes, and his smoothed-out Oklahoma twang. "I didn't write that story, Mr.—"

"My apologies." He smiled mildly. "My niece must be wondering where I got off to. But again—congratulations. I like to see smart people get what they deserve."

"Never got your name, friend."

He saluted, then threaded through the throng, out the double doors that fed into the main corridor. I told Ida to wait and dodged between well-lubed revelers, quick-stepping down the hallway to the lobby. Oklahoma was reclaiming a topcoat and hat from the checkroom girl.

A ravishing young redhead—Devin or Dulcie, who could tell which?—waited at his side. She spotted me across the lobby and showed off a razor-thin smile, honed from emulating her mother: cold, dismissive, confidently superior.

"Stanford or Radcliffe?" I asked, negotiating the thinning crowd.

She gave no reply, hooking the old guy's arm. He set a perfectly blocked Homburg atop his head and likewise ignored me.

"Lovely night to walk, don't you think?" he murmured to the redhead, strolling with her to the club's entryway.

"You've got *some* stones, Threllkyl." I grabbed at his free elbow.

He gave me a befuddled look. "I'm sure you'll excuse me," he said with practiced pleasantry, shaking me off. "My name is Glass. You've mistaken me for someone else."

They passed through the doors and onto Post Street. He waved off a cabbie eager to squire them away.

I grappled for some tart and telling line to throw at their departing figures. The perfect kiss-off to the whole intrigue. But to my shame, I came up empty. Speechless.

So I let them go. Point of fact, I let it all go.

Could I really gripe?

I was *Mr. Boxing* again, full-time.

It paid to remember what Marty English said, when he slapped the William Sonlich byline on those stories:

"Who the hell's gonna believe a sportswriter?"

—30—

About the Author

As the son of a famed boxing writer also named Eddie Muller, the author grew up in newspaper offices and boxing arenas and has an insider's knowledge of both worlds. He is the founder of the San Francisco Historical Boxing Museum and an honorary member of the California-based World Boxing Hall of Fame. He is the author of several books of nonfiction, *Dark City Dames: The Wicked Women of Film Noir* (ReganBooks, 2001), *Dark City: The Lost World of Film Noir* (St. Martin's, 1998), *Grindhouse: The Forbidden World of "Adults Only" Cinema* (St. Martin's, 1996), and *The Art of Noir: The Posters and Graphics from the Classic Era of Film Noir* (Overlook Press, 2002) as well as the first Billy Nichols crime novel, *The Distance* (Scribner, 2002). Eddie Muller lives in the San Francisco Bay area.